TV GODS
SUMMER PROGRAMMING

EDITED BY
JEFF YOUNG
LEE C. HILLMAN

FORTRESS PUBLISHING, INC.
WWW.FORTRESSPUBLISHINGINC.COM

TV Gods — Summer Programming
© 2017 Fortress Publishing, Inc.
All stories copyright by the respective authors
All artwork copyright by the respective artists
ISBN: 978-0-9887991-4-1

Cover Art: Dirk Shearer

Edited by: Jeff Young & Lee C. Hillman

This book is available for wholesale through the publisher, Fortress Publishing, Inc.

PUBLISHED BY:
Fortress Publishing, Inc.
1200 Market Street
Unit 17 / Box 137
Lemoyne, PA 17043
WWW.FORTRESSPUBLISHINGINC.COM

CONTENTS

From the Editor

A good idea sells itself. Take your favorite pantheon and your favorite TV show and mash them together – that's usually as far as I get. I'm pitching the idea to an author and about there the lights go on. I can almost start to see the idea percolating in the gray matter. In fact half the time I'm expecting them to push me out of the way mumbling, "Can't talk, must write," and stagger away bemused. One of our authors staked her claim on a TV show at the book launch for the original *TV Gods*, she was that anxious to start again.

So the best news I can give you reader, if you've stumbled upon this collection by accident, is there's a whole other one out there as well. In fact just like *TV Gods: Summer Programming*, it has 18 stories and different artists illustrate each one. Just like last time we've got a collection of work from established authors and illustrators as well as up and coming writers and artists. We've found brand new participants and welcomed back familiar favorites. Our creative folk have taken on TV shows both brand new and classic, mixing them with pantheons as diverse as Hindu, Native American, Norse, Greek, Egyptian, Celtic, Meso-American, and Japanese. Co-Editor Lee C. Hillman did her usual fine job of prose wrangling to ensure each story was ready for you to enjoy. Dirk Shearer returned to cook up another amazing cover for us.

So fire up the barbecue, get out the red plaid tablecloth, load up a cooler of cold ones, and grab the hot dogs and burgers. It's time to beat the heat with *TV Gods: Summer Programming*.

Cheers,
Jeff Young, Editor

Poseidon's Island
Maria V. Snyder

"Just sit right back and you'll hear a tale…," Pilligan sang to himself as he wound the anchor's rope into a neat coil on the ship's deck. The white wood shone in the warm tropical sunshine. He'd done a fabulous job of scrubbing it, if he did say so himself. In fact, the S.S. Mini Cooper gleamed. It bobbed in the gentle waves like a seagull about to take wing.

When he finished with the rope, Pilligan set the sign out on the pier. Shaped like a ship's wheel, the sign read: Island Charters. Exotic Trip. Free Lunches. Before they added free lunches, they hadn't had a customer in months. But now —

"Pilligan!" Captain's voice cut through his musings. "Clients at two o'clock."

"But Captain, you said they'd be here at eleven." Pilligan scratched his temple in confusion.

The Captain's big belly expanded as he sighed. The motion stretched his royal blue shirt almost to the ripping point. Taking off his captain's hat, he ran a big hand through his thick white hair. Pilligan flinched, expecting to be swatted by the hat, but Captain just pointed to the end of the dock.

Five passengers stood on land, appearing confused. They peered at the rows of sailboats, fishing trawlers, pleasure cruisers and yachts docked at the Tropic Port.

"Go help them," Captain said.

"Aye, aye, Captain." Pilligan saluted.

"Oh, Pilligan?"

"Yes?"

Captain gestured to Pilligan's red shirt and white pants. "You're supposed to instill confidence as my first mate."

"Oh. Right." He raced below decks and looped a coil of rope around his right shoulder, tied on a flashlight and a fanny pack filled with... well, he wasn't sure, but it must be something important. When he returned, he held his arms out and asked Captain how he looked.

"Like a mighty sailing man," Captain said drily.

Pilligan preened. He hustled over the dock's wooden boards to greet their clients. As he neared the group of three women and two men, he slowed.

The red-haired lady was gorgeous. Her gold evening gown glittered in the sun and hugged her curves. And boy oh boy, her figure put an hourglass to shame. The other girl had her brown hair pulled into pigtails and her complexion was farm fresh and milky pure. She wore a cotton half-shirt and short shorts. An older man and woman bickered good-naturedly. The woman's copious amount of jewelry flashed sparks of sunfire and Pilligan was surprised the seagulls hadn't attacked her. And the older man wore a straw hat with his three piece suit. The last man stood a little bit away from the group. He clutched a stack of books to his chest, wrinkling his white button down shirt. His sandy brown hair matched his tan pants.

Pilligan introduced himself to the passengers.

"About time, my boy," the older gent said. "I'm Phorbas Howl the three hundred and thirty third and this is my wife, Mrs. Lovey Howl." He pointed to a stack of luggage. "If you'd be so kind to carry these to your ship...," Mr. Howl pulled out a wad of cash. "I'll add an extra hundred if you avoid the puddles of rotten fish guts."

The red headed lady sidled up to him. "Pilligan," she said in a breathy whisper. "I'm going to need a big strong man to carry my suitcases."

"Uh, Miss…?"

"Lampetia." She fluttered her long fake eyelashes at him.

"No. No," interrupted the sandy-haired man. "He needs to ferry my crates of books without getting them wet. I'm Aepytus." He shook Pilligan's hand.

"I can carry my own bags," the pigtail lady said. "I'm Euryte."

Pilligan looked at the mounds of luggage and bags. "Ummm. Do you know it's only a three hour tour?"

"A THREE HOUR TOUR." The words echoed all around them, but only Pilligan was startled by the booming voice. He peered at the passengers. They were a strange group of minor gods who now looked nervous.

"Then let's go, my boy," Mr. Howl said, waving cash in front of his face. "Time is money!"

They seemed anxious to leave. Pilligan shrugged and hefted a heavy suitcase, making the first of many trips to the S.S. Mini Cooper.

After stowing all the luggage — a miracle, considering there was a reason the ship was named after a tiny car — they set sail. An hour into the trip, the weather started getting rough. The tiny ship was tossed like lettuce in a salad. If not for the courage of — oh, who was Pilligan kidding? He blew chunks into the heaving ocean, curled into a fetal position, and cried for his mommy while the Captain was brave and sure and steered them straight into the rocks, causing them to shipwreck on an uncharted tropical isle.

With suitcases and luggage piled around them on the lagoon's beach, the storm-weary group dried out on the sand. The passengers sat around a campfire eating their soggy free lunches when Captain told them the bad news.

"We were blown miles off course, our shipboard communications are dead, and there's no cell signal." The last comment caused a collective gasp of dismay. "All we have is a survival kit and this old radio, but it's busted." Captain held out a white box with a bent antenna.

Aepytus raised his hand. "I can fix it. I've a Master's degree in electrical engineering." He took the radio, drained the water from it, straightened the antenna, and muttered something about using the salt in the ocean to build an alkaline battery.

Pilligan tuned him out. "What are our chances of being rescued, Captain?"

"Well, Little Minnow, I'm sure the Coast Guard is out searching for us right now."

Panic boiled in his chest. They were marooned and doomed. Captain only called him Little Minnow when things were bad. Like, getting a lollypop right before an injection bad.

"Of course they're coming," Mr. Howl said in a rich baritone. "I'm the Wolf of Olympus, a billionaire *after* taxes, and I've suitcases full of money."

"And I'm having tea with the mayor's second ex-wife tomorrow!" Mrs. Howl pressed her hands to her chest in dismay. Not a smudge of dirt sullied her white silk gloves.

"I've an audition," Lampetia said. Desperation laced her voice. When she noticed everyone staring at her in pity, she fluffed her hair and purred, "It's a mere formality."

"My cows won't milk themselves," Euryte cried.

Static crackled through the air. Another storm! Pilligan hunched over and pulled his white floppy hat down over his ears, but the sound came from the radio. Aepytus fiddled with a knob as he tuned in to an active frequency.

A whistle sounded, then a male announcer said, "This just in... authorities have launched the search for the S.S. Mini Cooper. We received a passenger manifest...," The man continued, listing their names and their minor accomplishments. As each bio was read, the passengers brightened. "Every effort is being made to find these lost gods, who no one knew existed until now."

"Do you know what this means?" Mr. Howl asked.

"That we're going to be rescued," Pilligan said.

"No," Lampetia said. "We're going to be famous!"

Cries of happiness echoed all around. Pilligan shook his head — minor gods were worse than demi-gods. Just then a faint whine of an airplane engine sounded.

Captain jumped to his feet. "It's the search plane. Quick, Pilligan! The flare gun."

Pilligan ran right into the Captain and bounced off. "Sorry, Captain." Then he stepped on Captain's foot as he rushed over to the survival kit.

"Hurry up." Captain urged him as the drone of the plane grew louder.

Fumbling with the flares, Pilligan dropped them on the beach. They rolled toward the waves lapping at the sand. He dove and grabbed one right before it reached the water. Whew.

The others waved their arms and yelled as the plane passed right over head. Pilligan loaded the flare into the gun, aimed it at the sky, and pulled the trigger. A woomph sounded as a bright red spark streaked through the sky and… hit the airplane. Dead center. It exploded in mid-air.

Mouths agape, the others stared at Pilligan.

"Oops." He swallowed. Loudly.

Aepytus pointed to the sky. "Look."

A man dangled below a blue and yellow parachute that floated toward the island.

Pilligan's knees gave out and he plopped to the sand in relief.

"Let's hope he radioed in his position before ejecting," Mr. Howl said.

They watched as the pilot came closer, but then a strong wind gusted over the island. Palm trees shook and coconuts fell as the pilot was blown far out to sea.

After a moment of shocked silence, Aepytus said, "If my calculations are correct, he's going toward the shipping lanes. He's bound to be picked up."

They waited on the beach for another plane or ship to arrive. One day turned into two, then into three. On the third day, the radio suddenly crackled to life.

The same announcer said, "This just in… the Coast Guard has found the pilot of a rescue plane that had disappeared while searching for the S.S. Mini Cooper. Other than a concussion and dehydration, the man is in good shape. When authorities asked him what happened to his aircraft, the man claimed he has no memory of the incident. The doctors confirmed the man has a classic case of amnesia. In other news, the search for the S.S. Mini Cooper has been called off."

Hostile glares focused on Pilligan. He made himself scarce.

Two weeks later, they were still stranded on the island, but they had built huts and chairs and hammocks and tables and dishes and beds and… it was amazing what they were able to construct from the island's natural resources. Plus the suitcases seemed to have an unlimited supply of clothing and accessories. It was almost magi—

"Pilligan! Stop daydreaming and help me put up the umbrella," Captain ordered.

"Aye, aye, Captain."

That night after Mr. Howl drank too much fermented coconut milk, he offered a million dollars to the person who discovered a way to get them off the island. They all brainstormed ideas, but Aepytus came up with the winning design. Actually, it wasn't all that impressive. Even though they built huts and chairs and hammocks and tables and dishes and beds, no one, until now, thought to build a raft. Captain and Pilligan would sail it out to the shipping lanes and bring back help.

The girls sewed a sail, while Pilligan collected branches. He dropped his load onto the growing pile in the lagoon and checked in with Aepytus. The man worked at a complex still. White smoke puffed and a sweet odor fogged the air.

"What are you doing?" Pilligan asked.

"Since I have Master's degrees in botany and chemistry, I'm making an adhesive for the raft from coconut sap, sugar, and—"

"What's an adhesive?"

"It's glue. We're going to glue the branches together."

"That's a good idea."

"I know. Now, if you don't mind…."

Pilligan returned to his task and soon they had enough branches to construct the raft. With everyone assembled on the beach to help, Aepytus sent Pilligan back to his hut to fetch the glue. He ran

13

the whole way and was hot and thirsty when he arrived. There was a coconut filled with milk and Pilligan downed that before grabbing the other coconut with the glue. He raced back to the lagoon. They built the raft and Captain and Pilligan launched it, jumping into the small craft before it could leave without them.

They sailed approximately ten feet before the branches floated apart, dumping them into the lagoon. They swam for shore. Standing on the beach, soaking wet, Captain growled at Aepytus.

But Aepytus was staring at Pilligan. "Did you get the adhesive from my hut?"

Pilligan opened his mouth to reply, but his lips were glued shut. Guess that wasn't coconut milk he drank. Oops. He made himself scarce.

Aepytus brewed another batch of glue and they launched the raft again.

"Good bye!" Lampetia waved a white handkerchief.

"Bye!" Pilligan called.

"Good luck," Euryte said.

"Thanks." Pilligan tipped his hat.

"Bon voyage!" Mr. Howl said.

"Uh… bon voyage back at you," Pilligan said.

"Watch out for sharks," Aepytus said.

"Sharks?" Pilligan tried to turn the raft around.

"Pilligan," Captain growled.

Twenty feet into the journey, the glue dissolved in the water and dumped Pilligan and Captain into the lagoon. This time Aepytus made himself scarce.

A few days later, Pilligan found a large rectangular crate that had washed up on the beach. He raced to get the Captain, but the entire population of the island followed Pilligan back to the lagoon.

Captain used a pry bar to open the crate. Inside was a robot. Constructed from a shiny silver metal, the automaton had a cone-shaped head with an antenna sticking out the top. Two square panels extended to each side of the robot's head, looking like ears. It had a rectangular body with lights and a control panel. It stood on metal legs, but its arms were made out of that flexible piping used in ducts.

"What do you think, Aepytus?" Captain asked.

"It's a robot."

Captain grabbed his hat, but didn't take it off. "Can you turn it on?"

"Well… I studied robotics when I was in school for—"

"For money's sake, my good man," Mr. Howl said in frustration. "Yes or no?"

"I was getting to that, Mr. Howl." Aepytus frowned, but he reached into the crate and pushed the fist-sized button labeled "power" on the robot's chest.

A rumble sounded from deep within the metal… er… man? Yes. Pilligan decided it was a man. Lights flashed and he sat up. They all jumped back a couple feet. But the robot didn't move.

"Now what?" Pilligan asked.

"Now what," the robot echoed.

"Hey, he can talk!" Pilligan inched closer.

"Hey he can talk," the monotone voice repeated.

"I might be able to program him to do some simple tasks," Aepytus said.

"Oooohh," Euryte said. "He can do the dishes and sweep the sand out of our huts."

"He can do the laundry and iron my gowns," Lampetia cooed.

"He can gather the coconuts and carry them back to camp." Pilligan rubbed his lower back, he was tired of fetching coconuts for everybody.

"Now see here, I'm a Howl and I'm used to certain luxuries. He can be *my* valet."

"*We're* used to living in luxury," Mrs. Howl corrected. "He can be *our* butler."

"That's a fine idea, Lovey." Mr. Howl kissed the back of her gloved hand.

"Now wait a minute," Captain said. "He can chop the fire wood."

An argument broke out as each person tried to shout over the others. The radio crackled to life, silencing them.

"This just in…," the announcer said. "A very expensive T.X. 14 robot has fallen off a container ship in the south Pacific. Massive search efforts along the shipping lanes are underway."

"Or we can program him to swim out to the shipping lanes and report our location," Aepytus said.

Cheers and back-slaps erupted.

Boy, Aepytus is smart, thought Pilligan. *He's like a person that teaches stuff at one of those schools for smart kids.*

While Aepytus worked on the program, Pilligan was given the job of teaching the robot how to swim. All four men struggled to lay the robot on a narrow table belly down. Pilligan lay on another table right next to him.

"Move your arms and legs like this, Robot," he said, demonstrating how to swim the freestyle.

But Robot couldn't rotate his arms over his head, which also ruled out the butterfly stroke. And the breast stroke proved too difficult as well. So Pilligan taught him the only thing that worked. The doggie paddle. Or in this case, the robot paddle.

Once Aepytus uploaded the program, they directed the robot back to the beach. After a bon voyage party and a kiss from Lampetia, the robot started doing the robot paddle with his arms as he waded into the lagoon. The water rose up to his knees, then his waist, up to his chest and… over his head.

"It appears the robot cannot float," Aepytus said.

"You think?" Captain snapped.

At least no one blamed Pilligan. This time. They waited on the beach, but the robot never resurfaced. Disappointed, dejected, and depressed everyone shuffled back to their huts to drown their sorrows with coconut wine.

A week later as they ate lunch, the radio sizzled to life. "This just in… the missing T.X. 14 robot just walked onto a beach in Hawaii."

The castaways applauded. They were going to be rescued!

"…scientists examined the T.X. 14's data banks, but salt water corroded the files. We'll never know where the T.X. 14 was after if fell off the ship and before it walked onto shore."

Gloomy silence. Then. "Aepytus?"

"I'll brew up another batch of wine." Aepytus headed for his still.

"Better make that *two* batches, my good man," Mr. Howl said, staring into his empty mug.

A couple days later, Pilligan rested on the beach in a lounge chair. He'd fetched hot water for Mr. and Mrs. Howl, collected plants for Aepytus, helped the girls wash dishes, and fixed the holes in the grass walls of the huts. He was beat. The sun warmed him. The soft lapping of the water lulled him to—

Whap!

Wide awake, he jerked upright. A giant white net covered the island.

"Captain. Captain," Pilligan shouted, trying to stand, but something was hooked around his neck, prevented him from moving. He struggled to free himself.

"Be still," an unfamiliar voice hissed. "You'll scare off the *Pyrgus malvae tropicae regionibus.*"

"The pyra-what?" Pilligan pushed the net off his head.

"Drat," the man said with a British accent. He hefted his net and stalked away.

Pilligan was annoyed at the stranger for interrupting his nap. He settled back on the chair. A second later he realized that a stranger was on the island. A stranger! Jumping up, he scrambled after the portly man wearing a pith helmet, khaki shirt, and khaki shorts. An orange belt, green knee socks and brown boots completed the outfit. The man appeared as if he were on a tropical safari.

"Mister, wait!" Pilligan cried. "What are you doing here? How did you get here? Do you have a boat?" The questions tumbled from his mouth in a rush.

"Do be quiet," the man said, peering through a pair of binoculars. He crept through the bushes and then swung his net. "Drat." Then he crouched down and crawled through the underbrush.

Unable to get the man's attention, Pilligan fetched Captain and the others. They finally managed to get a response from the stranger.

"My name is Lord Papillon. I'm hunting a very rare *Pyrgus malvae tropicae regionibus.*" At their blank looks, the Lord sighed. "It's a

Tropical Grizzled Skipper butterfly, recently only thought to live in the United Kingdom. Once I capture it, I will fire my flare gun and my ship will come and pick me up."

"Will you take us with you?" Captain asked.

"Of course."

They celebrated. Pilligan jumped up and down. They would be rescued. Finally!

"But not until I find that butterfly," Lord Papillon said.

"How long will that take?" Mrs. Howl asked.

"Days, weeks, months, years... I will stay on this island until I've captured it! Even if it takes forever."

They ceased celebrating. After a few days of frustrated waiting, they plotted how to speed things up. Aepytus made seven butterfly nets for the castaways. They spent an entire day hunting the Tropical Grizzled Skipper with Lord Papillon.

When they returned, they plopped onto the chairs in exhaustion.

"My blisters have blisters." Lampetia rubbed her feet.

"I'm probably two inches shorter," complained Euryte.

"That man is obsessed," Mr. Howl said. "We need a new plan and more coconut wine."

"That's it," Aepytus said.

"What's it?" Pilligan asked.

"I'll brew a stronger drink from berries and we'll get him drunk. While he's unconscious, we'll steal his flare gun and signal his ship."

The next day, the castaways invited Lord Papillon to a special tea in his honor. They poured cups of berry tea for everyone and toasted butterflies, the British Empire, and Pilligan's Aunt Beatrice, because by that time, they were all a bit drunk. They toasted to everything they could think of until they could think no more.

Pilligan woke... hours later? His head throbbed and Lampetia had drooled on his red shirt. His only red shirt, which still looked brand new despite—

"Owww... my head," Captain groaned. "How long were we asleep?"

"According to my watch, only ten minutes," Mr. Howl said.

"According to my *calendar* watch, we'd been asleep for ten minutes and two days," Aepytus said.

"Where's Lord Papillon?" Pilligan asked.

They searched for him, but he was not on the island. Dejected, they sat around the table.

The radio buzzed to life. "Today we are interviewing the world famous butterfly collector Lord Papillon who has netted the rare Tropical Grizzled Skipper. Tell us how you found this unique beauty Lord Papillon."

The castaways leaned closer. Pilligan's heart tapped like the woodpecker that liked to peck on his head. Would Papillon mention them? Would they get rescued?

"I've no time for this nonsense," Lord Papillon said. "There's been reports of an extremely rare *Frigidum Callophrys rubi* in the Artic and I must leave right away before the creature freezes to death."

"Good hunting, Lord Papillon," the radio announcer said.

A collective groan ringed the table. Mr. Howl picked up an empty cup. He shook it. "Perhaps more of that *tea*?"

Pilligan slumped in his chair. So close. Again. How many times had it been? A lot. He straightened. "Does it seem like one of those endless punishments to you?" he asked the others.

"What do you mean?" Euryte asked.

"You know, like that Sissy Pus guy who has to push the boulder up the mountain, but it keeps rolling back down."

"That's the dumbest thing I ever heard, Pilligan," Captain said.

No one else said a word. They looked everywhere but at him and the Captain.

Standing, the Captain crossed his arms and peered at each of them. "All right, who pissed off Poseidon?"

Cheeks turning red, they stammered and fidgeted under his scrutiny.

"What did you do?" he demanded.

"I turned down a marriage proposal from his son," Lampetia said.

"He hired me to find a way to clean the contaminated water in the Bay of Olympus," Aepytus said.

"But that's a respectable thing to do," Mrs. Howl said.

Aepytus hunched his shoulders. "I turned the water into gelatin."

"Which flavor?" Pilligan asked.

Captain swatted him on the head with his cap. Pilligan rubbed his temple, he thought it was a good question.

"I was swimming and encountered a sea cow. It appeared to be in distress." Euryte wrung her hands. "When my cows are in pain it means they need to be milked. What I tugged on was not a teat."

"What was it?" Pilligan asked.

No one answered.

"I foreclosed on Atlantis," Mr. Howl said.

Groans all around.

"That's it. We're never getting off this island. He's going to keep torturing us with the possibility of rescue." Captain slammed his hat onto the table. "I knew I shouldn't have offered free lunches."

Pilligan didn't think it was fair of Poseidon to punish him and the Captain, but he was just a mortal — what did he know? The island would now be his permanent home. He glanced around at their huts, the lounge chairs, the still, and — hey!

"This place isn't so bad," Pilligan said. "We have everything we need. It's warm. It's beautiful. No telemarketers. No taxes. No political debates."

They brightened.

"My dear boy, I think you may have something there," Mr. Howl said.

After that, the mood on the island was downright jubilant. For the next few months, they sunned on the beach, surfed the waves, drank lots and lots of coconut wine and berry tea. With two beautiful single girls and three bachelors, there was quite a bit of hooking—

"Pilligan!" Captain called from the lagoon. "Pilligan!"

He raced to the beach with the others close behind. Captain pointed out to sea. Bobbing on the waves was a large Coast Guard cutter. A smaller boat jetted toward their lagoon.

"A rescue boat," Captain said.

"You all know what to do," Aepytus said.

"Hide!" Pilligan dove for cover.

The X-Scrolls
Larry Ivkovich

Edo, Japan, 1650
Shitamachi Undercity, Adachi Ward
Hour of the Rat

Yakoto Kenta sipped a cup of sake, kneeling in cushioned comfort at his kotatsu table. Long past his bedtime, and with his wife sound asleep, he waited impatiently for his new business associate to arrive. Absently, he rubbed one sweaty palm over his rotund belly. The tightened obi of his kimono barely kept the garment fastened around his ample girth.

Kenta sighed contentedly at the momentous deal he had negotiated. Supreme good fortune would now come his and Mari-chan's way due to his great courage, cunning, and business acumen.

Mari-chan. Kenta licked his lips in anticipation of seeing the young courtesan again. Together, with the payment he would receive tonight, they would....

A noise outside the house interrupted his lustful reverie. The time for the secret exchange-of-goods had come. But, with the sake cup halfway to his lips, Kenta cocked his head, puzzled. This sound was not what he expected. There it was again! A fluttering, like that of bird wings... No, no, something else.

It sounded more like rustling paper. Why would that be? Kenta put the cup down and rose from his pillow. Stepping around the bamboo trays of silkworm cocoons he would sell to his late-night visitor (for a great profit!), he approached the entry panel.

He slid aside the shoji screen to look out on his modest-sized courtyard. A half-moon lent a shimmering luminance to the gardened landscape. Nothing. He heard nothing and saw only the flowers, shrubbery, mulberry trees, and rock sculptures he had paid to have designed and installed.

A movement near his household kami shrine caught Kenta's eye. Squinting, he discerned a strange-looking object hanging from the lower crossbeams of the small-scale torii gate, which stood over the shrine.

He walked closer, curious and emboldened by drink. The object seemed to move jerkily under its own power. How...?

He gasped, horrified by the sight of a horse's leg tied to the gate. A horse's leg without the horse! As if alive, it kicked at him with its large, wicked-looking hoof.

Kenta cried out and stepped back. What madness was this? He whirled, as, once more, the fluttering, papery sound emanated behind him. There, hovering in the air like a giant butterfly was... a paper parasol! Spear-like, it shot toward Kenta and impaled him in the shoulder with its tip.

"Aaieeeeee!" Kenta stumbled backwards against the torii gate. He swung desperately at the parasol with flailing arms, clutching and ripping at its fabric. Before his fear-widened eyes, the horse leg lashed out once more.

Adachi Ward
Hour of the Snake

Muridaoru Kitsune, Imperial Investigator of the Yoshima Samurai Clan Investigation Collective, studied the murder setting in the mid-morning sunlight. The victim, Yakoto Kenta, kept an unpretentious household in Edo's Shitamachi Undercity. Surprisingly, however, a beautiful garden had been commissioned to enhance the otherwise humble abode.

Now Yakoto, a silk merchant by trade, lay dead in that flowering beauty.

"Muridaoru-san."

Muridaoru turned at the soft voice of his colleague, Imperial Investigator Kempo Sikurie Chie. He bowed. "What have you discovered, Sikurie-san?"

Sikurie bowed in turn. Though Nipponese, her flaming red hair, tied in a topknot, marked her as an interesting and unusual-looking individual. Muridaoru was lucky to have her as a fellow investigator. It was true they sometimes disagreed in their analyses, but Sikurie's skills at healing and deductive techniques were beyond reproach.

Like himself, she stood garbed in the dark gray, long-sleeved jacket and trouser-skirt all Imperial Investigators wore. However, unlike the katana longsword and the metal gunsen war fan sheathed through Muridaoru's obi, Sikurie wore the shorter wakisashi blade sashed to her waist. "I have examined the body," she said, "and would like your opinion on my findings."

"Ah." Muridaoru felt gratified Sikurie would respect his opinion on such matters. They approached the corpse where it sprawled before a household shrine. Two members of the Edo Dōshin Police moved aside, bowing in deference to the higher-ranking samurai.

"I found this clutched in the victim's right hand," Sikurie said, holding up a torn and crumpled piece of paper. Part of a colorful image inked its surface.

"Hmmm," Muridaoru said. "Intriguing."

He and Sikurie knelt at the blood-soaked body. "He had been stabbed in the shoulder but that is not what killed him." Sikurie indicated the wound on the man's forehead. "The fatal blow was struck here, as you see."

Muridaoru grunted. Sikurie often spoke calmly during these examinations. Trained as a medical Kempo, Sikurie seemed impervious to such grisly scenes. In this case, the victim's brains protruded from the gaping slash on his forehead; his eyes bulged. His mouth yawned bloody and slack, tongue protruding.

"Can you tell what weapons were employed?" Muridaoru asked, averting his eyes. Though he had also witnessed the results of violent deaths, he had never fully gotten used to them.

Sikurie grunted. "That is where I am troubled."

"How so?"

"The shoulder wound was not caused by a blade. It is too circular in shape. The head wound looks to have been caused by the hoof of an ungulate, perhaps from a horse or donkey."

"Hmmm," Muridaoru murmured. "There are no hoof prints here in the courtyard."

"As you say. In fact, no footprints are visible at all except for Yakoto's. Perhaps a ninja did this? An agent of the 'art of invisibility'? We have run up against their wily sort before."

A sharp tingling ran up Muridaoru's spine, indicating the presence of the arcane. The realm of the inscrutable had been a fascination, a calling, since his childhood. He sensed it at once. "No, Sikurie-san, I fear not."

Sikurie sighed, her eyes darting in his direction. "I know what you will say. This looks like an X-Scroll. Hai?"

"Observe." Muridaoru indicated the torii gate. "This wooden crossbeam has been damaged as if a weight hung from it, perhaps animated in some fashion. Could it have been uma-no-ashi, the dangling, kicking horse's leg?"

"Aieee, Muridaoru-san..."

Muridaoru persisted. "And the shoulder wound? A rounded tip? Consider the paper fragment in the man's hand. Could it be from kasa-obake--a possessed paper parasol monster?"

Sikurie, ever the logical realist, shook her head. "Legends, myths. In any case, why would a supernatural entity possess a parasol, of all things? Again, you jump to fanciful conclusions."

"Perhaps. But were not ninjas once thought to be fanciful?" Muridaoru appraised his colleague. Once more they differed but he welcomed such disagreement. It kept his wits sharp and, he had to admit, allowed some delight in bantering with his colleague.

Sikurie nodded, her expression bland, though Muridaoru detected a flash of amusement in her eyes. "As you say. I will agree we have seen things which have been difficult to explain."

"Hence, the creation of the X-Scrolls. Still, I defer to you for the moment. Let us reserve judgment until after we talk to the merchant's wife."

Sikurie Chie knelt on a square zabuton cushion in the Yakoto abode's sitting room, surrounded by flowering ikebana arrangements and bonsai. A sweet odor of incense lingered.

Yakoto Ayaka, the "grieving" widow, seemed perfectly calm and unaffected by her husband's death. That in itself looked suspicious, but Sikurie did not quite believe the merchant's wife had been involved in her husband's murder. She sensed their marriage had not been a happy one. Had there been some trouble between them with

Ayaka's demeanor indicating relief? Or was it nothing more than shock and denial?

Muridaoru Kitsune stood, his lanky, unusually tall frame bent in rapt concentration. He had found a silkworm cocoon on the merchant's wooden floor and studied it assiduously. Since the victim had been a purveyor of silk, this didn't seem of great import to Sikurie. Mulberry trees were grown in the courtyard and a search of the abode's topmost level revealed stacks of additional trays containing the mulberry leaf-eating worms. But Sikurie's otherwise brave and introspective colleague often concentrated on seemingly unimportant details. Such meticulous attention had served them well in the past and might do so here.

Sikurie faced the silk merchant's wife and bowed her head. "Honorable Ayaka-san," she began. "We share your grief at your husband's violent demise and pray the sun goddess Amaterasu admits him to the Plain of Heaven. But it is necessary to ask you some questions."

The older woman turned a stony gaze to Sikurie. "He had a young mistress," she admitted matter-of-factly. "A yūjo. He was planning something. I know it. He schemed to leave me for that filthy whore. He even took my jade amulet to give to her. He denied it, of course, but I knew."

Yūjo. Sikurie thought. *A woman of pleasure. Even more motive for her to commit this crime.* "I see. My apologies, but do you know the name of this mistress?"

At that moment, the lodging's entry panel slid open and three men entered. All bowed and removed their sandals. Two of the men were the Dōshin policemen who had arrived at the crime scene. The third was the investigators' superior, the samurai commander Sikinuru Norio.

Sikurie looked incredulously at Muridaoru, who also registered surprise. She bowed her head to her superior, stood, and, along with Muridaoru, faced the head of the Yoshima Clan Investigation Collective.

"Sikurie-san, Muridaoru-san," Norio said in his usual gruff tone, nodding. Broad of shoulder and chest with stern features and shaven head, he wore his customary black kimono. He radiated a commanding, if surly, presence. "Accompany me."

As Sikurie and Muridaoru walked with Norio to the entry panel, the two policemen took up positions on either side of the merchant's wife.

Norio turned and directed a steely gaze at his two subordinates. "New evidence suggests this crime is simply an attempted robbery gone awry. It is not of our jurisdiction. We are turning it over to the Edo police. Do you understand?"

"No, Lord, I do not," Sikurie replied, confused. "What is this new evidence you speak of?"

"Sir, perhaps you are not aware that there are some discrepancies..." Muridaoru began.

"Just follow my orders," Norio interrupted. "This is not an X-Scroll." He paused, his brow furrowing. "I... I will be at my abode for the rest of the day." He bowed, donned his sandals, and exited the house.

Sikurie frowned. This abrupt reversal of investigative assignments was unlike Sikinuru. It surely seemed their superior had been pressured to make this precipitous decision. And why was he returning to his home and not to Clan headquarters? Her concern and curiosity increased.

Muridaoru walked to the shoji screen entry panel and pulled it partially open. "Sikurie-san," he said, peering without. "Observe."

Sikurie joined him. Outside, Sikinuru entered a covered palanquin. The conveyance's window curtains pulled aside for a moment, revealing a glimpse of a silhouetted figure seated within. Curling tendrils of mist surrounded its head.

"Smoking Sama," Muridaoru whispered. "He is behind Sikinuru-san's reluctance to allow us to investigate. Again, this shadowy personage interferes with the X-Scrolls."

"We have no choice but to obey Sikinuru-san," Sikurie said reluctantly.

Muridaoru raised an eyebrow. "When has that ever stopped us before?"

"Ah," she said, allowing herself a slight smile. "Indeed."

Yoshiwara Pleasure Quarter
Hour of the Goat

Imoo Mari stood impatiently in the alleyway, holding a handkerchief to her nose. Ugh! The smell of garbage and urine was overpowering. Why did that besotted fool, Kenta, want to meet here in this foul ghetto instead of in her own rooms as they always did? And interrupting her lunch in the process!

They had reached an agreement, made a plan. What did he want to discuss now? Now, before the final part of their scheme was to be put into motion? They would leave Edo and start a new life--at least, until she tired of him. Which, she knew, would be sooner rather than later.

Nervously, she touched her finely-coiffed hair, and ran a hand over the silk kimono that clung to her firm, voluptuous body. She could have any man she wanted once she got her hands on Kenta's newly-acquired fortune. She had performed the correct rituals and offered the proper gifts to the kami. She would....

A clucking sound startled her. She shifted her attention toward the dark end of the alley. A chicken strutted out of the shadows.

Stupid bird! How had it survived in this slum? Surely someone would catch it soon, wring its neck, then pluck and cook it. Perhaps she would do so herself, if she could keep from ruining the lacquer on her fingernails.

Mari stepped back, blinking in confusion. As the chicken approached, she could see it more clearly. The fowl wasn't really a chicken but a chicken-like bird.

No, not a bird either. The creature was much bigger, covered in feathers and scales like a fish....

Mari shrieked as the beast-bird ran up to her. It spread bat-like wings, opened its wide beak, and...

Spewed fire.

Muridaoru's informants, the Lone Swordsmen, alerted him to the second murder. The three scholars had assisted him and Sikurie on several cases with their own research into the arcane. Now, this fortuitous information enabled him and Sikurie to arrive at the crime scene before the police. Unofficially and clandestinely, of course. They had, after all, been ordered off the case, had they not?

The second victim's charred remains lay in a cobblestoned alleyway in the Yoshiwara Pleasure Quarter. The smell of burnt flesh was horrifying. Muridaoru stifled the gag building up in the back of his throat. The corpse looked like crispy pork belly! Sikurie, as usual, appeared unruffled.

"This is...was a woman," she said. "But I do not have to tell you she burned to death. What could have done this?"

"This was the work of a basan," Muridaoru said.

"A large, fire-breathing chicken creature." Sikurie's eyes narrowed. "Again, you fantasize, Muridaoru-san. What evidence do you have of this...conjecture?"

Muridaoru pointed. "Observe, Sikurie-san, these bird-like footprints in the dirt where the cobblestones have been upheaved. And...." He bent down and picked up a brightly-colored feather. "Do you see what is stuck to the quills?"

Sikurie looked closer, a thoughtful expression transforming her pale features. "A scale as if from a lizard."

"Just so." Muridaoru pursed his lips. "Are you not a devout believer in the sun goddess Amaterasu, Sikurie-san? Why is the existence of this creature any less viable?"

"Well said, Muridaoru-san, though not exactly the same thing. At any rate, I think this poor woman was the yūjo whom Yakoto's wife spoke of."

Muridaoru cocked an inquisitive eyebrow. "Indeed. And how can you be so sure of this, ah, conjecture?"

Sikurie pointed to the body's charred feet. "Here. The feet are bare, and her geta had very high platforms. Only yūjo do not wear stockings. And this amulet about her neck? Look closely at its surface beneath the blackened soot. I believe this is that jade amulet Yakoto Ayaka mentioned her husband taking to give to his mistress."

"Hai, I concur. But there is more here than meets the eye." Muridaoru moved closer to his colleague, speaking quickly. "Sikurie-san, the three creatures that killed the merchant Yakoto, and this woman...."

Sikurie held up a hand. "*Alleged* creatures."

Muridaoru grunted. "Alleged. The basan, the kasa-obake, and the uma-no-ashi. They are all of a lesser class of mythological beings, are they not? Laughed and scoffed at even by children because of their absurd-sounding aspects."

"Dangling horse leg, possessed paper parasol, and fire-breathing chicken-creature." Sikurie smiled. "Hai, I would agree."

"Then consider." Muridaoru paused, knowing what his next words would sound like to his ever-doubtful comrade. "Does this observation not imply a relationship among the three, perhaps a common cause or a powerful mastermind which unites and controls them to do its murderous bidding?"

"Again, I will agree, that is possible," Sikurie replied, surprising him. "If these creatures are truly real. What then, is the significance, of the silkworm cocoon you found?"

"What indeed?" Muridaoru paused, then admitted, "I am not certain yet but I feel it is essential to our investigation."

"And what of Smoking Sama? What is his role in this?"

"He is crucial to this case, more than any other we have worked on. I sense it strongly. Smoking Sama is more than he seems."

"So you have often said." Sikurie sighed. "What, then, do you suggest? Contact the Lone Swordsmen again?"

"I do not think the Lone Swordsmen can help us at this point."

"Your Shogunate contact, Deep Maw?"

"No. Not even Deep Maw, with all of his government resources, could help us in time. I fear Sikinuru-san may be in danger. Did he not tell us he would be at his home for the remainder of the day, which was strange in itself?"

"Hai, I found it odd, too."

"I am convinced he is in thrall to that same unknown mastermind and tried to send us a message. We must go to him at once."

Hongō Ward
Hour of the Monkey

"By Amaterasu!" Sikurie exclaimed as she and Muridaoru rushed into their superior's domicile. Though they had gone swiftly to Sikinuru's abode, it appeared they were too late. She and her colleague had drawn their weapons but Sikurie wasn't prepared for the horrific sight that greeted their eyes.

Sikinuru lay convulsing on the floor of his sparsely-furnished main room. An abnormal viscous aspect hovered over him, churning like an errant storm cloud. "It *is* Smoking Sama!" Sikurie cried.

"Not so," Muridaoru said. "The man we have known as Smoking Sama was never a man at all. What appears before us is enenra, a mythical smoke beast."

A chill ran up Sikurie's spine as she tore her gaze away from the beast. "Behold Sikinuru-san!" White, fluffy strands entwined their superior's face and chest, pinning his arms to his sides and suffocating him.

"Quickly, Sikurie-san!" Muridaoru pulled forth the gunsen with his free hand. "I will distract enenra!" He unfolded the war fan and waved its metal width at the smoke beast, dispersing its misty essence away from Sikinuru.

Sikurie rushed to Sikinuru's side. She dropped her wakisashi and yanked and ripped the strands of strange fabric from the helpless samurai. Rushing to a kotatsu table, she threw the writhing mass over the candles, which burned there. The fabric burst into flames and dissipated. Sikinuru gasped, breathing hard, but he lived.

"An isumade!" Sikurie exclaimed as she joined her comrade, who faced the smoke beast. "A possessed roll of smothering cotton." She glanced at Muridaoru and shrugged. "You are not the only one to know a little esoterica."

As if from nowhere, three other unearthly figures appeared within the room and took up positions on either side of enenra. The basan flapped its wings, a small flicker of flame sparking within its beak. The kasa-obake opened and closed, the parasol's surface showing the tears rendered by the silk merchant. The uma-no-ashi kicked and flexed as it hung from the ceiling.

In other circumstances, Sikurie would have laughed at such ridiculous-looking creatures, but she knew all their lives were very much in peril.

Before they could act, the air between the investigators and the Lesser Ones crackled and sparked. A shimmering nimbus blossomed, pulsing with an eerie light. A figure coalesced within its roiling mass. Two red glowing eyes affixed a baleful gaze upon the Imperial Investigators.

"Ama-tsu-Mikaboshi!" Muridaoru cried. "The God of Primordial Chaos!"

The being cocked its amorphous head as if studying the investigators. "Well done," it rumbled in a dark, deep voice. "You two humans are very different from other Earthlings I have dealt with since my entrapment on this planet. I am impressed."

"It speaks!" Sikurie exclaimed.

"Planet?" Muridaoru asked. "Earthlings?"

"I am from another world, another cosmos, far, far from your puny star system," the voice intoned. "I have been stranded here for millennia, exiled for certain, shall we say, crimes. In times immemorial, my occasional forays into the Nipponese world gave birth to the persona of the God of Primordial Chaos, a role I readily accepted and cultivated."

"So you played at divinity?" Muridaoru stood transfixed. A being from another cosmos! One who shaped the mythology of his people. He felt awed, yet angered and betrayed. "As Ama-tsu-Mikaboshi you have caused untold sorrow and despair. Now you reveal yourself as a meddling fraud!"

The star-being rumbled. "What do you know of that? I did what was necessary for my survival. But now things have changed. I have received a message from my supporters on my home world: The ruling class has been overthrown and I have been forgiven of my crimes. I can now return to my own universe."

Muridaoru's anger rose. "Then depart! Too many have suffered because of your wars and deceit, you foul creature."

The star-being made a noise like laughter. "And so I shall, now that my depleted starcraft has been repowered by the essence of the creatures you call silkworms."

Muridaoru couldn't help casting a knowing glance at Sikurie. "So," he said to the star-being, "the merchant Yakoto cultivated a special supply of the worms' cocoons in return for riches."

"Indeed, but then, he and his mistress became greedy, overconfident, desiring more wealth and power, as all Earthlings do eventually. He threatened to expose my presence before I could leave this wretched rock."

Muridaoru fumed. "So you silenced them by controlling the Lesser Ones to do your abhorrent work just as you now commanded the isumade to kill Sikinuru-san. Why? Are you not an all-powerful god? Why delegate such acts to those pitiful creatures and a mere merchant?"

"Hai," Sikurie said. "I suspect your starcraft is not the only thing depleted. You, too, are sorely weakened, your power diminished after all these centuries. You need to return to your own world quickly or you will die here."

"I have no time for this!" the star-being howled. "My launch window is at hand!" With that, the creature vanished. Around the two investigators, the Lesser Ones also evaporated.

A groan emanated from Sikinuru. Muridaoru and Sikurie knelt at their superior's side. "Smoking Sama..." Sikinuru muttered. "He...he bespelled me."

"Still, you bravely warned us, Lord," Muridaoru said.

"The threat is ended," Sikurie added.

Sikinuru sighed and fell into unconsciousness.

"His injury is minor," Sikurie said momentarily. "He will recover. But Muridaoru-san...."

"Hai," Muridaoru replied. "The star-being mentioned its...'launch window.' I wonder if that means it has left our world."

"I pray that is so."

Muridaoru pursed his lips. He realized he wasn't sure how he felt about that. Indeed, a surprising disappointment arose within him.

Nihonbashi Mercantile District
Hour of the Rooster

That evening, Sikurie and Muridaoru relaxed in the Teahouse of Flying Storks. Sikurie sipped her rock tea reflectively, her lower legs tucked underneath her upon the tatami mat floor. As candles and incense burned with the lilting melody of a samisen drifting in the background, she reflected on the most recent news she and Muridaoru had received.

The sun goddess Amaterasu worked in strange ways.

Sikinuru had recovered and requested a meeting at Clan headquarters the next morning. The Lone Swordsmen reported multiple accounts of a flaming arc streaking into the sky above the countryside outside of Edo. Like a firework, or a falling star in reverse. Muridaoru had been summoned by Deep Maw, his secret Shogunate contact, who hinted at "singular X-Scroll investigations." It seemed they would not lack for cases for some time.

"So, Sikurie-san, what do you say now?" Muridaoru interrupted her musings, startling her. "Not only have we encountered mythic beings but an entity from the stars." Muridaoru's expression could barely conceal his self-satisfaction.

Sikurie nodded and admitted, "I shall concede this one, Muridaoru-san. However, I will continue to look for a rational explanation in all things."

"Or course you will."

She glanced sideways in his direction. "And, no doubt, this... star-being and his milieu will hereafter become part of our X-Scrolls investigations. Hai?"

"No doubt?" Muridaoru grunted. "But Sikurie-san, I thought you were the doubting one."

Sikurie smiled and raised the teacup to her lips.

Behind the Wheel
a tale of Cassie Zukav, weirdness magnet
Keith R.A. DeCandido

"Welcome back, race-car fans, to another episode of Behind the
Wheel. *I'm your host, Naza Mireles. Today we'll be taking a look at Jamie
McIntyre.*

*"Jamie burst on the scene out of nowhere five years ago, and has
quickly earned a spot in the top echelon of NASCAR drivers. At this rate, he
may be in the conversation for all-time great alongside Petty, Gordon, and
Earnhardt.*

*"Everyone knows that Jamie won his first eight races in a row, and
there was talk that he'd challenge Richard Petty's record of twenty-seven
wins in one season. He didn't quite manage that, though he did vault past Jeff
Gordon into second place when he won his fourteenth at the Pennsylvania
400. Everyone knows that he's continued to stay on the NASCAR leader-
board, recently taking first place at Daytona. Everyone knows that he wears
his racing gloves 24/7, like it's his good-luck charm. And everyone knows that
he does all this with a minimal pit crew, the smallest crew of anyone in NAS-
CAR history.*

*"But what everyone doesn't know is who the real Jamie McIntyre is.
After his Daytona win, he came to Key West, Florida, with his pit crew, and
lately, whenever they're not at a race, they're at the southernmost point,
mostly at a bar called Mayor Fred's Saloon."*

I knew something weird was going on when I saw a camera
crew in Mayor Fred's. And I had a feeling what it was when I recog-

nized the woman the crew was surrounding. She was sitting at the bar, chatting with the new bartender.

As I entered the open-air bar, I passed by the manager, Ihor, who said, "Hey, Cassie."

I pointed at the bar. "What's Naza Mireles doing here?"

Ihor just stared at me. "Take a wild guess."

"She's profiling Jamie, isn't she?"

"Yeah, and since he's been hangin' out here since Daytona, they wanna talk to his drinking buddies."

Wonderful. The word was out that Mayor Fred's was a NAS-CAR star's new favorite watering hole, which meant my favorite bar was becoming a Key West hotspot.

Which, I gotta say, was really annoying. One of the best things about Mayor Fred's was that it didn't get the nutsy crowds that Sloppy Joe's and Irish Kevin's and the like got.

But that had been changing, to the point where Ihor had to hire a second full-time bartender along with the part-timers he had working on Fridays and Saturdays.

That bartender, a cheery redhead named Meredith, was saying, "Oh, Jamie, Eitri, and Brokkr are just regulars like everyone else. We don't treat them any different, which is probably why they keep coming back. But I've only been working here about a month, so I haven't really gotten to know him as well." She caught sight of me, and I immediately started to head for the women's room.

Too late.

"Hey, Cassie! You'll wanna talk to Cassie, she's been a regular here, like, forever."

I sighed and glowered at Meredith.

Mireles immediately jumped off her stool and walked over to me. She was wearing a scoop-necked black shirt that emphasized her cleavage, which made it the same as every other top she wore on camera. Couldn't really blame her, since *Behind the Wheel* catered to NASCAR fans, who were mostly redneck white guys who loved them some boobs.

She was also only about five feet nothing, which you couldn't tell from watching *Behind the Wheel*. Since I'm almost six feet tall, this made for a hilarious visual as she put out her hand and said, "Hi, I'm Naza Mireles. We're profiling Jamie McIntyre for *Behind the Wheel*. Would you mind sitting down with me for an interview?"

My instinct was to say no, but it was mostly because I knew that, once this aired, Mayor Fred's was going to become *more* popular, and it was gonna become impossible to even sit in here.

But that was gonna happen whether I talked to her or not. So I returned the handshake. "I'm Cassie Zukav. And yeah, why not?"

Mireles grinned. "Excellent. Have a seat, Ms. Zukav."

I plunked myself down on one of the stools. As soon as I did so, Meredith placed a pint of beer in front of me. It was good to see that the newbie was as prompt as Ihor always was when it came to providing a drink without even having to ask for it.

Mireles noticed this as she sat on the stool next to me. "You definitely are a regular."

"For almost two years now, yeah."

"First of all, what's your name and what do you do for a living?"

"I'm Cassie Zukav, and I'm a dive-master at the Seaclipse Dive Shop on Stock Island, and I also work at the Bottroff House Bed and Breakfast on Eaton Street here on Key West."

Shaking her head, Mireles said, "Everyone here has two jobs."

"Price of living in paradise," I said with a shrug.

"You said you've been a regular here two years. Is that how long you've lived in Key West?"

I nodded. "I'm from San Diego originally. After I finished school, I road-tripped across the bottom of the country. I was planning to do a two-week vacation here and then turn around and head home. Still haven't gotten around to the second part yet."

She chuckled. "So you met Jamie here?"

I nodded and sipped the beer. "It was after this year's Daytona. Eitri and Brokkr came down first, then Jamie, and then they kept coming back."

"What do you think brought them here in particular?"

For a second, I hesitated. There were, of course, several very good reasons why they came here, and why they kept coming back, but it wasn't the kind of thing that should really go on a nationally televised profile of a stock car driver.

Then I decided, *aw, what the hell.* It's Key West. Crazy is what we do here. I'm living proof of that.

I pointed to the ficus that was at the center of the bar. "See that tree? That was Key West's hanging tree in the nineteenth century. Later, they built this bar around it — the tree's stayed intact this whole time. And the reason for that is that it's also a root of Yggdrasil."

Mireles's studiously perky face fell. "Of what?"

"Yggdrasil. The world-tree. See, Yggdrasil links the Nine Worlds together — you can read up on it in Norse myth, or just watch the Marvel movies, I guess. Anyhow, Jamie McIntyre isn't his only name — he also goes by Tyr, one of the Norse gods, and the reason why he came here is because of Yggdrasil. Same reason why Eitri and Brokkr came here — they're both dwarves — and also Loki and Odin and Sigyn up there." I pointed at the stage where 1812, the bar's house band, was setting up. Sigyn — a.k.a. Ginny Blake — was the drummer.

"She was actually Loki's wife once upon a time. A little over a year ago, Loki tried to destroy the world by sundering Yggdrasil and causing Ragnarok — remember that weird snowstorm we had here last April? That was part of it. Luckily, I was able to stop him. See, I'm a Dís, a fate goddess. That's part of why I was drawn here, also. Well, that and it's a fun place. Good beer, good people, and wait'll you hear 1812 play, they're the best cover band on the island."

Somewhere in the middle of my colloquy on how Norse mythology intersected with Key West, Mireles's face went from confused to incredulous to wondering who this nut job was, exactly, and finally to amusement.

"You know, every time I come to this island, I hear a lot of crazy stories. And yours needs a better hook. I mean, Norse gods? Seriously? The *Thor* movies aren't even all that good."

"Oh, I don't know, I wouldn't kick Hemsworth or Hiddleston out of bed," I said with a grin.

"*Oh* yeah." Her expression got feral for a second, and then she put her professional interviewer face back on. "But seriously, what *really* brought you to Mayor Fred's?"

I took another sip of my beer. I kinda figured that would be her reaction — which also confirmed that everyone else she'd talked to had kept the truth under wraps.

You see, everything I said to her was a hundred percent true. Jamie McIntyre really was Tyr, Eitri and Brokkr really were the dwarves who forged (among other things) Thor's hammer, and Ginny really was Sigyn. Odin and Loki both used to come here, too, but the former died helping me stop a crazy ghost from killing people, and the latter died at the hands of a mermaid who wanted vengeance for a thousand-year-old prank he'd pulled.

"Honestly," I said, only partly meaning that adverb, "what drew me in here was 1812. They really are the best cover band on the island. I don't know if anyone told you, but they were the band backing John Robertson up on his last CD before he died."

"Really?" Mireles said. "That's impressive."

"Oh yeah, they're fantastic." I didn't mention that Robertson only died because I stopped him from sucking 1812's souls out of them.

"How well do you know Jamie?"

I shrugged. "Hard to say. We're bar-friends, y'know? I mean, there are people who come in here every night, and I couldn't tell you what their favorite color is or what their religion is or even what they do for a living. I *can* tell you their favorite beer or which sports team they root for or what their favorite song is."

"So what's Jamie's favorite song?"

I chuckled. "Well, he keeps asking 1812 to play Black Sabbath's 'Feels Good to Me.'"

"So he likes power ballads," Mireles said with a nod.

"I guess." I pointedly didn't mention that that song was on the Sabbath album entitled *Tyr*.

"And his favorite beer?"

"He doesn't drink beer — he mostly goes for whiskey. Eitri and Brokkr, though, they order stouts every time."

She asked a few more innocuous questions, and I gave the most boring answers I could think of. Then she stopped a second, tapped the bar with her index finger for a second, and then said, "Okay, maybe you know the answer to this — no one seems to have any idea, but I've heard a rumor that Jamie has a brother. There's no record of him, but I keep hearing references to him here and there from the pit crew and from a few of his other racing buddies."

I didn't even know Tyr had racing buddies. I also was now *really* glad that I never mentioned Thor when I was telling Mireles the truth she didn't believe.

Because if she was having trouble with Tyr, Sigyn, Loki, and Odin, the reality of Thor didn't bear talking about, and the idea of her meeting Thor didn't bear thinking about. Especially with her showing off all the cleavage...

"Um, no, no brother that I know about. Bar-friends, y'know? I couldn't tell you who the only children are and who has siblings. People here only know I have a twin brother 'cause he visited last Thanksgiving."

"Huh. Okay."

Then Larry came out of the men's room and stared dolefully at Mireles and me. "You're still here," he said.

"Yes, and I still want to talk to you."

"Forget it," Larry said, and he veered off toward the pool table.

"What is with him? Everyone else is jumping at the chance to talk about Jamie."

"No, they're jumping at the chance to be on TV," I said with a smirk. "But Larry's kinda special."

"Let me guess, he's a Norse god, too?"

I grinned. "No, an immortal, thanks to a love affair he had with a water elemental."

Mireles rolled her eyes. "You people and your scary stories. Last time I was down here, I took a ghost tour — saw that creepy doll at the museum, heard about all kinds of crazy stuff. Is it something in the air here, or what?"

"Ah, those ghost tours are weak. They don't even mention the ghost in the Bottroff House."

"You know I'm not gonna be using any of this crazy stuff, right?"

I grinned. "I know, I just like seeing all the funny facial expressions you make."

"I'm not gonna use those, either."

But she also laughed when she said it.

I had sworn up, down, backwards, and sideways that I would never set foot in the bungalow on Summerland Key again.

And yet, here I was driving up to Thor's place in my battered old Ford F-150 pickup truck.

I was only a little surprised to get to the end of the long dirt road off Ocean Drive to see Jamie McIntyre's stock car parked in the bungalow's driveway.

Normally a stock car wouldn't be drive-able on regular roads. But normally a stock car isn't tricked out by two dwarves out of Norse mythology who can literally work magic. So yeah.

I could hear the argument before I even walked in the door.

With a sigh, I threw the screen door open to see Tyr and Thor standing on either side of the sofa that was in the middle of the living room that the front door opened up into, screaming at the tops of their lungs.

"Look, this interview's important, all right?" Tyr was saying. "Could get me more endorsements, and—"

"And what do such things matter to me? I will speak with whom I wish, dear brother, and no strutting fool will tell me otherwise!"

"For once in your life, Thor, will you *think*? Just for a change?"

"I think all the time, braggart! Right now, I'm thinking of how I may thrash you if you do not leave my home!"

Tyr finally noticed that I'd walked in. "Cassie, maybe y'all can explain it to him." As soon as he saw me, he got heavier on the fake Southern accent that he used as "Jamie McIntyre."

Thor turned and broke into a big grin under his thick red beard. "Ah, Cassie! It is well that you have once again chosen to grace my home with your presence! Let me toss my imbecile brother out on his ear, and we may converse in private."

"No point, Thor, 'cause I'm here to talk about the same subject."

"*Thank* you," Tyr said.

"Look, Thor," I said, moving into the living room and standing between them, which was probably not the smartest thing I ever did, "you can't go telling Naza Mireles that you're the god of thunder and your brother here is Tyr."

"Why not? Is not the purpose of this — this program to aggrandize yourself? Why not boast of our accomplishments? We have slain many a foe together and apart, and those battles should be chronicled!"

Tyr stared at the ceiling in supplication. "'Cause they ain't watchin' *Behind the Wheel* t'hear about the time we fought the Fenris Wolf or the frost giants, they wanna know about my racing career."

I chuckled. "Well, actually, they want to know what you like to drink and what songs you request, but yeah."

"Bah!" Thor started stomping around the bungalow. "The people of the former mayor's tavern know of our exploits!"

Shaking my head, I said, "Yeah, those are the patrons of a bar in Key West. They've seen all kinds of shit weirder than you two, and they also don't care, as long as there's a sunset, good beer, and live music. But *Behind the Wheel* is gonna show *all over the world*, and is gonna be watched by people who like their lives simple and uncompli-cated."

"Fie on them! We were worshipped once!"

"And now you're a comic book. Worse, they're going to think you're *copying* a comic book. Besides, Mireles will think you're nuts. I tried telling the truth, and I got laughed at."

Thor and Tyr both whirled on me. "You did *what*?" they both cried out.

I took half a step back and held up both hands. "Damn it, calm down, will you? I figured it was better coming from me first — worst case, I was some crazy in the bar. But Mireles just laughed it off and asked for the *real* story."

"Bah," Thor said again, and he turned away from me and wandered toward the galley kitchen that was at the back of the living room. "Just because *you* were not believed—"

"Hey, fate goddess, remember? I know from truth, and I can see through artifice. And I'm telling you, they won't buy any of the Norse god stuff."

"An' even if they do," Tyr added, "I don't want you talkin' 'bout the good ol' days. Last thing I want is people knowin' about my hand."

I stared at Tyr's hands. One of the weird things about Jamie McIntyre was that he never took his racing gloves off, but that's because a long time ago, Tyr stuck his right hand in the Fenris Wolf's mouth, and the wolf bit it off. Thanks to Eitri and Brokkr, he had a fancy-shmancy prosthetic, but he didn't want the general public to know that.

"Nonsense!" Thor bellowed as he went to the fridge to pull out a beer. "Your exploits should be told far and wide!"

"In Mayor Fred's, sure," I said. "Then it's just a crazy story in a bar, just like all the other crazy stories you hear on the island. But you put it on TV, and people start thinking we're all nuts or something."

Tyr walked over to his brother and put a hand on his shoulder. "Please, Thor, I'm *beggin'* you. As a favor to me, just stay away from Mayor Fred's until the crew's gone."

"And what possible reason do I have to do favors for you, brother?" Thor asked with a sneer.

"Then do it for me," I put in quickly before they started shouting at each other again. "Trust me, it will end *really badly* if you start talking about brave exploits and slaying dragons and how big your hammer gets to this woman."

Thor almost dropped his beer. "Wait, this inquiry is being held by a member of the fairer sex?"

I put my head in my hands. "This is exactly what I was afraid of."

"Is she perhaps a comely wench?"

"Ugly as sin." Tyr looked like he'd eaten a lemon.

Thor grinned. "Ah, she is *very* lovely then! Now the truth comes out! You wish to steal her from my bed!"

"She isn't *in* your bed, dumbass, which puts her in company with all sensible women." *Including me*, I didn't bother to add. Thor had tried to seduce me once. That was the first time I came to the bungalow. "Fine, do whatever you want, but I guarantee that if you talk like you usually do, she *won't* go to bed with you. She *will* have you committed."

Tyr snorted. "Wouldn't be the first time. 'Member that time in New York on Roosevelt Island?"

"Od's blood!" Thor cried and threw his beer glass against a far wall. It shattered, tossing beer and bits of glass all over the wall and linoleum floor. I was glad I didn't have to clean up after him, lemme tell you. "Very well, Cassie, in deference to the services you have performed as one of the Dísir, I will accede and avoid the tavern for the nonce."

I breathed a sigh of relief. "Thank you."

"I'll be goin', then," Tyr said. "Thanks, Cassie."

Grinning widely, Thor said, "Since I am granting you this boon, Cassie, might you remain a bit and allow me to grant you another?" And then he waggled his eyebrows, something I'd never seen anyone do in real life before.

"One boon's plenty, thanks." I high-tailed it out right behind Tyr.

I walked into Mayor Fred's bracing myself for another onslaught of camera crews, but there was no sign of Naza Mireles or her crew. Or of Tyr, Eitri, and Brokkr, for that matter.

Larry was nursing a Coke in his usual spot at the bar, wisps of white hair sticking out from under his Rays ballcap. Larry's immortality was contingent on staying awake, so he was always drinking something caffeinated.

"What's the word, Cassie?" he asked when I sat on the stool next to him, just like he always did.

And as always, I came up with a word. "Surprise. I figured the TV folks would be back."

"Not anymore, thank goodness. Once Thor came in—"

I felt the color drain from my face. "What!?"

Larry turned and blinked at me. "Yeah, Thor came in, made a beeline for the TV girl, and turned on the charm."

I winced. "Oh shit, he flirted with her?"

"Well, what passes for flirting in that old duffer's gray matter, anyhow. They chatted over by the pool table and then they took a powder."

"Together?"

Larry nodded.

"Damn."

Meredith placed my usual beer in front of me, but I didn't even notice it. I had to figure out where they went.

Then my phone rang. Pulling it out of my shorts pocket, I saw a number I didn't recognize. Most people wouldn't answer a call from an unknown number, but as a dive-master, I got calls from Seaclipse clients all the time. I never bothered to save them in my phone because I usually only saw them a couple three times while they were here on vacation and then they went away never to be seen again.

So I answered it.

The voice on the other end said, "I guess you think this was funny, Ms. Zukav?" It took me a second to realize that it was Mireles.

"I'm sorry?"

"Figured your jokes in the bar weren't enough, you had to send some jerk to pretend to be Jamie's brother? Even said his name was Thor for Chrissakes."

"Um, I really don't know what you're talking about." That was even almost the truth.

"Don't give me that crap. Once I realized he was full of it, I had to call hotel security on him. Of course, by the time they got here, he'd passed out on my bed. I figured him being drunk would make it easier to get the scoop, but I guess the whole brother thing was a load of crap, wasn't it?"

"Um, well, I—"

"Forget it." She hung up.

I stared at the phone for a second and then laughed.

Larry just stared at me. "What's tickling your funny bone?"

I grabbed the beer Meredith had brought me and took a big sip. "It's too much to explain. Let's just say I'm not worried anymore."

"Didn't realize you *were* worried..."

Later that night, after 1812 finished their second set, Tyr came into the bar. Nobody made a fuss about it — Meredith had told Mireles the truth about that, as far as the regulars in Mayor Fred's were concerned, he was just another customer, and the tourists generally kept their gaping to a minimum — as he headed straight for the table by the ficus, which I'd grabbed after the first set when the tourists who'd been sitting there left.

"I shoulda known you'd have it all in hand, Cassie," he said as he sat down uninvited.

"I don't know what you're talking about," I said, grabbing my beer to take a sip.

"I mean Thor. Shoulda known you told the TV lady the truth so she'd think it was just a joke. Meant she didn't even take Thor seriously. It was perfect."

"Uh, sure." I hadn't planned it that way, but whatever. Let him think I used my fate goddess mojo.

"She called me up earlier to get him outta the hotel parking lot. She had him up to her room in the Hyatt up on Front. My brother prob'ly thought he was gonna get lucky, but she just wanted to grill him. After he passed out, she had security toss him, but he was just snorin' in the driveway till I came to grab him. Got him back to the bungalow to sleep it off."

"Good," I said, though I would've been perfectly okay with him snoozing in the Hyatt parking lot all night.

"And she's headin' out in the a.m. She said there wasn't nothin' interestin' down here in Key West. So looks like you ain't gonna be on TV."

"I'll live. This place has gotten too crowded as it is."

Tyr chuckled and I raised my glass to him.

"It doesn't look like anyone will ever know the real story of Jamie McIntyre. Everyone has a different tale to tell, and they don't all add up right. But maybe it doesn't matter if he wears his racing gloves all the time because it's an affectation or a good luck charm or a case of psoriasis he doesn't want the general public to know about. Maybe it doesn't matter if he has a long lost brother or not. And maybe it doesn't matter why he spends so much time in an out-of-the-way bar in Key West. What matters is that he's one of the NASCAR greats, and we get to see him in action.

"For Behind the Wheel, *I'm Naza Mireles. See you at the raceway!"*

The Show Killer
Hildy Silverman

"Under the world where Earthmaker lives, there is another world just like it and of this world, he, Trickster, is in charge." – **The Winnebago Trickster Cycle**

I.

Once upon a time there was a television network that was presided over by a chief who was preparing to go on the warpath.

He used to be another kind of chief, who planned to go on other kinds of warpaths (but never actually got around to it), but that was very long ago — long before television, long before white people, and long before he made a simple mistake that led to his current torment. Back then, his younger brothers and sisters of this world also knew him as Trickster.

The speaker on his desk buzzed. He jabbed a button and said, "Yes, Miss Snipe?"

"Hello, sir. Your brother's calling. Shall I send him through?"

Despite his indisputable greatness, Trickster shivered. "P-please do. Line 1."

A moment later: "Hello, Chief… what *are* you calling yourself these days?" Younger Brother's grating voice disrupted Trickster's enjoyment of his latest triumph. He should have sent his fist through the ether to pummel Younger Brother for that alone.

Why don't I just kill him and be done with all this again? Trickster mused. The problem was his convoluted plans were so difficult to follow, he often found himself just as confused as everyone he meant to fool. But then he remembered. *Oh, yes. The children. I owe him for the children. And Trickster repays what he owes, for good or ill.*

"Did you see the show?" he asked, ignoring Younger Brother's question.

Even Younger Brother's silences were grudging. But at last he said, "Yes, I did. My son's spirit lives on, for now. But what of my daughter's? *Vampire Journalists in Love* airs its finale next week."

"Oh, don't worry," said Trickster, breezily. "I already have a new lodging prepared for her on one of our longest-running soap operas."

Younger Brother grunted. "Just how long do you think you can postpone my vengeance, Chief?"

Trickster considered his question. How long would television exist? At least another few lifetimes. And after that some other means of sharing stories would surely follow. "As long as possible. And since I am Trickster, *possible* lasts as long as I wish it to."

Younger Brother grumbled. "Yeah, well, as long as it takes I'll be watching. And waiting. You will not cheat justice forever."

Despite who he was and what he was, Trickster shivered again. Younger Brother's murderous, albeit understandable, intentions had kept him alive well beyond a regular mortal's lifespan, and probably would continue to do so until Trickster abandoned this world for another. But although Younger Brother couldn't be escaped, he *could* be stalled. And so long as Trickster controlled the TB Network — much as he had always orchestrated mankind's narratives — he would remain safe.

"I will speak to you again, Brother," said Trickster. His finger hovered over the speaker button.

"Until then, child-slayer."

Trickster leaned back in his creaky chair and sniffed. *That was an unfair appellation*, he thought. After all, he didn't kill two of Younger Brother's children on purpose. They'd only died because they decided to starve to death after Trickster forgot to feed them for months. Younger Brother should have known better than to lend them out in the first place. Besides, he had kept a couple spares for himself. How many children did one man need, anyway?

Trickster buzzed Miss Snipe. "Schedule Bear Corazón for nine a.m. tomorrow. Tell him I want to discuss an exciting new addition to the *Days of Our One Bold Life* cast."

II.

Robérto "Bear" Corazón blinked rapidly at the fifty-five inch T. V. screen as though his eyelashes could sweep away its images like wiper blades clearing bird shit off a windshield.

"So? Wasn't she just something?" The Chief grinned and leaned back in his vast leather executive's office chair.

"Something," repeated Bear, bewildered. "I'm not even sure… what did we just watch? That wasn't today's episode."

"Well, of course it was." The Chief chuckled. "You don't think I had the whole cast come together to tape a full dress rehearsal just to show *you*."

"But — we tape three months ahead." Bear ran his fingers through his gel-spiked hair, pulling out a few strands along the way. "That… *actress*… wasn't even on set back then!"

"Oh, now, you probably just forgot." The Chief waved his hand.

Suddenly, Bear found himself questioning his memory, even though he was always on set when episodes were being taped, and just a moment ago he'd remembered this day of filming with absolute clarity. "Maybe," he said, dubiously. "But I just don't see how I could have forgotten a performance like *that*." He cringed. "Why bring in a competing love interest for Beau? His relationship with Charmaine has been the centerpiece of the show for almost two decades!"

The Chief sighed. "You know as well as I that happy couples are the kiss of death on a soap. Audiences want to see the on-again, off-again, on-again of romance. Third party spoilers are a staple!"

Bear drummed his fingers on the rubber armrest of the swivel chair for visitors. "Yeah, but, she's so much *younger* than DeeDee Luciano."

"May-December romance is also 'A Thing' in soaps."

"She's younger than May," said Bear, holding his hands out in supplication. "She's, like, April. Maybe even March."

DeeDee, who'd played vixen-turned-heroine Charmaine Santiago since the premiere of the soap his parents created, was going to go absolutely ballistic over the insertion of this ingénue into her character's romance. As soon as she found out, she'd mobilize her army of Twitter followers to war against the show — and him, directly.

As though reading his mind, The Chief said, "Come on. Don't let Deedee make you nervous. After all, what's she going to do? She's *w-a-a-ay* past the age where leaving's an option. There are, what, three soaps left on the air? Her alternatives are slim to none."

"There's always prime time," said Bear. He remembered DeeDee's turn on *Fandango with the Famous,* and the hue-and-cry that erupted when her character spent six weeks in a coma to accommodate her leave from *Days.* "We ignore her fans at our peril."

"Eh," said The Chief, shrugging. "They'll come to love Misty. She's such a sassy little thing."

Bear rubbed the bridge of his nose between his thumb and forefinger, feeling a migraine coming on. "She delivered her lines flatter than a truck-squashed squirrel."

"Okay, so she's a little green. She'll learn. They always do."

"She obviously missed her mark halfway through her second scene. The camera was on the back of her head!"

The Chief's eyes twinkled. "I gave her great hair this time, did I not? So thick and blonde."

Bear struggled to maintain his chill. The Chief was right that triangles were the hallmark of soap romances. In the end the most popular pairing would win out, and this no-talent addition would be sent upstairs to find her skis and never be seen again. "We'll see who the audience sides with, but you should prepare this young lady for disappointment. *Barmaine* are a supercouple. Destiny, you know?"

"Destiny?" The Chief rolled his eyes. "It's not a thing, my brother. No, Misty's going to win this battle. After all, *Days* has been in a rut. We've got to break 'em up to shake it up." Bear opened his mouth to object but The Chief plowed on. "Their portmanteau, what do you think it should be, *Bisty* or *Meau*? I'm partial to *Meau*, myself, but that's because I'm a big Three Stooges fan. Also, it sounds like *more*. More *Meau*, yeah. Get that hash trending on the Tweeter."

The oncoming migraine was giving Bear tunnel vision. Through it, he envisioned his parents' legacy spiraling down the toilet.

He stood fast enough to spin his chair and slammed his palms down on The Chief's expansive, mahogany desk. "This girl's got no chemistry whatsoever with Beau! They might as well have not been in the same scenes; there was so little connection. Plus, she doesn't have as much talent or charisma as DeeDee has in her left pinky toe. And… and… that blonde dye job is *uneven*!"

The Chief arched one beetle-like eyebrow. "There is one soap opera left on this network," he said, slowly. "Just. This. One."

Bear opened his mouth then snapped it shut. The Chief was right: the days of at least three soaps on every network were over. The remaining shows were clinging by their fingernails to ratings under constant threat of cancellation in favor of yet another cheaply-produced gabfest.

He inhaled and exhaled several times, using the breathing technique learned in his bi-weekly Bikram yoga class to bring his temper back under control. Only when he was certain he could speak without committing professional seppuku did he say, "I suppose we could get her an acting coach. That one who came in last summer worked wonders with the teen set."

"Now *there's* the team spirit this business requires!" The Chief's rosy, round face split into a toothy smile. He glanced at his Rolex. "Now, I've got an appointment in the commissary. It's Barbecue Thursday, you know. I l-o-o-ove a nice barbecue." He licked his lips while eying Bear as though he were the one slathered in sauce and roasting on a spit. "Wanna join me?"

An electric shiver coursed down Bear's spine. "Er, no, thank you. I'm vegan."

The Chief snorted. "Oh, wait. You're serious?" He shook his head. "My little brothers and sisters these days."

Bear wavered between offense and bewilderment, and came down on the side of abject misery. He turned and walked his throbbing noggin out of the office without another word.

He wound up in an elevator with Shawnda Mink, showrunner extraordinaire, undisputed queen of Tuesday night programming. She spared a look at his face and said, "I see you've met Cousin Ted."

"Uh, who?" Bear felt like his brain had been tossed in the wash and was trapped in the spin cycle. He struggled to focus on Shawnda's words.

"The Chief." Her lips twisted around the title like a lemon she was being forced to suck. "They call him Cousin Ted because he's a show killer. Cousin Oliver, Ted McGinley... legendary show killers? Hence Cousin Ted."

"Okay," Bear mumbled.

"He randomly inserts unnecessary elements that tank otherwise solid shows." She leaned in and added in a conspiratorial tone, "Only it isn't actually random."

"Isn't it?" Normally, he'd have been thrilled that someone of Shawnda's caliber would deign talk to him. But now all he wanted was to go home, toss back a Xanax or three, and forget everything for a while.

"Haven't you noticed?" Shawnda continued, seemingly oblivious to his woe. "He only goes after top shows, the ones with high ratings and rabid followings, albeit usually little critical acclaim." She crossed her arms and nodded, as if in vigorous agreement with herself.

Despite his abject state, Bear managed, "Why would he do that? Surely he's destroying his own reputation as much as anyone's."

She waved one glossy-nailed hand in dismissal. "You know how it goes. Execs like him screw up one network, they just strap on their golden parachute and jump to another. So, what'd he throw at you?"

The elevator dinged their arrival at the glass-enclosed lobby and they exited. "He cast some no-talent bimbette as a romantic rival for my nine-time daytime Emmy nominee, that's what. And he pretty much ordered me to write the newbie as the victor." A thought struck

65

him. "Is this Misty related to The Chief somehow? Is *that* what this is, nepotism?"

Shawnda nodded. "I think so. And it isn't just your girl, oh, no. Seems every show he pegs as successful he tosses some no-talent into the mix and, well, kills it."

Bear stopped in front of the security booth and frowned. "Why would the network put up with his crap? TBN used to be on top and now it's what, number three?"

"If that," said Shawnda. "Which makes it all the more mysterious how he keeps getting away with the same B.S. It's like he never heard of jumping the shark. Or maybe—"

"It's deliberate." Bear sucked in a breath. "Either he just wants to secure jobs for all his friends and family on the hottest shows no matter the outcome—"

"Or he's working for a rival network on the D.L., taking down TBN from the inside. Probably with a sweetheart deal waiting for him as soon as things get to the point the other execs can't keep ignoring his track record." Shawnda's dark brown eyes flashed with rage. "Well, either way, if he thinks he's gonna take down even one show in *my* powerhouse Tuesday night lineup, he's got another think coming!"

"Would he dare even try?"

"He already left me a message saying he wants to meet with me to discuss his 'vision' for Tuesday night." Her fingers tightened around her Gucci leather clutch until her knuckles cracked. "Let me tell you, right now. As you and whatever gods-may-be are my witnesses, I'll use every bit of influence, every relationship I've forged, every favor I'm owed to take the bastard *down!*"

She stalked over to the revolving door and exited, leaving Bear with no doubt The Chief was going to regret messing with Shawnda. The thought buoyed his otherwise leaden spirit as he followed her out into the still-warm LA nightfall, where he awaited an Uber to whisk him home to his waiting pill bottle.

III.

"Ms. Mink," said The Chief as Shawnda strode into his office. He jiggled to his feet and indicated the dumpy chair facing his desk. "Please, take a seat."

"Thanks, but I'd rather stand." She folded her arms over her chest and tried not to feel like a defiant child facing down a bullying principal.

If her stance bothered The Chief, he didn't show it. He simply sat again and stared at her over a steeple formed by his fingertips. "As you like, Younger Sister."

She fought the impulse to curl her fingers into fists. Who did he think he was calling sister? *Racist, sexist, incompetent son of a—*

"So, let's get down to it," he said. "I've been going over the dailies for Tuesday nights, and quite frankly, I'm concerned."

"The ratings for all my shows, from *Anatomically Correct* to *Presidential Mistresses*, have remained consistent if a little lower than in previous years. Tuesday on TBN still dominates television. I fail to see an issue."

"They're not a little lower, now, are they? From their highs in the first two years, viewership's fallen off by about ten percent." The Chief tapped his computer screen. "That's cause for concern."

Shawnda ground her molars. He wasn't entirely wrong, but there were perfectly good reasons for the drop-off, and none having to do with quality. "Real-time viewer attrition is the new normal. Appointment television is a thing of the past, what with DVRs and binge-watching on streaming services." *Am I really explaining the realities of the modern television landscape to this fool?*

He shrugged. "Nevertheless, even high-quality shows need refreshing from time to time."

Here it comes. "And just how do you propose to do that, huh?" Before he could respond, she raised her hand in a halt signal. "Wait, let me guess. You've got some new talent you think would be just the shot in the arm my shows need."

He clapped his hands in seeming delight. "Ah, I knew you would get it! Your reputation as one of our best and brightest is confirmed, Ms. Mink."

"Here's what I get," she said through gritted teeth. "You are not going to add some talentless underwear models or unfunny brats to *my* programs! Don't think I'm unaware of your reputation, Chief."

He flattened his palms against the shiny, deep red of his desk. The wide smile on his face remained, but it seemed forced now, as though flash-frozen in place. "Do tell. What reputation is that?"

"Hm, let's see." She rubbed her jaw and gazed at the ceiling as though struggling to remember. "Oh, I know." She snapped her fingers and glared. "The reputation that comes from adding that agonizingly humorless boy to *The Meany*, letting him monopolize every episode until the axe fell in a record three months on a sitcom that ruled Thursday night for seven years. Or how about the picketers I had to navigate through on my way in to meet you here today? They were foaming at the mouth over DeeDee Luciano walking off the set of *Days* after being relegated to the back burner in favor of that talentless blonde starlet you cast. *That* reputation!"

"So hostile," he murmured. "And all I did was provide opportunities to a couple of promising youngsters."

"Not a couple, oh no." She foraged through her Italian leather tote until she found the printouts of her meticulous research in preparation for today's meeting. "According to what I found, you've been at this for years, not just at TBN. When you were at MBC, you cast no fewer than *twelve* unknowns on a long succession of ruined hits during your tenure. Then, when you turned up on DBC, you managed to insert a whopping *sixteen* into one doomed show after another. And don't even get me started on your cable years." She tossed one printout after another onto his desk to emphasize her points. "Those in the know say you're the sole reason the entire Cinetime outlet doesn't exist anymore!"

She waited, chest heaving with righteous fury, anticipating his defensive response, his inevitable excuses. But he just gazed at the scattered papers across his desk without blinking or saying a word. Finally, when the silence and the staring reached the point she thought he might have had a stroke, he looked up and said in a tiny voice, "What is it you think I'm doing wrong?"

So many possible responses bobbed up that the words collided and formed a logjam in her throat. She opened her mouth, but only a weird choking sound came out.

The Chief slowly shook his head then buried his face in his hands. "At first, I thought Younger Brother was sabotaging me somehow, convincing viewers to tune out. But that's not within his power. I suppose it's because they're just children, no matter how I make them appear. I mean, they do try, but the result is always the same. I get their little souls attached to surefire stories that should keep them alive for years, only to watch them die again and again." He lowered his hands and rubbed them over his desktop, revealing eyes awash in unshed tears. "Ms. Mink, the proverbial ice is cracking beneath me. For all my power I don't know where to go or what to do next. And I... I don't want to be kicked out of this world."

Dear lord, he did *have a stroke.* It was the only thing she could think of, as nothing he was saying made any kind of sense.

Regarding the ridiculous lump of a man with his sad eyes and nonsensical words, her anger ebbed. She sat down across from him, and after only a brief hesitation, laid her hands atop his. "Look, Chief. I've been in the business for a long time, too. I started as an assistant to an assistant producer and rose through the ranks. I know it's tough and I know it's a damned miracle when any show not only gets green-lit; it actually succeeds and lasts more than a season. What I... what *we* do is hard. That's why people like me, and Bear and the rest; we're so protective of our properties. It's also why some folks just aren't," she chewed her lower lip before deciding *just say it,* "cut out to make the decisions that make or break those shows. It's not a slam on, um, them," she added, hastily. "It's — well, we can't all be good at every-thing, right?"

"You don't understand," he said, dejectedly. "Of course not, how could you? But I have to keep the children existing in some form. Films only give them hours, tops. I need *series,* long-running stories. But every single time I find them lodging, the show falls apart." He pulled his hands out from under hers and scrubbed at his round face. "I'm so tired. This is not how I want to exist anymore. I have so many other adventures I could be enjoying. All this staying in one place, worrying and plotting and comfort eating is quite literally weighing down my spirit."

She latched onto the only thing he'd said that made any sense. "Well, Chief, then maybe you should find someone else to, ah, create opportunities for those kids you want to help out." She offered a one-shoulder shrug. "Then you'd be free to pursue other — interests."

He straightened abruptly in his chair, which groaned in pro-test. "Why, Ms. Mink. I believe you are exactly right! That's what I need to do. I don't need to cast shows. I need to cast *life!*"

She blinked. "I don't think I—"

"You!" He stood up so fast his chair shot back and slammed into the wall. She jumped out of her seat, caught up in a sudden panic that he might fling himself across the desk and go for her jugular. But all he did was jab both index fingers at her and nod wildly. "Yes, it's you. You have experience. You've had a string of hits. Oh, my dear Ms. Mink, it's *you* who should be vegetating on this side of the desk, not I!"

This conversation was making her dizzy. But then a crystal-clear image of herself sitting in that cushy chair, behind that expansive desk, with her ankles crossed atop it while filing her nails and talking via speakerphone to some other network honcho filled her brain like someone had switched on a projector behind her eyes. Her pulse throbbed.

"Yes, that's it," crowed The Chief. "You're seeing it too, aren't you?"

"I, well," she said, dreamily. "Yeah. Maybe I am."

The image evaporated and she staggered, blinking. "What was that?" she asked, grasping the edge of the desk against a wave of nausea.

"That, Younger Sister, is the future. Yours and mine, which, with your able assistance, will be assured." He grinned so widely it looked as though his face might split along its equator. "Ms. Mink, I resign, effective immediately. You should expect a call from the network in, oh." He glanced at his watch.

Her ringtone, *I am Telling You*, sang out from the depths of her tote. Her gaze met his.

He winked. "Now."

She pulled out her phone, movements as slow as a dreamer's. "H... hello?"

A few minutes later, The Chief gathered up his few personal effects, tossed them into a large leather case, and strolled out of his office after a final, vigorous shake of her hand between his.

No, not his office.

Hers.

She had no idea how it had happened. Everything that had transpired over the past hour defied reality. But somehow she was certain that all the *T's* had been crossed and all the *I's* dotted, and that she was now, indisputably, the new network chief of TBN.

She stumbled around the huge desk and dropped into the leather chair that could accommodate at least two of her, waiting for the real world to snap back from the fantasy universe into which it had retreated. And when it did, she put her Jimmy Choos up on the desk, crossed her ankles, and activated the intercom.

Trusty Miss Snipe answered, "Yes, Chief Mink?"

"Please arrange a meeting with the whole staff for tomorrow morning. I want to be brought up to speed on plans for the fall schedule." *What else? Oh, right!* She grinned. "Get Bear Corazón on the line. Time we gave those protestors what they want and get *Days* back on track. Then bring in a couple of the more promising sizzle reels for my review. We need some new blood coursing through our place from the top down."

"Yes, ma'am, right away."

Shawnda leaned back in her chair, folded her hands behind her head, and smiled up at whatever gods had granted her this favor, vowing in her heart to make them proud.

IV.

"Ms. Coyote!" Shawnda exclaimed, extending her hand across

the expanse of her desk. "Thank you for coming in on such short notice."

The tall, slim, elegant brunette's face had an ageless quality that came from either nature or really skilled Botox injections. She gave Shawnda a surprisingly firm handshake. "But of course, Ms. Mink. I was delighted to hear from you about my pilot so soon."

Shawnda indicated the visitor's chair and sat. Ms. Coyote sat down and rested her right ankle atop her left knee. Shawnda blinked, surprised by the inelegant casualness that seemed at odds with her guest's posh outward appearance, but then brushed off her reaction as internalized misogyny.

"I won't keep you hanging on tenterhooks," said Shawnda. "I watched your pilot, the other execs reviewed it, and we're all in agreement that it's a winner."

Ms. Coyote grinned ear to ear. "So, you liked it then? Oh, good. I spent a lot of time on getting everything right, from the script to casting. Especially the kids' parts."

Shawnda felt a strange, niggling doubt tickle the back of her brain. She gave her head a quick shake to dislodge it and said, "It shows, Ms. Coyote." She glanced down at the notes provided by faithful Miss Snipe. "May I call you Kunu? Such an unusual name, I love it."

Somehow, Kunu Coyote's grin stretched wider. "I wish you would. It's Winnebago in origin."

Yes! The other suits would be thrilled that they could now claim a Native American among their diverse stable of showrunners. "Well, like I was saying, we were especially impressed with the cast. Those kids are simply terrific. So natural. Wherever did you find them?"

"You might say I've been keeping them in a pouch around my

waist." Kunu snorted. "Ha, just kidding. We held open auditions and got lucky."

"Well, however you found them, I foresee a long run ahead for their show. We're picking you up for a full season, starting in September. How does that sound?"

"It sounds like I've won again," said Kunu, hugging herself. "Oh, Ms. Mink, thank you! You have no idea how long I've waited to find *Olivia and Teddy's Misadventures* secure lodging. Once I was less distracted, I had time to realize the trick was letting the kids play themselves instead of pretending to be others, and everything just fell into place."

For some reason, an alarm bell rang in Shawnda's head. *Why does this woman sound so familiar? Not her voice, but her words?* The answer kept slipping away, like she was standing in a fast-moving stream trying to catch a particularly slippery fish.

"Those other shows I put them in? Let's be honest, the quality just wasn't there, popular or not," Kunu was rambling. "I forgot my bigger purpose, you see. I do that sometimes. But it's my job to make things better for *all* my younger brothers and sisters, and though they didn't realize it, they deserved better stories than those dominating their airwaves. Once I had time to wander about and learn which shows resonate and why, I remembered this purpose. I put all the pieces together — the children and a quality tale that will enjoy lasting popularity, and soon my debt will be satisfied and this world improved. Even Younger Brother must accept this and finally leave for the Second World."

"That's... good?" offered Shawnda, uncertainly. *What's with all the talk about purpose and siblings? Must be an Amer-Indian thing.* "Anyway, I wanted to tell you in person how much I enjoyed your show and look forward to watching it on Thursday nights."

She rose and Kunu joined her, still smiling her toothy smile that seemed so at odds with her otherwise polished appearance. "Please stop by Miss Snipe's desk on the way out and she'll review the next steps for arranging soundstage time, a shooting schedule, and the like. Your representation will receive the contract before close of business."

"Thank you again, Ms. Mink," said Kunu. She extended both hands and grasped Shawnda's between them then shook the resulting hand sandwich energetically. "I knew you were the right person the second I met you. I look forward to a very long, mutually-beneficial relationship."

"Uh, huh," said Shawnda, retrieving her hand as politely as possible. She smiled despite a growing sense that she'd somehow been had. "Yes, well, you know even the best shows sometimes fail to find an audience. We have high hopes for *Olivia and Teddy*, but it's ultimately up to the viewers."

"Oh, I understand, believe you me." Kunu shrugged. "No worries. If for some reason this one doesn't catch on, I've got at least a hundred other ideas that will. Why, I dare say, I have the time and freedom now to come up with enough shows to fill TBN's schedule until this world ceases."

"That's... wow. Great, I guess." Shawnda shook her head slowly. Who did this odd woman remind her of? *It's not her looks or her voice. But the way she talks, what she says. I knew someone else who—*

"A pleasure to meet you, Chief." Kunu winked.

Shawnda grasped a revelatory thought and held onto it for almost a full second. But before she could say anything, Kunu Coyote waved and it swam away.

Two Horses
Elektra Hammond

"Why don't I have a horse to ride, Nanahuatl?" Hildr asked in a quiet, reasonable tone, as she trudged along behind Huat's horse. That meant she was plotting something. Again. The quieter she got, the closer he'd have to watch.

"There's only one horse. When I bring you back to your lug of a brother Thor, you can ask *him* for a horse to ride. And I told you to call me Huat."

"Or I can kill you in your sleep, *Huat*, and take *your* horse."

"You could *try*."

They'd had this argument before. Huat was almost sorry he'd spotted her alone in the woods and grabbed her, thoughts of ransom filling his head. There was more than a little one-upmanship in there, too, what with the competitive nature of his bloodthirsty extended family, everyone carving out their little piece of things. His brother Tecuciztecatl chasing around just added to the chaos. And her family! Fatalists, the lot of them, always Ragnarok this and Ragnarok that. It didn't stop them from squabbling with every other family in the meantime.

"It's your turn to make dinner," Hildr interrupted his not-so-very-deep thoughts.

"I made dinner last night. The squirrel, remember? *Your* turn tonight."

"Then let's stop early so I can fish."

"If we stop early we'll never get to the Dopplegangers."

Now where was he? If he was being honest with himself, it was

77

about the cash. He hadn't created the damn situation—he just wasn't above taking advantage of it. They'd barely escaped an altercation with the Greeks, so holier than thou....

"It's not *my* fault you're stuck out here," he said, trying for a conciliatory tone. "You were being escorted to the Bifrost. You would have been safe there. Your bastard brother Tyr is a Sentinel—he would have seen to your safety."

"My *escort* was corrupted by Huehuecóyotl," Hildr said, voice rising as she lunged at Huat. "He would have betrayed me."

"So you ran off to the woods. Brilliant. Now he's chasing you, my brother's men are chasing you, even your family is chasing you.... Is there anyone that doesn't want to kill you, ransom you, marry you, or ravage you?"

Hildr just stared at him. "My father loves me."

"Right. If Odin hadn't been so damn stubborn—by all that's holy, he gives new meaning to the word inflexible! Refusing to bend just got him banished from this plane of existence."

"My father. Is a. Man. Of. Honor," Hildr said slowly, through gritted teeth.

Nanahuatl pulled the horse around so he could look her in the eye. "What good is honor? It doesn't keep you warm at night. You can't eat it or drink it or screw it. He has his damn honor, but it forced him to abandon his family, leaving you and your sister Eir among the enemy."

"I can take care of myself," she snarled.

"I know. That's why I found you hiding in the forest with no supplies." He turned the horse back around and started moving again. He could feel Hildr staring daggers at his back.

Several minutes later, she spoke up again, "Eir can take care of herself." But she said it quietly, and her voice held no conviction.

As they came around the bend, Huat could see a wagon a ways down the road, an old man staring stupidly at the cracked wheel lying on the road. He turned back to Hildr, chuckling in disgust. "Stupid peasants. Can't even figure out how to fix a broken wagon."

He stopped laughing, though, when she changed her pace from trudge to run in a single step, bounding toward the wagon. He looked at where she was headed, and saw a ragged figure with an up-raised club heading purposely toward the old man.

"Look out!" Hildr gasped out.

Huat sighed, and kicked the horse into a canter, passing close enough for his leg to brush against Hildr, earning him a dirty look. He drew his sword—in seconds he was swinging on the old man's attacker....

... who heard the horse coming, turned, and fell to his knees. "Please, please don't hurt me."

He pulled back his sword. He'd make it quick. He swung, and—

Hildr grabbed his arm.

"What? I was helping. I nearly cut off your arm."

"You wish."

He pointed. "The sneaky little creep you didn't let me kill is running off."

Hildr took off again and tackled him. He had to admit, she was pretty agile for her size. He rode over and dismounted, interested in what she would do.

She smacked the ragged man. A boy, he saw, height and dirt making him look far older than his years. "Why were you going after that old man?" she said, putting a bit of snarl in her voice as she hit him again.

That's all it took to break the boy down. *Nice technique*, Huat admitted, grudgingly.

After a few sobs, the boy said, "I was hungry. I just wanted something to eat."

"What's your name?"

Huat and Hildr both turned to look at the old man, Huat to the side, and Hildr awkwardly up from her position on top of the boy. He'd made no noise walking up to them, and probably could have wounded at least one of them, if he'd been so inclined. Fortunately for them, he didn't seem to be.

"Rast. I'm Rast."

The man looked at the armed figure of Huat, and the more diminutive, but no less dangerous Hildr, as well as Rast and the club now a safe distance away. He said, "I'm Benet. Thankee. My place is near, but my wagon's broke. I'll feed ya if you get it going." He turned to Rast. "I knew your kin. I got room for ya, but you'll work for your keep."

Rast nodded, tears still running down his face, but slower now.

Back over at the wagon, Benet directed the others to efficiently get the wheel back on the axel.

"That'll hold for a bit," Benet said, when they were done. "Fix it better later."

Benet led them to his "place": a small one-room farmhouse, snugly built against the winter. They made quick work of feeding the cart horse and Huat's mount, leaving them in the equally snug barn.

He showed them proudly around the surprisingly tidy room, then stoked up the fire, put on a pot, and quickly added vegetables from a basket, dried herbs from a shelf. "Wife died last winter. She was better at this. Sorry."

Huat glanced around—he was observant by nature and his training had honed it to a fine art. Benet had next to nothing, and he was still willing to share. Despite the lack of meat, the stew smelled ... good. "Back soon," he said, and *looked* at Hildr, "wait."

Outside, he silently slipped into the woods, listening carefully. A rustling to his right—he popped a dagger into his hand and tossed it. He walked over and picked up the bird. Not very large, but better than nothing. He brought it back to the farmhouse and quickly plucked it and passed it to Benet, who nodded and cut it up and added it to the pot.

Dinner was the best they'd had in a long time.

The next morning, they set off in a much better mood. It was even sunny.

"Can I ride the horse today?" Hildr asked.

"Let me consider that request," said Huat. "No."

Well, at least *Huat* was in a better mood as they trundled along the road.

He tried again later, "It's a good travel day, the more ground we cover, the sooner I can get you to Thor. And I can get a fresh start. Someplace far away from here."

"I'd move faster if I had a horse."

"Do you ever talk about anything else? I haven't got a spare horse tucked into my saddlebag, you know."

Could be worse, Huat thought. She could be whining about a horse in the rain. He was musing about where he would go after he ransomed Hildr; maybe take passage on a ship somewhere that the winters weren't as harsh, away from family politics.

"That's an inn up ahead," Hildr announced, knocking him out of his reverie.

"A small one," he agreed. "So?"

"We could get a decent meal, sleep in a real bed."

"We had a decent meal last night."

"Yes, but a real bed."

"We don't have extra coin to pay for a bed. We can sleep in the woods. Tonight will be dry."

"And cold."

"No." And it was settled.

Or so Huat thought. Until Hildr resolutely ducked into the inn before he could grab her, and sat down. He tied up his horse and followed her. He stopped short when he saw the men already in the common room, they were wearing his family colors. He quickly sat with Hildr, his back to the other occupants.

"We need to leave," he said, urgently. "Now."

"Quiet," Hildr said, just as urgently. "Listen."

One of the men on the other side of the room was saying, "Best job ever, working for the Hill on a Horse. All we have to do is take what we want. If they don't give it to us, we kill them."

"And the pay ain't bad, either," chimed in another.

"That's the group that killed my friends," said Hildr, quietly. "You need to kill them."

"Too many of them," he said. "And they work for my brother Tecuciztecatl—you heard them—the Hill on a Horse."

"Are you scared? They're drunk. And stupid. I thought *you* were a great fighter. I'll do it myself."

"You? You've never killed anyone."

"I have." Hildr reached over the table and plucked his dagger from his belt, then walked quickly over to where the men were drinking. She caught one's eye and crooked her finger at him, holding the dagger behind her. He slipped down the bench and tried to pull her on to his lap. She checked to be sure his friends weren't watching, and slashed his throat.

"Damn," said Huat from right behind her. "Now I have to kill them all." He pulled his sword and made short work of two of them, the last one ran for the door. Hildr tripped him, and put the dagger in his back.

"See," she said, "that wasn't so hard."

Huat nodded. "Didn't think you had it in you." He looked around, then turned to the innkeeper, quivering by the door. "Two bowls of stew." He quickly searched the bodies, keeping the coins.

When the food came, he looked pointedly at the innkeeper while putting a coin on the table. "For the food." Another joined it. "We were never here." He pointed at the bodies. "I'd throw those in the river." Two more coins. He looked at Hildr. "Time to go."

Outside, he pointed at four horses tied in a row outside the inn. "Those belong to the thugs inside. Which one do you want?"

Huat nominally led the way to the Dopplegangers, Hildr riding beside him, for once a smile on her face. He did not return the smile. "We should make it to Thor soon."

"Well, yes, now that I *finally* have a horse."

"It's your turn to make dinner."

"It was *my* idea to stop at the inn— so your turn."

Some things never changed.

The Sisters Three Approximation
Russ Colchamiro

"What's up, peeps?" Rav said, strutting into Lonny's spacious, two-bedroom apartment. Lonny was in his armchair, while their mutual friend Henry sat across from him, on the center of the couch.

"Hey, Rav...," said the diminutive, bowl-haired Henry Wallenstein, who turned to face the door. "Who, uh, who do we have here?"

Posing with black-tinted rock star sunglasses, even though they were indoors, Rav Kurapati smirked. "Boys ... say hello to my new friends. Maddy, Euri, and Thini. The Sisters Three. Ladies ... this is Henry and Lonny."

A brown-skinned, casually well-dressed transplant from New Delhi with a soft Indian accent, Rav was accompanied by three young, beautiful women. He threaded his arms along their backs.

Undone by Rav's new posse, Lonny Heffsnorter tried—and failed—to speak coherently. "Where ...?"—the experimental physicist adjusted his dark-rimmed glasses as his voice cracked and then fidgeted awkwardly with the drawstrings on his hoodie—"where did you meet them? Who are they? How ...?"

"They're visiting lecturers at the University," Rav said. "They all have PhDs in Greek mythology. They're working with me," he added, and smirked again, "in my lab. My job *is* to study heavenly bodies. To really get to know them. I am an astrophysicist, after all."

The three young ladies giggled, the two immediately next to Rav on each side of him giving a kiss on the cheek.

"When you s-say *helping in the lab*," quivered Henry, an MIT-trained aerospace engineer, who, like Rav and Lonny, was a scientist at Caltech, "you mean...?"

"Relax, you tiny man-child," Rav said. "I completed my cross-referenced research project based on the new star coordinates to match NASA's report on the constellations. It started from the brouhaha about the change in Astrological signs, but it gave us a chance to promote Caltech's relationship with the University of Athens. We're giving a lecture here next week. I'll be discussing the astronomy, and my brilliant new colleagues from the exotic Greek islands will address the mythology behind each constellation."

"Much like the stars that guide the Cosmos," said Maddy, a raven-haired stunner with milky-white skin, light green eyes, thick, pouty lips, and a honeyed voice, "the company a man chooses to keep reflects the constellation of his truest desire."

"Rav praises your friendship and hospitality," said Euri, a tall, oval-faced blonde with hazel eyes, and a silvery cadence. "You orbit him, as much as he orbits you."

Thini, a curvy brunette with brown eyes, olive skin, and thick, well-groomed eyebrows, continued. "In our culture," said the loudest of the Sisters Three, "a man who opens his home and heart to travelers is to be showered with respect. Civilization is but a collection of strangers who unite in their pursuit of the gods."

Regaining his composure, Lonny found his manners. "Henry," he said, gesturing with his hands for Henry to scoot over. "Be polite. Give our guests the couch."

"Are you kidding me? I'd give them my *lap* if I didn't already have a weekly appointment with Human Resources. You make one remark about the Dean's wife and they label you a pervert."

"You said she should visit the astrophysics lab because perfectly shaped moons orbit her chest," Lonny said. "What did you *think* was going to happen?"

Henry shifted into a chair, while Rav took the couch's center cushion. He gently, and gentlemanly, guided Maddy and Euri to share the right side cushion next to him, while Thini sat on the arm of the burgundy leather couch. The far corner cushion closest to Lonny was left unattended.

The seating arrangements scrupulously followed the conventions of the compulsively well-tended apartment, decorated with framed movie posters, classic comic books sealed in protective plastic bags with backing boards, superhero and SciFi action figures, and several computer stations and gaming consoles.

"Can I offer you something to eat?" Lonny asked meekly, curling his hands as he spoke. "We're a little low on supplies right now, but we've got Hot Pockets, squeezy applesauce, gluten-free chocolate chip granola bars, and assorted juice boxes?"

"Not to worry," Rav said. "I'm taking my girls out for dinner at *Italiana Rosana*."

"*Italiana Rosana*?" Henry said. "A meal there costs more than the new argon laser we installed in the engineering department."

"Yes," Rav said, grinning. "It does. But the University is picking up the tab, so ... Champagne and strawberries all around. (He pronounced strawberries as straw-buhr-ees.) Right ladies? How does a little bubbly sound?"

"What better way to bond new relationships," Euri said, "than by sharing a luxurious meal and all the delights that come with it."

"Devouring the soul of what once was alive," Maddy added, "is to experience its rebirth."

"And we love to eat," confessed Thini, whose silk blouse revealed a plunging neckline. "Our appetites are boundless."

The apartment door opened in just then.

"I know it burns a little, Bridget, but that's what happens when you let Ming Mae wax your eyebrows. She's got a wicked..." Lonny's wife Rose, a yoga-toned blonde with a perky figure, stopped mid-sentence. She stared at Rav and his new friends. "Lonny? What, uh ... what's happening right now?"

"Wow," said Bridget, her companion. Short and busty, she was a high-pitched microbiologist who worked as a pharmaceutical company researcher. "You girls are really pretty. Are you sure you're in the right place? Rose. They're even hotter than you."

"Yes, yes," Rav said with an extra lilt to his smile. "Sure, they're more attractive than a yacht full of supermodels, but they have brains, too. They all have PhDs."

"Them, too?" said Rose, who smirked, shaking her head with an amused chuckle. "Wow. Henry. That's gotta be killing you."

"Hey!" Henry exclaimed, with the gravitas of an eight-year-old declaring before his parents that he was, in fact, a big boy. He puffed out his nearly concave chest. "I may be the only one of us with a terminal Master's—except you, Rose—but I'm an Astronaut? That's right! I'm an Astronaut! Ladies, did Rav tell you I'm an Astronaut?! I went to *space*. I'm an Astronaut!"

They shook their heads *no*.

"Yeah," Rav said, grinning with a sly sense of masochistic pleasure. "Funny, how I forgot to mention that."

"I'm sorry," said Rose. "I'm Rose. Lonny's wife ... for now."

"I'm Maddy. And this is Thini and Euri. Rose, are you a scientist, too?"

"Well ... not really," she said. "I'm a pharmaceutical sales rep. I drink a lot of wine then fake my *interest* in science. Does that count?"

"Ha. You're funny. Lonny. You're very lucky to have such a beautiful and witty wife. Did you know that Aphrodite, the Greek goddess of love, was often depicted with roses around her head, feet, and neck? Rose is a glorious name. It suits you."

"Aw. That's so sweet," Rose said, and swatted Lonny on the arm. "See that? I'm a Greek goddess of love. And don't forget it." She chuckled at herself. "Not that I'd ever let you."

"And you must be...?" Maddy said.

"I'm Bridget. I'm married to the Astronaut."

"Henry visited the stars," Thini said. "Like the Gods before us, he stared into the great expanse. You must be very proud."

"Yes. I am. I'd be even more proud if he would stop staring at your cleavage."

"I wasn't, you know ... staring," Henry said. "I was concentrating on her ... intellect."

"And you girls are with Rav?" Rose asked.

"Yes," Euri said. "He's been wonderful; so romantic. He speaks of the stars with the elegance of Homer himself, our greatest poet."

"Three years ago he couldn't even *speak* to women without a cocktail," Rose said. "And now he's nailing triplets like the Fonz. Those must be some sonnets."

Rav shifted in his seat. "As I'm sure you know, Rose, from our crazy night of love when you got us drunk and took me into bed, I am indeed a passionate man, whether the beauty is right before me," he said proudly, nodding at his Greek guests, "or if I'm examining the Universe."

Lonny's roommate Shelby entered the apartment just then, holding two comic books, and talking to his girlfriend Audrey. "After all these years," the lanky, baby-faced Shelby said, "how can you not differentiate between the *Hulk* and the *Thing*?"

"They're both huge superhero monsters who smash things as a general form of communication," said Audrey, a dour-faced brunette dressed in an oversized wool-knit sweater and heavy clogs. "Forgive me for missing the nuance. I see no difference."

"No difference? No *difference*?" Shelby placed his keys in the bowl near the front door and dropped his shoulder bag on the floor. "Lonny. Is Rose similarly dense? Oh, who am I kidding? Of course she is. Oh ... hello. Who are all these strange people in my apartment?"

"Shelby," Lonny said, "these are—"

In unison, the three visiting women rose from the couch, mesmerized.

"Shelby?" Maddy inquired, batting her eyes.

"Shelby Copper?" Thini said, also fixed on Shelby.

"Caltech's lord of theoretical physics Shelby Copper?" Euri said.

Shelby was suspicious but intrigued. "You've heard of me?"

"But of course," Maddy said, walking away from Rav, and approaching Shelby. "You are the greatest mind of your generation. Your theories on black hole gravitational fields are revolutionary."

"Well, yes of course," Shelby said with half an aw-shucks nod. "And you are ...?"

"These wonderful ladies—" announced Rav, but was immediately cut off.

"We are the sisters three," the Sisters Three said.

"Maddy," Maddy said.

"Thini," Thini said.

"Euri," Euri said.

Shelby studied them. "Fascinating. And if I'm detecting your accents correctly ... and I'm sure that I am ... do I hear a Greek inflection, from Athens?"

"Oh, yesssss," said the Sisters Three with an extended lisp.

"You are even more observant than we had heard," Maddy said. "We have PhDs in Greek mythology. But as you know, while mythology is the study of collected stories of a shared culture, constellations were named for the Greek gods in reverence to the Universe itself, and the celestial bodies inhabiting a realm deemed worthy only of those very gods. Your studies in the field of quantum physics—and thus the stars—have advanced our own understanding of mythology far beyond what we had thought possible."

The socially oblivious Shelby did a quick survey of the others in the room. He paused, contemplating the appropriate response. "Welcome to my humble abode," he said finally. "Rav. Extricate yourself. Make room for my guests. And why are you wearing sunglasses? You look more ridiculous than usual." Shelby took to the cushion at the far corner, the prominent spot on the couch. His spot. "Maddy. You sit here, next to me. Thini, Euri. Please. Join us."

"Hold on," Rav said, left to stand on the opposite side of the room, separated from the Sisters Three. "These are *my* lovely ladies—"

"Pipe down, Dr. Dre," said Audrey. "Shelby. Aren't you going to introduce me? You're being very rude."

Shelby nodded. "Yes … very well. Sisters Three, this is Audrey. Audrey, these are the Sisters Three. They are brilliant and insightful and worship my mind, which, I suppose, is redundant. Nevertheless..."

"Yes, Shelby. But I'm also a neurobiologist at Caltech. And your girlfriend."

"Oh, pish-posh. I'm sure they're not interested in that."

"Oh, but we are," Maddy said. "Any woman to capture the heart of such an intellectual warrior is either brilliant herself, or a specter assuming familiar form."

"I can assure you," Shelby said. "Audrey is quite temporal. Although her constant chirping about my *need to be right*, which—let's face it, as a certified genius—I usually am," he huffed, mocking Audrey, "can be quite banshee-ish, now that you mention it."

"Hey. I have something to say," Rav interjected, and tugged on his sport jacket, which he wore open and over a thin sweater and collared shirt. "I've worked *extremely* hard to attain a certain level of standing, respect, and expertise in astrophysics. *I'm* the one who's giving a lecture at the University, and these three ladies have traveled all the way from Greece to accompany *me*, on *my* talk, because of the work that *I've* done. I'm getting a little tired of being dismissed here. I'm a sensitive and soulful man, and my feelings are hurt. Today isn't about Shelby. It's about, well ... me."

The room went momentarily silent, reflecting a shared acknowledgment that Rav had, in fact, been unfairly pushed aside.

After a long pause: "Sorry," Lonny and Henry said.

"Yeah," Rose and Bridget said, "sorry."

"Ssshhheldon," Maddy said, becoming even more animated. "Rav has made a testimonial, a claim to prominencsssse, before witnessezsssses, in defiance of your standing. This is *your* dominion, and you are its *lord*. Do you let this transgression go unanswered?"

Unprepared to be challenged, much less on a grandiose level, Shelby gathered himself. The group waited again in anticipatory silence, staying clear of the fracas lest they be drawn in themselves. Sheldon rose from his spot.

"Rav," the former child prodigy with a genius level IQ offered gently. "You are a most amusing acquaintance—I daresay even, my friend. You have indeed achieved some notoriety in the field of astrophysics, and for that, you should be commended. Being asked to give a talk at the University is an honor."

Rav nodded, smiled. "Thank you, Shelby. That means a—"

"However, my strangely sun-glassed friend," Shelby continued, stepping forward, physically plying his authority over Rav, "let me set a few things straight, as if they really need to be unspooled. First ... your research," Shelby said, making air quotes in reference to *research*, "is nothing more than a recitation of someone *else's* work. Not exactly what the Nobel Prize committee looks for when it comes to advancing the understanding of the Universe. Second ... if you require accolades for rewriting derivative data, then I'm afraid you are already on the accelerating down slope on the y axis of your career. Aaaaand last ... of *course* today is about me. It is, after all, my apartment, and, let's face it, I'm a genius, and you are, how should I say ... not."

"Shelby," Audrey said, "don't you think you're being harsh?"

"Actually," Maddy said, her eyes glowing yellow as she spoke, "Ssssshelby is acting as the lord of his dominion should—asserting his prominence."

"Yesssss," Thini said. "In ancient Greece, Hera ordered the creation of the lion. It lived in a cave in the Nemean Mountains and killed interlopers and cattle down in the valley. Hercules strangled the lion as one of his tasks. He wore the sssssskin as a trophy."

Shelby perked up. "So you're saying that, in this analogy, I am Hercules and Rav is the lion?"

"That isssss correct," Euri said.

"Well, I am nothing if not a dead ringer for Hercules," Shelby said. "But Rav? A lion?" He chuckled. "Fheh-heh-heh. Oh. I don't think so. Although ... I did just skin him raw." Shelby pawed at his shoulders—limp, droopy pads that anyone other than he quickly recognized were about as un-Herculean as a grown man's body could support. "My, this skin *is* a perfect trophy, though."

"You know," Rav said, pouting, "you guys really suck. I'll just sit over here like a mute."

"Ahhh," Shelby said, basking in triumph, "back to your old ways with the ladies, I see. Atta boy."

Shelby took a moment to enjoy his victory before Rav spoke again.

"Fine," the Caltech astrophysicist said in defeat. "You're right. But at least," Rav continued, and subtly reached into a gift bag he had brought with him, "allow the Sisters Three to discuss their findings. As I'm sure you'll agree, Shelby, they have made tremendous inroads into further connecting the origins of Greek mythology with the science of Astrology."

The apartment went silent, preparing for the inevitable, forthcoming lecture filled with exasperated derision they had all come to begrudgingly accept as being part of the Shelby experience.

"Astrology, Rav? *Astrology*? Really? Why oh *why* must you make things worse for yourself? Isn't it enough that I just gave you a proverbial atomic wedgie for uttering your nonsense? And now you insult my guests by correlating their brilliance in Greek mythology and the examination of the constellations to a summary of the Big Dipper as described on the back of a cereal box that Rose eats? The cereal, that is, not the box. Although sometimes I can't tell."

"Hey," Rose said. "I don't eat the box."

"Actually," Lonny said, "last week you tore the box top off of *Count Crunch & Munch* and ate it thinking it was a piece of chocolate."

"Hey. I was drunk. And it was dark."

"It was noon, and you forgot to take off your sleep mask."

"Thus proving my point," Shelby said. "Astrology is to science what Rose's only movie, *Killer Penguin Streetwalker Seven: A Love Story* is to classic cinema."

"You know not what you sssssspeak," said the Sisters Three, who stood up, confronting Shelby. Their eyes glowed yellow. Their shiny, immaculately groomed hair morphed into thickets of live, venomous snakes.

"There is much to be gleaned from the position of the sssssstarzsssss," said Maddy, whose front-most serpent snapped at Shelby.

"Yesssss," Thini said. "Even Zeusssss studied the sssssstarzsssss." Seven of her head snakes hissed at each other, and then at Shelby.

"Do not underesssssstimate the influence of the sssssstarzsssss," Euri said. "They are the power of the Sibyls. Their prophecies were influenced by divine inssssspiration. They tell ussssss about the future."

"Oh, not you, too," Shelby said. "I've heard of women getting their panties in a bunch, but your hair coming alive? Speaking in tongues? That's a bit much, even for your gender."

"What do you mean?" Maddy said, her glowing eyes now burning crimson.

"Yesssss," Thini said, whose eyes did the same. "Exsssssplain yourself."

"Exsssssplain yourself to the Sisters Three," Euri said.

"Indeed," Rav interjected, and from within the gift bag quietly handed each of his friends—except Shelby—a pair of black-tinted sunglasses, which they now wore. "Show respect to these superior minds. Explain yourself."

"Them? Superior? To *me*? I don't know who you think you are, but any so-called *doctor*," Shelby said, making quote marks once again, "who not only believes in but actually *endorses* Astrology as an actual science is a Doctor of Poppycock from the University of Hooey, Hogwash, and Humbug."

Just then the entire apartment began to shake and tremble, as if under the spell of an Earthquake. Or forces far more deadly.

"WE," the Sisters Three proclaimed, "DO NOT JUST SPEAK OF GREEK GODS AND MYTHOLOGY. WE *ARE* ANCIENT GREECE INCARNATE."

"Medusa," Maddy said.

"Stheno," Thini said.

"Euryale," Euri said.

The Sisters Three grew taller. Their eyes glowed red with the flames of Zeus's stolen fire, their head snakes unleashed poisonous fangs, and their skin, no longer desirable human flesh, transmuted into green, prickly, decaying scales reeking of ancient, unholy death.

"AND WE ARE GORGONS," the Sisters Three continued. "THE DAUGHTERS OF PHORCYS AND CETO. WE DO NOT TOLERATE THE TRANSGRESSIONS OF MERE MORTALS. WE ARE THE GODZSSSS. AND YOU SSSSSHELBY, ARE NOTHING BUT FLESSSSSHHHHH AND BONE WITH A PAGAN'S PETULANT TONGUE. DO NOT TEST OUR PATIENCE."

"Now listen here," Shelby said. "You don't come into my home and …" He nearly erupted into a fit of intellectual rage as Medusa took her place on the corner of the couch reserved for Shelby and Shelby alone. He jabbed his finger sternly and with mortified intolerance towards the apartment door, instructing the Sisters Three about where to take themselves across the spectrum of mythology itself. "Don't make me get all Perseus and behead you evil wenches. Get out! Get out of my *spot!*"

With that command, the Sisters Three and the hissing lethal snakes focused their combined, ancient power at Shelby. Their eyes flashed with incendiary illumination. The air around them shuddered. And Shelby, who had just insulted the very essence of the Sisters Three, instantly turned to stone, permanently captured in his pointed pose. His face was locked in a puckered-lip scowl.

The others, protected by the sunglasses, stared, their jaws hanging open.

"Well then," Rav said as the Sisters Three resumed their gorgeous human forms. Rav placed his arms at his sides, and bent his elbows. "Ladies? Shall we?"

Maddy and Thini each took Rav by the crook of his arm. Euri snatched Thini's free elbow.

"Rav," said Lonny, gratefully wearing the shades Rav had supplied, "how did you know to bring the sunglasses?"

"What can I tell you? Do not underestimate my powers."

"Try again," said Rose, making her own quote mark gesture, mocking both Rav and Shelby, "your *powers* come and go pretty fast."

"It could also be that Kripco tried soliciting the Sisters Three at the University," Rav confessed. "They responded pretty much how'd you think. Although … Kripco *does* make a great coat rack."

"So who's in the mood for Italian?" Henry said as the gang spilled out into the hallway. "I'm feeling like a veal parm."

Rav offered a slight nod. "Ladies? Do you concur?"

"Oh, yes. We love to feast with friends. Especially with ones as cute as you."

"You'll get no argument from me," Rav said, leaving the apartment—and stone statue Shelby—behind. "I'm all yours."

"Yesssss," the Sisters Three said, smiling as their eyes glowed yellow. "Yesssss you are."

Out of Sight
Cliff Ackman

Knock – Knock...

Knock – Knock...

Slumber retreated and the muse opened his eyes to gloom. He felt heavy and lethargic making standing and walking difficult.

Knock – Knock...

Stumbling to the picture window, he swung open the curtains revealing a town of winding narrow streets lined with small, colorful apartments – a town he had never seen before.

Knock – Knock...

Turning back to the room, he saw the morning light illuminate a room of muted black, off-white and grey that reinforced his mood. He made his way to the entrance, opened the door, and looked down.

A dwarf dressed in a tuxedo raised his top hat. Without a word he reached into his vest pocket and presented a card.

The muse accepted it and read, *Questions and answers exchanged. House #II One Post Meridian* He inhaled preparing to ask a question, but the dwarf was already walking down the short flight of steps to the lane.

An energetic, middle-aged goddess walked up the steps passing the dwarf, "Good morning, Number VI!" she said in a cheerful, melodious voice as she edged past the muse.

Using his anger to drive away the slumber and lethargy, the muse followed her back inside. "Who are you? What is this place?"

"I'm Number XXXVII." She opened a window, letting in a breeze. "And this is The Polis."

"Where am I?"

"The Polis." Number XXXVII smiled as she repeated the obvious answer. She fluffed pillows and straightened up the room.

In determining his location, the muse thought – distance, speed, time. "When did I get here?"

Still cheerful, Number XXXVII paused in her duties and looked up. "I don't know, Number VI - a few days ago?"

"Why do you keep calling me Number VI?"

"That's your name."

"How do you know that?"

Number XXXVII puffed out a short laugh and spread her hands. "This is Number VI's Cottage." She opened a closet to present a grey jacket with a large pin prominently displaying the number VI. "These are Number VI's clothes." She reached into the pocket, pulled out a plastic identification badge and handed it to him. "And this is your picture."

The muse looked at his image underneath a glittering, multicolored numeral VI. "I am *not* a number! I am..."

She cut him off. "Yes, yes. I've heard that before. But we're all deities here. Lesser ones to be sure - no omnipotence or omniscience but we all have our fields of expertise. The local shop is run by the god of profit. The park and square are maintained by the god of spring. Then there's me – goddess of cleanliness and order." She motioned to the dust-free room, regimented in its tidiness and perfect dullness. "And you? Where in the pantheon do you fall?"

The muse grit his teeth. He turned toward the door to leave.

"Wait!" the word came with an urgency inconsistent with her introductory politeness.

He stopped.

She relaxed and continued calmly, "You should change first. And never leave your room without identification."

He stared at the goddess unsure of what to ask without getting an obtuse answer.

Number XXXVII held out his grey jacket with darker grey collar and his number VI badge. "Nonconformity is frowned upon. And they do like to impress that on newcomers, no matter who you were."

Curious of the reaction for a display of individuality and to the consequences "they" would impress upon him, Number VI studied the goddess before him. She smiled, a well-rehearsed smile that quivered from years of practice but not of happiness. His actions were his own and he accepted their repercussions. But his actions should not be seen as a failure on her part. He accepted the clothing. "I understand and should experience normal Polis first."

Number VI strode through The Polis looking for an information exchange. He passed dozens of demigods from multiple pantheons – Greek, African, Asian, Pacific. All were polite, well dressed and filled with the same grey color of his apartment. He merely nodded in response to their greetings.

Coming across a small shop, Number VI opened the door. An overhead bell rang.

"Good morning to you, Sir." The shopkeeper, Number CXXXIII according to his tag, put down a duster.

Straight to business, Number VI asked, "Do you have a map of the area?"

The shopkeeper glanced at his guest's button. "Maps are free and on the counter, Number VI."

The muse opened the top copy from a neat stack to reveal a map labeled 'Your Polis'. The surrounding countryside had a similar naming convention: The Mountains, The Beach, The Forest, The Sea. Number VI folded the map and returned it to the counter. "Do you have anything larger?"

The proprietor handed Number VI a color copy from behind the counter.

A customer from the back of the store came up to the counter and handed his purchase to the shopkeeper. He casually watched while Number VI looked over a map larger in scale but not in area. The deity deposited several bills on the counter, accepted his now bagged purchase and left the book shop.

"Until tomorrow." Number CXXXIII waved after the customer.

"No, no. Not larger in size, larger in area." Number VI refolded the map.

The shopkeeper accepted the map back. "Sorry, Sir. Just local maps."

Frustrated, Number VI opened the door. The ringing bell announced his departure.

"Until tomorrow." Number CXXXIII called after Number VI.

The muse glared at the shopkeeper considering the phrase an odd farewell.

Outside the book shop the other customer waited. "Good day to you, Sir."

Number VI ignored him and turned down the lane.

The customer followed. "Number VI is it?"

Number VI continued to walk.

"Having trouble remembering how you got here?"

That question stopped him. He turned to look at the book shop customer. The man's suit was similar to his, grey with a darker grey trim. A large button displayed the numeral XX.

Reaching out his hand the customer introduced himself. "Number XX. I was a hero from the Nordic Pantheon. What was your position in the Cosmos?"

"Number VI. I was... no, I am a muse."

They shook hands.

"Been here long, Number VI?"

"I woke up here this morning."

Number XX turned his head left and right looking for anyone interested in their conversation. "That's understandable. New arrivals aren't complacent. Not like these other good citizens devoid of internal color." He tilted his head to the right.

Number VI saw a man standing on a street corner, noticeable in his attempt not to be noticed. "I haven't seen The Beach yet. Doubt there are corners to stand on there."

Number XX nodded.

A short time later, the two non-complacent citizens walked along The Beach under a noon sun. Number VI asked, "How long have you been here?"

Number XX shrugged his shoulders, "Two months maybe. They don't have calendars. And I've tried etching the days in my apartment wall. The marks change from day to day -last week was day one hundred, today was day forty-one." The hero changed the subject. "Were you important in your pantheon? Will others come looking for you?"

"I don't know." Number VI picked up a rock and tossed it into the surf. "I don't know where we are, to have someone look for us. All pantheons are represented, so The Polis isn't theologically specific. Do you know how long The Polis has been here? I've never heard of any place like this."

"No idea. Eons? There are no noticeable characteristics of creation, duration, acclimation or organization. The stars are different every night. Tides don't correspond with movement of the sun or moon. The days don't seem to have a set number of hours either. Perhaps you can see some order in the day-to-day structured chaos. What is your talent, anyway?"

Number VI frowned and nodded his head. "Well, if today is any indication then I don't have a talent or an area of responsibility any-more.

"Then it should be easy for you to leave."

Number VI threw another rock into the surf. "I'm not so sure. Not all prisons have bars we can see."

"Hmm..." Number XX lingered on the verbal pause. "So you're a god of prisoners or captives. Is that right?"

Number VI pondered his answer for several moments before an-swering, "No. I don't think they could hold that sort of deity here."

"Why do you say that?"

"Deities derive their strength from followers – daily prayers, songs, hymns. Everyone here would befriend a god of prisoners for what he could do for them, meanwhile his energy levels coupled with his talent for helping prisoners would free everyone."

Number XX stopped. "Could a god of prisoners be behind this place?"

Turning to his companion, Number VI chided, "That's ridicu-lous. They help captives, they don't imprison them." He resumed his walk. "Anyway, we have to leave as soon as possible."

Taking some quick steps to catch up, Number XX asked, "Why is that?"

"I told you. Gods get their strength from worshippers..."

A high-pitched, metallic hum caught their attention. Together they turned to see a large white sphere bounding toward them.

"Run!" Number XX set off at a sprint.

Number VI followed the hero but the sphere gained on them ig-noring wind and ground. The sphere of samite shimmered as it rolled, bounced and undulated narrowing the distance between it and its tar-gets. Brushing against Number VI, the sphere numbed his shoulder throwing him off-stride. He stumbled to the sand. The sphere envel-oped him and his perception went blank.

"Hello."

Number VI opened his eyes on an older deity with a calm smile.

Attired in a grey suit but with a button displaying the number II on his lapel, the deity sipped tea from a china cup with matching saucer. "Welcome to my home, Number VI. I can tell we're going to be great friends."

Rubbing his forehead Number VI asked, "How do you figure that?"

"We both uh..." The wall clock chimed one. "...appreciate punctuality." Number II set his cup and saucer down. He motioned toward the pot and a second cup and saucer.

Number VI sat up and shook his head, dismissing the tea. "My arrival wasn't planned."

"Ah, yes. But it was scheduled. Sorry about your collection method. Your walk on The Beach was... taking you in the wrong direction."

"I didn't think casual walks had a right direction."

"Nonsense. Everything has a purpose. We just have to find it. You for example – inspiring the human race, even gods I would gather. Now I know, you and all the muses work on your individual responsibilities but when mortals the world over give you praise does that activate your talent or does your talent just naturally flow into them?"

Number VI suppressed a smile. "Yes and no. But let's talk about you. What is your purpose here?"

The deity stood. "I help to orient new arrivals, get them acclimated, talk with them in what, for most, is a... disconcerting time in their existence." He approached a door situated between two sunlit windows and motioned to it. "Shall we?"

Number VI looked at the other doors in the room, wondering where they lead but instead stood and followed his host.

"Excellent. We have so much to do. I'm sure you'll find our time together... enlightening." Number II opened the door, but rather than an open air, sunlit yard, a darkened room lay beyond. Walking through, the deity continued, "You've met several residents. How do they seem to you?" He turned expecting an answer but his companion stood near the door.

Number VI examined the windows. The visible 'exterior' was a painting lit to mimic a building's view in daylight. Crushed flowers and cut grass lay in a trough to provide an aromatic dimension and expand the illusion. Gritting his teeth, he stepped into the darkness and pulled the door shut.

A light shone directly above Number II. Echoes from the darkness impressed that the room was immense. The muse walked calmly but purposefully toward the deity and answered his question, "Manipulated. Complacent. Egocentric. All with a touch of fear." Number VI stood close, staring into Number II's eyes.

Number II turned away. "Hmmm. I don't see it. And actually, I see a lot."

The room's distance remained in darkness but as they walked, overhead spotlights turned on and off illuminating their continually changing location. The doorway that was their starting point was lost in the past; their goal unknown. Only their current steps could be seen as they walked over the drab, concrete grey surface.

"So all-seeing, like Helios, Horus or Shiva?"

The deity scoffed. "No. I rely on my flock of ravens. And here they are."

The two approached a wide, circular pit excavated into the ground. Several people sat at desks, their heads at the same level as the floor. At the center, two men sat on opposite ends of a large teeter-totter that rose and fell as it rotated on a disc. The men stared into monitors set before them, seemingly oblivious to the actions occurring around and to them.

"Muninn, bring up Number VI's morning." Number II looked up. Images of Number VI waking, talking to Number XXXVII, looking over maps, and walking along The Beach flashed on a wall. "Quite an eventful morning you've had."

"It isn't my morning I'm interested in. Do you have anything on my previous day?"

Number II accepted a manila folder from a clerk at a sunken desk. He opened it and scanned both sides. "Hmm. This is interesting."

Number VI waited while Number II looked over the information. He asked with a calm but firm voice, "Care to share that?"

Number II turned the folder around. "Empty. Apparently anything you've done before today doesn't matter." He handed the folder back to the clerk. "I'm sure it's only a matter of perspective. You must've done something. No one is completely without benefit." He paused, waiting for the muse to add to the thought, but met only reticence. "Come now. There must be something you're proud of, something you smile about, something you want on your headstone."

"There is more to come and I'm certain you'll be there to write it down."

"We do our best." Number II turned from the pit and walked into the darkness.

Number VI took a few steps to follow, but all light went out, leaving him in a Stygian darkness.

A spotlight cracked to life some twenty paces behind Number VI. He turned around but did not move. With no other frame of reference, the circle of light represented safety, certainty and a lure into another mental game. Approaching the light would reveal a desire and need. Extinguishing the light demonstrates their ability to marionette him.

The muse turned away from the light; toward the pit and walked. He did not need light to remember where Number II stood or the direction the deity walked when he left. Following the known path was less of a hazard then walking into the lure of light.

Before Number VI reached the edge of the pit, a spotlight illuminated Number II standing by an open door. "Come along Number VI. No one likes being kept in the dark."

Number VI maintained a steady pace as he approached. He held his emotions in check, showing neither anger, desire, anxiety, nor hope. Referring to the door, he asked, "Is this another example of your operation?"

"Not at all. We've returned so I can finish my tea."

Number VI was surprised to see the room they exited a short time ago. He turned to the darkness, trying to get his bearings. He realized they had taken an indirect route on their walk, but the direction never turned back on itself. There was no circuitous route that could have brought them back to this room. Cautiously, he stepped into the room. Everything was as they left it: the wall clock (now at 1:15), the white lounge indented from his repose...

"Something the matter, Number VI?" Mock concern oozed from Number II.

...Number II's chair was the proper distance from the lounge, his steaming cup of tea oriented in the exact position as when it was placed on the table...

"You seem troubled." The deity followed him into the room.

...the steaming cup of tea...

Realization dawned on the muse. "I'm not." Growing conviction ignited his ire. "This... orientation... was a demonstration of control. Your games of disorientation, of ambiguity, of instilling doubt – that has been illuminated this afternoon."

"I assure you, I have no idea of..."

The muse answered quickly. "Of course your assurances don't mean anything. Your tea is steaming."

"What of it?" Number II picked up his tea cup and saucer.

"Your tea is still steaming after fifteen minutes. That is not the cup you had. This is not the room we were in. And I am in control of my destiny." Number VI walked to the door on the opposite wall. He placed his hand on the doorknob.

"Where are you going?" Number II's voice rose to a shout.

Number VI turned the knob opening the door to a Polis thoroughfare. He turned his head just enough to glimpse Number II's restrained anger. Number VI smiled – a wry, knowing, half-smile that more information flowed to him than from him. He walked into The Polis, leaving the door open.

Number II seethed. He watched Number VI blend into the crowd and walk away. He sipped the tea, uncaring that his mouth burned.

Number XX stepped in from the outside, pulling the door closed. "I told you he would be a tough conversion."

Sipping the tea again, Number II responded, "That doesn't matter. We need him on our side."

Blinking in confusion, Number XX shook his head. "Why? Who is he?"

"Mneme – Muse of Memory."

The hero exhaled, "Ah... or forgetfulness."

Number II finished his tea. "Exactly. And once gods are forgotten, they fade away."

The Ode Couple
Michael Jan Friedman

Sing, Muse, of Zeus's son Hephaestus, who on the thirteenth day of the eleventh month was asked to remove himself from his place of residence. That request came from Aphrodite, his wife. In his heart, the blacksmith god hoped to return to her some day. With nowhere else to go, he appeared at the doorstep of his fellow Olympian, the wine god Dionysus. Sometime earlier, Ariadne, the wife of Dionysus, had thrown him out in a similar manner, requesting that he never return. Can two members of the Greek pantheon share an apartment without driving each other crazy?

Tell us, o Muse, of Dionysus's inability to keep it in his pants. "All I want to do is have dinner with a couple of Maenads," he said, spreading rose petals on the floor. "Is that so much to ask? Try to have a good time, Hephaestus. No weeping, no sighing, no gnashing of teeth, no rending of garments, please?"

To this, dour, hunched Hephaestus replied, "I agreed to this evening for your sake, Dionysus, ivy-browed lord of the revel. I prepared a feast, slaving away in the fires of my blackened smithy. And how do you repay my generosity? You show up late, without so much as a phone call. We said seven o'clock for cocktails and eight o'clock for dinner. Now my brisket will burn like the towers of Troy under the torches of the cruel Achaeans."

To this, Dionysus replied: "This is no time for a quarrel, mighty-thewed and not-so-terribly-hunched Hephaestus. We have two beautiful Maenads coming over, ready to worship us, if you know what I mean. Can't you keep your meat moist?"

In response, Hephaestus said: "What am I, Poseidon?"

Before Dionysus could respond, the Maenads arrived. They were sisters and fair indeed, like sea birds flying free against a blue expanse of sky after it has been cleansed by one of Zeus's more violent storms; though in truth neither Maenad was quite a "10."

"I do hope we're not late," said Gwendolyn (an unusual name for a Maenad, but who are we to judge, o Muse?). "O, look at the flowers you've arranged! And smell the scented candles! And there are crackers! And dip!"

"Hephaestus made the dip," said Dionysus, placing an arm around his roommate's thickly muscled shoulders. "He's a regular little homemaker."

"Isn't that lovely," Gwendolyn cooed.

Gwendolyn's sister Maenad, Cisseis, added this: "And it's so cool in here." She closed her eyes and smiled. "It's hot as Hades in our apartment."

"Don't you have an air conditioner?" asked Dionysus.

"I'm afraid not," said Cisseis.

"Well, we do," Dionysus said with a wink. "If you like, you can stay here all night."

Cisseis laughed then, her lovely throat fashioning a sound like the music of Pan's pipes as he woos a beauteous maiden in a sunlit glen, his eyes gleaming lasciviously, his animal-like endowment...um, never mind.

"I told you about that one," said Gwendolyn, pointing a slender finger at the god of the vine. "He's naughty, he is."

"So," said Dionysus, "excuse me a moment while I get the wine. Entertain our guests for a moment, won't you, Hephaestus?"

And in the next breath, the party-god was gone, like the memory of a loved one after he has become dust and less than dust.

"Um, please, sit down," Hephaestus told the sisters.

As they sat on a flower-strewn divan, he eased his own misshapen body into a wooden chair. For a time, then, there was silence, and not of the comfortable kind, but rather the sort of silence that attends the funeral of a man no one liked.

"So," Hephaestus said finally, "Dionysus tells me you're Maenads."

The sisters laughed.

"Why, yes," said Cisseis.

"So we are," said Gwendolyn. "And you?"

To this, Hephaestus replied: "I'm the god of the forge. I make all the gods' armor. You know, Ares, Apollo…."

"Oh," said Cisseis, "how terribly exciting!"

"Yes," said Gwendolyn, "perhaps you can immortalize us on one of the gods' breastplates!"

"Well," said Hephaestus, "I guess if you do something spectacular."

"We've done spectacular things," Gwendolyn said, glancing mischievously at her sister, "but I don't think we'd want to immortalize them on a breastplate!"

The Maenads giggled then like…well, like two Maenads giggling. A lot. Giggling their bloody brains out.

Hephaestus, however, did not giggle. "My wife used to laugh like that," he said soberly. "Before, you know…"

"Did she perish?" asked Cisseis.

Hephaestus shook his head from side to side, like a great pendulum keeping time. "No. We're getting divorced."

Cisseis replied this way: "Oh."

"It's terrible about divorce," the smith-god continued. "You take two happy divinities and tear their lives apart..."

"You were happy with her?" asked Gwendolyn.

"Very happy," said Hephaestus. "I mean, she fooled around a lot behind my back. A ton, in fact. But when you're as beautiful as Aphrodite, you get a lot of offers."

"Is your wife as beautiful as Aphrodite?" Cisseis asked sympathetically.

Hephaestus responded to her question in this manner: "She **is** Aphrodite."

"Oh," Cisseis said again.

"Then she's beautiful, all right," said Gwendolyn. "Isn't Aphrodite beautiful, Cisseis?"

"Very beautiful," Cisseis agreed reverently.

"She was my whole life," said Hephaestus. A great sob emerged from him, as when a volcano erupts, spewing molten rock from the innermost bowels of Mother Gaia, which happens and isn't at all embarrassing at her age. "Please forgive me, I didn't mean to get emotional with you. It's just that...that..."

Cisseis and Gwendolyn left their divan then and put their arms around Hephaestus's shoulders.

"There, there," said Gwendolyn.

"It's all right," said her sister.

Gwendolyn sighed. "Now you've got me thinking about my poor Agapios. He died when...when..." Suddenly, she began weeping as well. "When he was gored by a boar."

Then Cisseis started weeping along with the others. "I was feeling so good a moment ago. Now I want to tear an enemy limb from limb and nail his extremities to his gateposts."

At that moment, Dionysus returned to the room with a bottle

in hand, and found himself in the midst of much wailing. "What in the underworld happened here?" he asked. "I'm gone three minutes and I walk into the formal mourning portion of the Protheis."

"We can't help it," said Gwendolyn, dabbing at her eyes with the hem of her garment.

"Hephaestus is just so sensitive," said Cisseis. "So fragile. I just want to take him in my arms and smother him."

Such was Dionysus's response, his brow arched in ill humor: "Yes. Smother him. Me, too."

Ultimately, Hephaestus's wife called him back to her bed, and he returned to her as might a loyal dog who has worshipped his master all his life but has been separated from him for a long time through no fault of his own. Yeah, like that.

Dionysus, on the other hand, never returned to Ariadne but succeeded in bedding Cisseis and Gwendolyn and many other Maenads besides. He was, after all, the god of revelry, and such fellows tend to do all right.

Swapped
KT Pinto

Sometimes a god's gotta go against his family to help a friend.

I mean, this wouldn't have been the *first* time I went against my family. Sometimes I just did it for the Hel of it. At least this time there was a legitimate reason for my little bit of fun. This time it was because of bonds stronger than the ones used to hold me down while I was tortured: the bonds of immortal friendship.

It took quite some time to plan this, but being immortal, the wait didn't bother me that much. I had to wait for just the right situation, become friendly with just the right immortals, and learn just the right ancient incantations…

The situation came in the guise of a bacchanal.

The Greeks and Romans aren't the only pantheons to have such an event, but I must admit that they host the best ones! So I waited until Bacchus announced the date of his upcoming Eostre party – inviting all the immortal families – to contact my trickster pals and start planning…

I know some people would take offense to their peers suddenly becoming silent and staring as you entered; I rather find it to be a commentary on my skills as a trickster god. Of course, the harsh and slightly drunken whispers that followed could have been from the fact that a crowd of trickster gods from all the pantheons followed behind me through the main garden gate. Under normal circumstances, this couldn't bode well… and whenever is a bacchanal a normal circumstance?

"My dear lords and ladies," I said with a flourish that would

117

make that Shakespeare fellow proud, "I apologize for our tardiness! We are here to provide some unusual and exciting entertainment for the esteemed Bacchus' guests."

An untrusting murmur went through the crowd, not that I could really blame them. I mean, I wouldn't trust me even with the Virgin Mary's blessing – and there was no way I was getting that anytime soon – let alone with over two dozen deceivers in my wake.

"We would like to play a game with you," I said as my cohorts started setting up four stations. "If you will let us. Something we will all enjoy…"

There was an obvious wave of confusion as the deities all looked towards their respective leaders for direction. Since this was a Roman event, the leaders in turn looked towards Jupiter. The long-bearded alpha-god turned to his Greek counterpart and then both of them looked to the god mistakenly considered my father. Of course, this silent discussion took too long for the more impatient among the gods in the various pantheons, and so the verbal debating started.

Have you ever tried to get a bunch of deities to make a decision? It's easier herding skogkatts. And then the fact that many of them were deep into the cups made the process even longer. I think that if it had just been up to the males, we would have been given the go-ahead without hesitation. But the goddesses… I was surprised at how adverse the females were to the Tricksters having control of the entertainment, even for a little while. Apparently they feared that we may have created entertainment full of debauchery and horrifying lasciviousness. That's right… the rulers of love, beauty, sex, passion, desire and lust were worried that we show would have too much gratuitous sex and nudity in it to be at a *bacchanal*.

I spent quite some time reassuring the goddesses that there would be no naked bodies, no full-frontal anything, no penetration, no means of ecstasy or heavy petting…

There would just be food.

That made the deities sit up and pay attention. This was the first time food had been mentioned, and – even in a party filled with wine and treats – deities from every culture love their eats.

It was a wild idea, but they really wouldn't expect less from us. It was to be a game, where contestants were given odd ingredients from which they had to make edible dishes, judged by three discerning palettes. The winner would receive various prizes, created by the craftiest (take that word as you'd like) of us. The contestants would be demigods (because pure immortal egos usually cannot handle losing to a peer), the judges, gods of my choosing. It seemed harmless enough – which is how I planned it – and we were eventually given permission to proceed.

As my friends continued to set up the game, I heard Woden say to his birds, "So tell me Huginn, Muninn: what do you think about this?"

"I think we should always be cautious where the Tricksters are concerned," Muninn answered.

Woden then turned his one eye to the other.

"I can't say for certain, Sire," Huginn said cautiously, "but I would definitely think twice about eating anything they serve."

Woden nodded thoughtfully as I walked away from them. "Very sage advice, my friend."

The judges were Anansi, Coyote and Laverna. The host was of course myself, to no surprise of any of the gods. The contestants were four obscure demigods who apparently had come to the party due to the good graces of their more powerful friends.

The other Trickster gods took on the task of choosing the mystery ingredients for the food bundles. During the first two rounds, it was

119

obvious to those who know their mythologies which god chose what. Coconuts, apples, beer, lettuce, nectar, sheep, goats, honey, fish and eels all made an appearance.

"Apologies for such simple fare," I said to our immortal audience as the second demigod lost round two and sat with the rest of the partygoers, "but it was, really, all we could whip up on such short notice so we would be able to entertain you this day. We saved the oddest ones for this last round."

The gods nodded in understanding, their mouths too full of the first two rounds of food to verbalize their consent.

"This final round will be our feast round, where our contestants will have to prepare – as is appropriate for this festive day – large, bacchanal-style meals in these cauldrons and using these secret ingredients." I turned to the last two contestants. "Please, open your bundles!

For this round we have: lobster claws, pickled eyeballs, octopus, blue and white chalk, and Babylonian figs."

The remaining two demigods looked at each other in confusion. What the hell were they going to make from that?

"Because it's a larger meal, we'll double the time for you to create."

The demigods tried to look like they were ready, but you could tell that they were stumped.

"How about this?" I said as two of my follow Tricksters brought out a huge cauldron. Judging from the looks one their mostly inebriated faces, I decided that none of them recognized the runes on the pot as anything more than decoration. "Why don't we change things a bit? Make things a little easier for our contestants. I mean, this was spontaneously planned and my cold heart feels that this might be a little difficult even for such excellent chefs."

There was a general murmur of consensus among the audience. It *was* a rather spur of the moment event; it was impressive they were actually able to do two rounds so far. It would be okay to bend the rules... this one time...

I continued, "So, if the judges would permit, I recommend that the contestants work together to make this final meal. And they'll be judged based on preparation, teamwork, presentation, and final result. Judges, what say you?"

Anansi tapped the tips of his four hairy front legs together. "Have them both use the same cauldron? Interesting idea."

Coyote nodded his furry head. "I think teamwork is essential. And then we'll add this result to their previous scores from other rounds."

"Brilliant!" Laverna said. They couldn't read her expression, because she had decided not to wear her head for the party. "Less chances for cheating and sabotage."

These were not surprising answers. My fellow gods were also friends with the one we were helping. They knew his plight and wanted him to get satisfaction just like I did. But I didn't want the blame to fall on us completely. "Because we are not the ones being entertained right now; this is not our event," I continued, turning to the audience, "I ask the opinion of my fellow immortals. Do you think this will be a good way to do a final round?"

The audience cheered loudly. I'm pretty sure that part of their excitement had to do more with the nectar, wine and ambrosia they had been devouring since the game began. Only Woden, who had taken the advice of his birds and had not eaten anything the Tricksters offered, didn't show any excitement at the prospect. He gave a slight nod as I looked in his direction, but I am certain it was more out of interest in what his mischievous foster son was going to do next than the actual goings-on.

I gave them a smile that most beings found trusting... unless you knew me all too well. Believe it or not, my family is not among those few. They knew me so little, they couldn't recognize me in a wig offering deadly mistletoe. They'd have no clue what I was doing if I told them step by step.

"Alright, so... to review... the ingredients in the bundles are lobster claws, octopus, pickled eyeballs, green soapstone, and Babylonian figs."

I had made the switch, and no one seemed to realize it... except maybe Woden, whose birds were whispering excitedly in his ears. From Woden's expression, they knew something was up, but they just couldn't figure out what. And since I wasn't going to tell them what was going on, they had no good reason to stop the game... especially since a false accusation may insult way too many pantheons for comfort. That's why I had my team helping me: not only extra hands, but an added buffer of protection.

The contestants didn't seem any more certain of themselves than they were beforehand, but they both leaned towards the one countertop set up behind the cauldron when I turned to them.

"We'll set 90 minutes on the digital sundial."

The audience leaned forward too, some not as steadily as others...

"Time starts now."

The contestants started chopping, peeling and shelling, creating a flurry of work to try to the disguise the fact that they had no idea what they were doing.

They had obviously decided to wait for the cauldron to boil before adding in spices, chicken broth, and various vegetables. It looked like they were hoping to make some sort of weird soup out of it... I knew soup was the last thing that was going to come out of that pot.

"Looks like they're making some odd kind of soup," Woden rumbled. If the wisest god in all the pantheons (I'm the shrewdest;

there's a difference) couldn't see past the chicken stock, then no one in our audience knew what was truly going on!

The contestants started adding the secret ingredients to the mix: the octopus cleaned and chopped fine, the eyeballs rinsed of the pickle juice and seasoned with saffron, the lobster claws shelled and diced the figs peeled, seeded and sliced, and then they started dropping in the soapstone...

Woden stood suddenly, startling the birds on his shoulders. He said nothing though; he knew it was too late...

Dark green smoke started pouring out of the cauldron, belching into the air and pouring onto the ground like an angry tide.

It took a moment for many of the deities to realize something was not right. The two innocent contestants had scurried to a corner of the room, holding each other in terror, not very much caring about the contest anymore. My fellow Trickster Gods had all assembled behind the judges table, eagerly watching the pot. I was standing alone by the garden gate, casually leaning against a tree with a wicked smile on my rather handsome face.

The ground began to shake and a huge crack started on the far side of the field and quickly traveled to and up the cauldron. It wasn't until the cauldron began to split that the majority of deities reacted to the situation.

They started to run.

Since they were all flying – some literally – for the gates in a very drunk and disorderly manner, most were blocked from leaving and saw the horror that started to emerge from the pot. Gigantic lobster-clawed hands gripped the sides of the cauldron and used it as leverage to emerge from the pot. A huge cephalopod head rose out of the pot, a few pieces of celery and carrots stuck to his skin. The eyes, tinted yellow from the saffron, scanned the bacchanal as the gods tried their damnedest to leave the area. A couple of soapstone-green tentacles oozed across the floor and wrapped around the legs of some fallen gods, raising them into the air as he stood to what looked like his full 15-foot height, although the lower half of his body was still in the cauldron.

He roared loudly as he lifted his claws and his victims into the air; it was an amazing sight, but sadly by this point he was performing to a nearly empty area.

I clapped as the roar died down, causing the last few gods in the area to jump slightly. "Great entrance, my friend," I said to the elder god.

The monstrous being bowed, his tentacles still holding his victims high in the air. "You don't think it was over the top?"

"Not at all!" I answered as my fellow Trickster Gods all cheered in agreement. Besides Jupiter and Bacchus, there were about a dozen deities left in the field – a few showing their true worth by being in a dead faint – and, of course, Woden.

The ruler of the Norse gods seemed unfazed by the creature in front of him. "After such interesting entertainment," he said to me, "how would you top it at the next party?"

"I don't believe we will have another opportunity to present our game," I answered. "Since an elder god such as my friend here is apparently not worthy enough to be at such events."

The monstrous being's tentacles drooped slightly. "I didn't get an invitation or anything."

"No invitation?" Bacchus asked with dramatic surprise, knowing better than to upset an elder god, "How could that have happened? I *must* have a conversation with Mercury about this oversight!"

The Elder One shrugged; I noticed he hadn't let go of his victims yet. "No one ever seems to want me at their parties. It gets… frustrating at times."

Eris called out from the judges' table. "I know just how you feel!"

Woden's one eye panned from her, across all the Tricksters behind the table, and then to me. "Maybe the Tricksters can plan the next event; make sure everyone is invited."

I nodded warily; what was the catch? "I see nothing wrong with that."

The elder god clapped his claws in excitement. "I'd like that very much!"

"And don't worry," Jupiter interjected. "We'll make sure *all* of the gods clear their calendars for your event. It will be a grand affair indeed."

"Excellent," Woden stood and headed towards the now-clear gateway, but paused and turned to his foster son. "Two things, Loki."

I hesitated, then turned to face my foster father. "Yes?"

"First," he said, "no more switching of ingredients. The name of this game isn't 'Swapped'."

I nodded, uncertain what exactly to call the entertainment. "And second?"

"Clean up this mess; your theatrics sent the cleaning gods running along with everyone else."

I watched my father leave along wish Zeus and Bacchus, then turned to my fellow Tricksters. "OK guys, let's start eviscerat... um... tidying up."

As the others got to work, the Ancient One dropped his victims with a thud and turned to me. "Do you think they got the message?"

I shrugged. "I would say yes, but being that that whole Troy situation didn't stop them from forgetting to invite people..."

The Old One climbed out of the cauldron and grabbed a broom. "Then, after this, let's start planning a party!"

Somebody's Got Talent!
Eric Hardenbrook

Richie Guns: Good evening America and welcome to this new season of *Somebody's Got Talent!* This is the show where the best and brightest compete for a chance to land a big time Vegas performance contract! I'm your host Richie Guns! We've got a spectacular show coming to you tonight from bright and shining LA. We've done live shows in the past to wrap the season up, but this time we're going to kick it all off live! That's right, LIVE! You'll see it just as we do, all the way from the front to the back!

We're all super excited to meet the new panel of judges this year, so let's get right to that!

First: our returning judges. Let's all welcome back the actor you know, the funny guy you love: Harry Vendal.

Next, the singer, the songwriter and all around 'scary' lady, let's welcome back Sam B!

And finally our new judge: among his many, many credits, he's said to be the giver of bliss. Let's give a warm round of applause for Shiva Cowl!

And now it's time to introduce tonight's first act. It's a duet from the Smith sisters. The Smith sisters have traveled all the way from Water Valley, Mississippi. They've lived their whole lives there. The town knows them for their dedication to the local music scene and particularly for the weekends when they sing in their home church on Main Street. Let's check out the song they composed just for our show!

Richie Guns: Shiva Cowl is jumping in first with his comments on the duet. Let's listen.

Shiva: Thank you, that's quite enough.

Sam B: Now, you don't have to be so harsh. They came up here and gave it their best.

Shiva Cowl: Their best clearly wasn't ready for our show today.

Harry Vendal: I'm going to vote for them. I think they've got a chance.

Richie Guns: Ever the spirit of hope, that Harry. It's two votes against one.

Shiva: You go right ahead and vote for them. I'm waiting to see the talent portion of our show.

Richie Guns: My goodness, Shiva Cowl is not giving anybody any slack today. So much for bliss! That's just the opener. After the break, we'll be back with our next talented hopeful.

Richie Guns: Welcome back, folks! Our next performer is a young man from a little town called Hamilton in New York State. Brian has been practicing his magic show for a number of years. He's using his show as a way to work through school. He's been struggling and really looking to make a move away from kids' birthday parties. He hopes to move forward to the prize money round as a way to get his tuition paid off. Let's see if he can wow the judges! Here comes a deck of cards - it's going to be some close up work for sure.

Shiva Cowl: That was not a very magical act.

Harry: Oh, come on now Cowl, don't be so mean to the contestants. I'm voting yes for him.

Sam B: No. I have to say no this time. I'm sorry.

Shiva Cowl: Can we move on? I do certainly hope something better is coming forward soon.

Richie Guns: Shiva Cowl is really not working well with what the show has to offer today.

Next up is Ronnie Rubber Chicken. Ronnie hails from Holton, Indianapolis. Oh my, he's a clown. Here he comes rolling in on a unicycle and juggling at the same time!

Shiva Cowl: NO, NO, NO, NO, NO! This is not a talent. This is not going to pass. Unacceptable!

Richie Guns: Shiva Cowl not even letting us get through the set up.

Harry Vendal: Now wait just a minute…

Richie Guns: Harry jumping to the defense of our performer.

Harry Vendal: I started off in comedy and it takes a lot of effort to get up there and do something like that.

Shiva Cowl: Significant effort is not the same as talent!

Richie Guns: Did anyone else feel that? I think we may have had a mini California trembler right there.

Harry Vendal: I think you're just afraid of clowns, Mr. Negative.

Richie Guns: Hold it there; I think that was another of our little quakes.

Sam B: I say we let Ronnie… whatever his name is go on and perform."

Richie Guns: Ronnie has hopped off the unicycle and does a quick handspring to land near the front of the stage. Doing his best to win over the judges!

Shiva Cowl: Fine. Tell him to do what he is going to do.

Richie Guns: It does not look like our judge is impressed at all. He is in fact turning away from the stage as if he simply won't watch.

Sam B: Ronnie, how long have you been performing?

Richie Guns: Sam B jumping in and taking over my job now.

Ronnie: Yo! I'm sorry he's so scared. I'm like a great admirer. I've been at this for real like 3 years now - WHOO!"

Richie Guns: Ronnie is off and waving to the folks off stage. The music is rolling and Ronnie has snatched the microphone from the stand. Here we go folks, the show is ON!

Ronnie is running back and forth on the stage rapping and pulling giant paper flowers out of his sleeves. WAIT, wait! He's jumped down the steps and he's running along the front of the judge's desk! What is he doing? He's throwing gold colored confetti into the air and across the heads of the judges! He's digging back into the pouch hanging from the front of his rope belt and going for another handful - and there goes Harry! Harry has leapt from his chair and dashed back from the table trying to avoid touching anything that Robbie has to offer.

Harry Vendal: No touching! There is no touching here!

Richie Guns: Harry looks skittish. He might run off the set! Oh, but there goes our clown back up onto the stage.

Ronnie: Yeah boyz! That's one the kiddies love every time YO!

Shiva Cowl: Now who is frightened Mr. Harry Vendal?

Richie Guns: The glitter doesn't seem to have had any sort of negative effect on Shiva Cowl. In fact he's actually looking a little better than he did before. The shimmer even seems to have extended to the fabulous trident necklace worn by our judge.

Harry Vendal: FINE! No to the clown! And NO TOUCHING!

Richie Guns: Harry hits the no buzzer and it looks like Ronnie won't be moving on to the next round.

OK folks, our next talent is another singer. Peter Valdez wants to break into music and go out on tour. His mother says he's got a heavenly voice and she loves to hear him sing, even when she doesn't understand what he's singing about. He's relatively local compared to some of our other performers. He's trekked on over from Peach Springs, Arizona to bring us his version of "Everybody".

Here he goes trying to get the crowd to join in with him…

Sam B: That was a bold choice to take on. There are multiple vocal parts. I did hear that you were trying to take on the various parts.

Richie Guns: Sam B certainly knows her music. She's crashed onto the scene a decade ago and is still working albums with her group when she's not going after her solo or television careers.

Sam B: I think there could have been some improvement in the middle…

Harry Vendal: I don't know if this was the best choice lyrically. I might have to vote no this time.

Shiva Cowl: Lyrically weak? Is that what you call it? That was somebody stepping on a cat for two minutes. It was painful to listen to and I felt sorry for the cat. This was a performance? Rubbish.

Richie Guns: Shiva Cowl blasting away with the negative comments and making the contestant rush off the stage.

Whoa, another trembler. This time even Sam and Harry looked around. Folks hold onto your hats, this is going to be a wild one!

We've got something special up next. Gary Ryan has come down the coast from Seattle. He's been working on and off as a street performer, but is looking for a way to break into the entertainment industry with his special physical abilities. Tonight Gary said he was going to 'Wow' us with his performance. I, for one, can't wait to see what he's got in store for us.

There goes Gary. He's headed to center stage where we've got a stand set up for him. On the stand is the suitcase he brought with him. It's a little smaller than normal, but otherwise looks like a regular bag you'd see somebody in the airport carrying. Oh my goodness - Gary has just bent and put the heel of his right foot against the back of his head. I saw him stretching out a little behind stage but this is crazy! I mean crazy! He looks close to being folded in half! I think he's going to try to fit himself into that bag!

Shiva Cowl: WHAT? You're going to bring this position to me! THIS is how you expect to impress me?

Richie Guns: Shiva Cowl has leapt up onto the judge's table ladies and gentlemen! He's roaring and waving his arms around in the air! He's going so fast I'd swear there were an extra set of arms there. Oh my goodness it's an earthquake! Take cover everyone! The other judges have scrambled under the table just in time! LOOK OUT! We'll be right back!

Richie Guns: Ladies and Gentlemen! I'm hoping the cameras are still rolling on this live show! The dust and smoke are starting to settle down some. It seems to me that the roof has actually collapsed and covered the stage. I can see Shiva Cowl still standing on the judges' table. He's looking around as if he's surveying the area for a good place to sit down. Harry and Sam appear to be safe under the table. All of the destruction seems to be centered around the stage. Let's see if we can get a look. I'm afraid for our performer since he was right in the middle of all that craziness!

A breeze. Thank heavens folks; we've got a breeze taking the dust and smoke away. OH MY GOD! There he is! Ladies and Gentlemen do you believe what we are seeing? Gary is still on the stand! Gary is still on the stand! He's standing on one hand with the rest of him folded inside the suitcase and using the hard back of the suitcase like a shield to keep the debris from the roof off of him! There he is STILL STANDING ON THE PLATFORM!

Shiva Cowl: Now THAT is a performance!

Richie Guns: I can't believe what I'm seeing! Shiva Cowl has just pushed the Platinum Paddle! Gary Ryan is moving directly through to the finals! What an amazing show! Gary's going through! Do you even believe what you have seen tonight?

I am just as stunned as our other judges look to be. That was our show. Join us next week to see what amazing and crazy talents come to the stage for this phenomenal season! This is Richie Guns signing off for *Somebody's Got Talent!* Good night everyone!

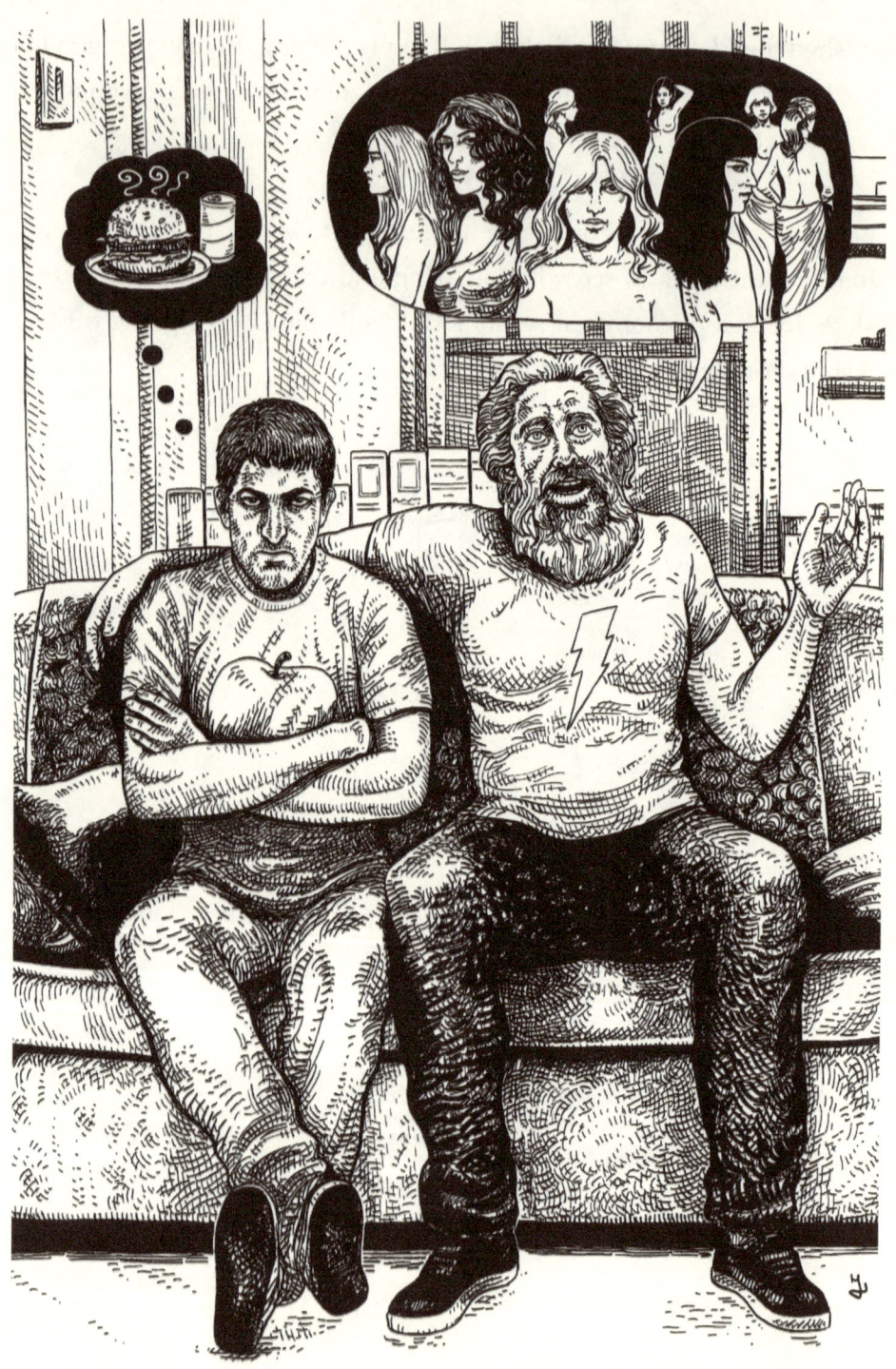

Godding About and Sleeping Around: Zeus' Conversation with Tatalus

Ian Randal Strock

"Son, I'm going to tell you an incredible story: the story of how I met your mother."

"But I'm already being punished."

"I know, but this is your break, so you can just sit there and listen."

"Uh, Dad, you caught me on the way to the kitchen. Can I grab a sandwich and get back to you?"

"Hang on, this'll just take a moment...."

I was soaring over the Saronic gulf when this cute little goat-nymph caught my eye. I just knew she was the one, but couldn't think of a way to separate her from the crowd of nymphs all around her. You know how those nymphs like to move in packs.

Anyway, I perched on a hilltop overlooking the meadow. I perched and I pondered, and then I saw a fast-moving shadow as an eagle flew by. Ah, inspiration comes from the strangest places, doesn't it, son?

So I turned myself into a giant eagle, swooped down, and managed to grab the object of my affections.

I carried her away, across the waters, to Oenone. After placing her gently on a bed of leaves, I transformed back into my more godly appearance, wooed the young lass, and had my way with her. Although I have to say, she had her way with me just as much. Let me tell you, son, those goat-nymphs really do know how to act like animals.

Although, animals is much more your Uncle Poseidon and Aunt Demeter's thing. But hey, different strokes....

At any rate, when we had finished with each other, I gave her dominion of this island (which, I later learned, was eventually renamed for her), and some time later, she gave birth to... your half-brother Aeacus.

In the fullness of time, Aeacus grew to manhood, and then to become king of what was then known as Aegina (after his mother). Well, you know how spiteful your step-mother can get. Hera was pissed at Aeacus, and sent a dragon, which carried off almost all the island's population. Really nasty dragon, that was.

So Aeacus, he was a king without a kingdom, and pleaded with me to restore his realm. Well of course I wasn't going to restore his lost subjects; they were covered with dragon saliva, which is just... yuck. Instead, I managed to repopulate the kingdom by turning the ants on the island into men. Aeacus again had his kingdom, Hera had her vengeance (for the moment), and the ants became the Myrmidons.

"But now that I come to think of it, the Myrmidons were there because of an earlier liaison of mine. Gee, I'm always planning ahead, even when I'm not doing it consciously."

"You planned to have an ant colony on the island?"

"Well, not precisely. You see, I'd been hanging out with your Uncle Hades—let me tell you, he has some strange tastes—and he started talking about zoophiles. And I said "you think that's strange? Let me tell you, I've been around, and I know that some chicks are turned on by the strangest things. For instance, there was Eurymedousa...."

Fetishes are almost without logic. Some people are turned on by feathers, some by the whole chicken. For some, it's a specific material, or position, or location. It's beyond reasoning, and not worth trying to figure out.

But for whatever reason, Eurymedousa was incredibly turned on by... ants.

You know, if you want someone badly enough, you can go along with whatever they want, at least for a little while. I wanted Eurymedousa, so I turned myself into an ant.

To this day, I can't figure out why it worked with her, but it surely did.

We had a son, Myrmidon, who married, as most boys do, and had children, who had children... but somewhere down the line—either it was her kink or my transformation—but Myrmidon's descendants eventually turned into a colony of ants. And so it was, that when Hera's dragon carried off Aeacus's kingdom, the Myrmidons were there for me to turn them back into people, to repopulate Aeacus's realm.

"That's really interesting, Dad. Ants, no picnic, I get it. I'm just going to slip out and grab a bite..."

"Wait, just a sec. Did I ever tell you about Alcmene? You'll get a kick out of this. Alcmene was stunning: tall, gorgeous, brilliant... She had wisdom surpassed by no person born of mortal parents. In fact, your Aunt Demeter—in her 'Law Bringer' guise—wanted to enlist Alcmene. But then Uncle Posei-

don distracted her, and, well… Anyway, Alcmene's face and dark eyes were as charming as Aphrodite's. And when she married, she honored her husband like no woman before her.

"But before that…"

Alcmene traveled with her betrothed, Amphitryon, to Thebes. He was on the road to redemption, and she was on the road to marriage. She wouldn't marry him until he had avenged the death of her brothers.

As they walked, they met a "beggar." "Stand aside, old fellow," said Amphitryon.

The beggar turned, and all but ignored Amphitryon as he ogled Alcmene.

"Mind your manners, grandfather," said Amphitryon, not unkindly, but sternly. He knew what Alcmene looked like.

The beggar, however, reached out and touched Amphitryon's arm, while staring at Alcmene. "She is marvelous," he mumbled. Then he turned away before Amphitryon could reach into his change purse.

The young couple passed out of sight over a rise, and I shook off the beggar image I'd been wearing. "I will have her," I said to myself.

Later, while Amphitryon was on his expedition against the Taphians and Teleboans, I visited Alcmene. But as the master of disguise, I was wearing Amphitryon's form.

"My beloved!" she greeted me at the door.

"I have returned. I have vanquished the Teleboans, destroyed the Taphians, and thought only of you." You know, as opening lines go, that's not too bad.

So I stayed with her for three nights, and then left. That night, the real Amphitryon returned, but Alcmene was already impregnated.

Several months later, I announced to all the other gods that a child would be born this day, a child of mine, who would rule them all.

Hera, once again showing her temper, prevented Alcmene's delivery, causing her great pain, and instead induced Nicippe to give birth (two months early) to Eurystheus. Alcmene later gave birth to Heracles, who grew to be one of the greatest Greek heroes.

"Sure, sure, I know all that, Dad. What's your point? And I'm getting hungry, you know."

"Just a moment, just a moment. What you don't know about that story is that Alcmene was one of my great-granddaughters, making Heracles my son and my great-great-grandson."

"Dad, you know, some of your relations—okay, a lot of your relations—are a little bit outre. Now, can we go to dinner?"

"Hang on. I haven't told you about satyrs. Do you know about satyrs?"

"Of course I know about satyrs, Dad. Everyone knows about satyrs."

"Yeah, well, but no. Everyone thinks they know about satyrs: goatmen, flutes, lust, but to really know about satyrs, you have to be a satyr. And once, I was."

"You were a satyr?"

"Let me tell you..."

It was all because of Antiope. She was in a garden, looking as wantonly innocent as you can imagine. If she'd been frolicking with woodland creatures in a Disney movie, she wouldn't have looked out of place. Well, except that this was before Disney, and nymphs frolicking in the woods were usually unclothed. And as I later learned, it was just an image for her.

Anyway, I looked at her, and I felt... well, I felt like a randy satyr must feel.

Rather than spooking her by just appearing in the garden, I transformed myself into a satyr, and then emerged from the trees. That was apparently the right move, because she wasn't shocked, wasn't scared, didn't bother trying to cover up. She looked at me, let her eyes wander half-way down my body, saw my desire, and came to me.

Let me tell you, those satyrs really have a way with themselves. I can't figure out why they call those little pills viagra, rather than just "satyr in a bottle."

She was almost insatiable. Almost. But eventually, we sated each other, and when she fell asleep, I limped out of the garden. She was a handful, let me tell you.

So anyway, after I left her, Epopeus kidnapped her. But she didn't scream, she didn't fight. No, not Antiope. She took up with Epopeus where she'd left off with me. Man, what a hussy, even with that innocent-looking face.

So, comes the time, Antiope gave birth... to twins: Amphion and Zethus. But it turns out only one of them was my son: Amphion. Zethus was Epopeus' son. What a mess. Well, fortunately, the twin-half-brothers got along with each other. But as you might imagine, she wasn't much of a mother herself, and left the boys to be raised by herdsmen. Eventually, after the boys were grown, they reunited with their mother, and got along. Amphion, my son, became a great singer and musician. Hermes—you know Hermes, right? always trying to join our gang in the bar? always trying to curry favor with me?—anyway, he gave Amphion a golden lyre, and taught him to sing. Zethus took after the men who had raised him, and became a hunter and herdsman. So yeah, you wouldn't think they'd get along, but sometimes opposites do attract, and the boys got on fine. Heck, they even got together to build the wall that fortified Thebes.

"So, a satyr?"

"Trust me, son. Would I lie to you?"

"Let's not go down that road, Dad. But satyrs are known for their appetites, right?"

"Well, yes…"

"Then let me tell you, my appetite is not being satisfied by this—"

"Unsatisfied appetite? Oh, that reminds me: the Arcadian king, Lycaon, had a daughter, and she was hot—"

"Did you ever met a woman who wasn't?"

"Hmm… not that I can recall. But anyway, Lycaon's daughter. She… well, she was like sex on a pair of legs; just oozing desire and desirability."

"But there was a problem."

"Of course there was a problem. If she was just ready and willing, it wouldn't be much of a story."

"The way you brag, Dad, it would be right in your wheelhouse."

"Very funny. But not this girl. No, she became a nymph of Artemis; took the vow of virginity and everything. Let me tell you, a girl like this, it was just a waste."

"But you weren't going to let that stop you."

"Ah, how well you know me, my boy. No, of course I wasn't going let an ill-considered vow stop her from experiencing the fullness of life."

"How noble of you."

"Right. Well…"

She was in this glen, probably praying to Artemis because, well, what else was there for her to be doing? So I figured it was my golden opportunity. I disguised myself as Artemis, and walked out from behind a tree.

I actually had to rustle the branches a few times and clear my throat before she looked up from her praying. Then her eyes got big.

"Goddess! I… I didn't expect… why… how…"

Not real fast with the words, but with a body like that, I wasn't really there for conversation.

"I heard you, my daughter. You may be my most devoted follower, and I just had to meet you in person."

"I'm… honored… not worthy, my goddess. How may I serve you better?"

"You are already a paragon, dear Callisto. I've only come to enjoy your company, to bask in your attention."

Flattery, let me tell you, son, will get you almost everywhere. And Callisto, she was a sucker for it. It took me, literally, a minute and a half to get her naked and on her back. If she'd been one of those modern monotheists, you'd have thought she was experiencing the rapture. I mean, she was hot, but completely inexperienced, so it was not quite the rapturous experience I was hoping for.

Anyway, I knew she wasn't leaving the sisterhood for greater carnal knowledge, so I left her dozing after the experience. But several months later, she was bathing with several other nymphs when Artemis herself actually did show up. And while Callisto was inexperienced, Artemis knew exactly what she was looking at: Callisto was pregnant.

Well, Artemis flipped out. Absolutely insane. Bam, boom, she changed Callisto into a bear, and then bear-Callisto gave birth to Arcas.

She ran off, he grew up, and then years later, bear-Callisto came back looking for her son. He of course didn't recognize her as anything but a bear, and went out to kill her.

I know, I know, they call me love-'em-and-leave-'em Zeus, but I try to take care of my own. I couldn't let Arcas kill Callisto, so I put them up in the heavens, as the Great Bear and the Little Bear. See? There they are now.

"And what's your point here? That it's cool to be a lusty god if sometimes you're going to fake it as a lesbian?"

"Well, no... Not quite. Um. Where was I?"

"You were telling me about this 'forbidden fruit,' Callisto."

"Right. Well, the mortals call it forbidden fruit. As Zeus, you know, nothing is 'forbidden' to me."

"Dad, at this point, the only part of that phrase that interests me is the 'fruit' part."

"By the way, have I told you that the phrase 'forbidden fruit' originates with Persephone's first visit to Hades?"

"At least she got something to eat."

"What are you mumbling? Anyway, forbidden. Like Danae, I'll get to her in a minute. But first, I have to tell you that—lies to the contrary—I never actually mated with Laodamia."

"You have to tell me that there's a woman you didn't have sex with?"

"Truth is truth, boy. I admit I got around, but not all the way around. Anyway Laodamia, she was married to Evander, who was Sarpedon's son. But somehow a story came about that I had my way with her. But that would have meant I was sleeping with my son's daughter-in-law, and I just didn't do it.

"Okay. You didn't seduce Laodamia."

"Right. There are some lines even a god just shouldn't cross."

"Great. Now let's go find the chow line."

"There'll be time for food later. But this, you should be paying attention, son. I'm imparting knowledge, the wisdom of my ages."

"Like sleeping with your grand-daughter-in-law?"

"Exactly. I mean, it's not like it was with Europa. Man, she was a babe...."

Europa was Phoenician, daughter of King Tyre and Queen Telephassa, sister of Cadmus and Cilix.

She was the daughter of a king, and gorgeous, but kings in those days, well, they weren't always living in Buckingham Palace. Tyre had to make ends meet in more pedestrian ways. He had herds of cows, and I realized that was my way in with his daughter.

I transformed myself into a white bull, and mixed in with the herd while Europa was out tending them. I know I cut a fine figure as a god, but I'm not bad as a bull, for all of that.

I caught her eye, enticed her a little closer, and soon she was caressing my flanks. Even as a bull, let me tell you, it felt pretty darn good.

Eventually, she was enchanted, and climbed up onto my back. And that was the break I was waiting for. Ran with her down to the sea, I did, and started swimming.

She freaked a little, at first, but soon calmed down, realized she wasn't going in the drink as long as she held onto my horns, and I swam her over to Crete. Climbed up out of the water, and she slid down to the grass, so, right in front of her eyes, I transformed back into this female-seducing form. Apparently, it worked. She wasn't the least bit frightened, but started batting her eyelashes at me, and she had me naked almost before I knew what was happening.

She may have been playing the innocent maiden at home, but here on Crete, with no one around, she let loose her inner slut, and nearly exhausted me.

I wound up staying with her for quite a while. Well, long enough to have three sons, anyway.

Of course, I couldn't stay forever. I had godding work to get back to. But Europa, she wasn't going back to Phoenicia. She had three new sons, and a new island, so I made her the first queen of Crete.

"Come to think of it, Europa was a descendant of mine, too. Great-great-granddaughter, I think, from my liaison with Io: Io's son Epaphus; his daughter, Libya; her son by Poseidon—that randy, water-logged... anyway—Agenor was Europa's father. Hmm, well, I guess that's an example of a bonding with a descendant that worked out well. Anyway, I'll tell you about Europa later.

"But usually, mating with a descendant just leads to problems. Which brings me to Danae, who was my g-g-g-g-g-great-granddaughter."

"You're stuttering."

"You want me to spell it out? Fine. Danae was my great-great-great-great-great-great-granddaughter. That's six greats. Upon Io, I sired Epaphus, whose daughter, Libya, mated with Poseidon. Their son, Belus, fathered Danaus, whose daughter Hypermnestra's son Abas sired Acrisius, who was King of Argos, and the father of Danae..."

Acrisius wanted a male heir. Heck, don't all kings want male heirs? Well, he was pretty unhappy. But he was man enough to not blame Eurydice, his queen.

Acrisius consulted the oracle of Delphi, and the oracle, in a rare fit of clarity, told him he wouldn't have a son. But, she said, his daughter would indeed have a son. Acrisius felt some relief at that, but the oracle kept speaking: "That son will one day kill you."

"Shit," said Acrisius. Well, with that kind of prophecy, you can pretty well understand his disappointment.

But Acrisius wasn't a bad man. He wasn't about to kill off his only, beloved daughter Danae. Instead, Acrisius had a tall brass tower built, and installed in it a gorgeous room, draped in silks and fancy woods and precious gems... but with no windows and no doors. He sealed Danae in that room, walling it up. But he wasn't completely cruel, so he had a skylight built into the room, to let in light and air.

Well, I wanted Danae. I figured six greats was enough generations between us that our kinship wouldn't matter, and she wasn't really in a position to be picky, being walled up in a gorgeous, but inescapable, tower.

So I went to her as a golden rain, streaming down through the skylight on a cloudless day, and entered her womb, and soon after, our son, Perseus, was born.

Danae was... I guess surprised is a pretty good word for it. But that was nothing compared to Acrisius; he about flipped out. Here he'd gone to the trouble of building an impregnable tower—get it? Im-*preg*-nable?—rather than killing his daughter, who was fated to bear the grandson that would kill him. And then she goes and has that child anyway. At that point, Acrisius was starting to get the message that there wasn't much he could do. But that didn't mean he was just going to roll over and die.

So he broke open the tower, hugged his daughter goodbye, and put Danae and Perseus in a wooden chest and set them adrift on the sea.

How he figured this was better than killing her outright, I'm not really sure. But Poseidon saw them on the sea—and in addition to being your uncle, he was Danae's four-greats-grandfather, remember. Yeah, we hang out in the bar, and we chase chicks together, but it still surprises me each time I remember our lineages have crossed and joined...

"Dad, you're going off on a tangent again, and I'm not getting fed!"

Right. Sorry. So anyway, Poseidon calmed the sea, kept the waves down to a minimum, and gave them a little current. They washed up on the shore of Seriphos, where the king's brother, Dictys, took them in, and helped raise Perseus.

Dictys's brother, King Polydectes, fell for Danae, and who could blame him? Heck, she was hot enough to attract me, and with that little bit of me running through her veins, well...

149

So Polydectes wanted Danae, but she wasn't interested. He was a king, so he felt he could make some demands. So he made a deal with her. He agreed not to marry her, but only if Perseus would bring him the head of the Gorgon Medusa.

"You know how this part goes, I'm sure. Heck, they did it in Clash of the Titans, *although I tell it better."*

"Dad...."

"Oh, right. Back to Perseus."

So, after Perseus committed his deeds of derring-do to become Perseus, he returned to Argos, and as soon as he got there, heard that King Teutamides of Larissa was holding funeral games to honor his father. Since Perseus had slain the Gorgon, slain Cetus, and slain Polydectes, he figured he'd outclass the competition, so he headed out to Larissa, and entered the discus throw, because it was something new and exciting to him.

But you know, sometimes you just can't avoid prophecies. In the audience was his aged grandfather, Acrisius. And Perseus, well, he was a world-class athlete, credit where credit is due, but he'd never actually thrown a discus before. So his throw was a good one—went farther than anyone else's—but it was so far off course that it went into the stands, and... well, you can see where this is going. Hit Acrisius in the head, killed him instantly, the poor old guy.

"So what's your point?"

"Well, it was 'better to avoid your descendants,' but now that I think about it, that whole being walled up in the tower puts me in mind of Rapunzel, except the Grimms hadn't yet borrowed Friedrich Schulz's 1790 story, because Mademoiselle de La Force hadn't yet written 'Persinette,' because this was before Giambattista Basile had first written 'Petrosinella,' which was going to inspire her."

"What?!"

"What 'what?' The literary history, or the anachronism? I'm a god, remember? Let it go."

"I get it. You were all over the map back then. Are you done? Can I get you a drink while I get myself one?"

"But wait a moment, son, I was going to tell you about Leda. You know Leda, right?"

"Leda? You mean Helen's mother?"

"Stepmother."

"Stepmother? That one I don't know."

"Then stop interrupting, and I'll tell you..."

Leda was a queen, married to King something-or-other... Tyndareus, of Sparta, that's it. She was one of the most fertile queens I ever met. Well, not exactly fertile. But eager... I guess if she'd been around in modern times, people'd have called her polyamorous. But back then, she was just really friendly, if you know what I mean.

So, Leda. It was like she had a big neon "Welcome" sign flashing over her bedchamber. I saw it one night, and decided to take her up on the offer.

Well, sometimes my timing is a little off. Turns out she'd just finished with her husband, who was snoring the loudness that comes from total satisfaction. But Leda, she was still up and about, wandering in the gardens.

I'm classy enough to know that some other guy wandering around wasn't going to get in there, so I transformed myself into a swan. You know, large, graceful, just the type of bird a girl would go for. Then I evoked an eagle, something to chase me, to get her sympathy going, and bang, there it was.

I fluttered down into the garden, this eagle chasing after me, and Leda, she scooped me up in her arms, petted me. "You poor thing," she cooed, chasing off the eagle. "You're so sweet. What a wonderful swan."

I was starting to get into this. The stroking felt good, her voice was all soft and loving, so I let my neck stretch a bit: long and sinuous, and snaking up her body, soft feathers stroking between her breasts....

It wasn't long before she got the hint, got a bit randy, and got goosed... so to speak.

Sometimes, my whims result in longer-lasting results than I'd intended. In the case of Leda, since I was a goose, she laid a couple of eggs. Not goose eggs, obviously, but people eggs. She didn't seem to think anything of it, and how she hid it from Tyndareus I'll never know. But one day, while she was dozing, I slipped another one in on her.

Nemesis and I had gotten together right about the time I'd been with Leda, but she wasn't interested in brooding a child-egg, so I took it and added it to Leda's clutch.

Then, right on cue, the eggs cracked, and out came the kids. For twins (well, quadruplets), the genetic mix-up was truly remarkable. There was Pollux, my son with Leda, Castor and Clytemnestra, her kids with Tyndareus, and Helen, my daughter with Nemesis.

So genetically, Castor and Clytemnestra were full siblings, twins. They shared a mother— and half their genetic complement— with Pollux. And Pollux and Helen were half-siblings through their shared father.

Fortunately for the kids, however, genetics hadn't been invented yet. Castor and Pollux grew up as twin brothers, knowing nothing else. And Tyndareus actually was a good guy; never showed that any of the kids might not be his, treated them all as beloved children, and they grew, as children will.

Later on, Leda and Tyndareus had a few more daughters— Timandra, Phoebe, Philonoe—all born in the more usual way: one at a time, viviparous births, and never a question about how the first four were born.

But Leda took to wearing feathers. All the time. Only feathers. Her silk gowns all went unworn; everything she wore was made of feathers. White feathers. Swan feathers. I guess she thought I was pretty good, eh?

"So you're saying any woman will fall victim to your charms, human or otherwise?"

"Well, not every woman, but I have to say my record is pretty good. And you know, I'm not the only one who gets around. Heck, at times it felt like a competition with your uncles Poseidon and Hades and me; like the only reason we got together in that bar was to discuss our conquests and see who was doing better. But that wasn't all there was to it. Although... where was

I? Oh, yeah: other than not having the term, we certainly had polyamory—don't roll your eyes at me; I'm telling you something."

"And telling me, and telling me... what you're not doing is letting me eat."

"Eat? What do you want with food? You can be feasting on my knowledge. Just listen, okay?"

Thyia was a naiad. She had a spring on Mount Parnassos, and her shrine was one of the first gathering sites for the Maenads. Well, except at the time, they were known as Thyiades... Thyades... whatever, the women who celebrated Dionysus with orgies.

Oh, speaking of which, I have to tell you about Dionysus and his mother. But I'll get to them.

Anyway, Thyia. She was a loving little naiad. Had a liaison with Apollo and bore him Delphos, for whom they named Delphi. She had an affair with Poseidon (like I said, sometimes they beat me to the punch). And she was "close friends" with the nymph Chloris.

Actually, now that I think about it, she wasn't so much polyamorous as just a proponent of the Free Love movement of the '60s, except this was a couple millennia before the '60s.

Well, by the time she got around to me, she was slowing down a little bit. Actually, her bed-hopping had slowed so much that I was in hers for two sons: Magnes, who became the first king of Magnesia; and Makednos, whose descendants became the Macedonians.

"But I was talking about Leda, and you distracted me. The point of the story with Leda is that sometimes, hooking up with your own descendants

brings a lot of disappointment."

"Didn't you already tell me that? And has that ever stopped you from having liaisons with your offspring?"

"One or two of them, but there were others."

"What is it with you, Dad?"

"Hey, I'm not unique. It worked for Lazarus Long, didn't it? Although I think Bill Compton was kind of squicked by the concept. But enough about twentieth-century literary characters; I want to tell you about Semele."

"Semele? Sounds familiar..."

"Semele, my great-great-great-granddaughter, from my son Epaphus and his daughter Libya—"

"You mentioned them before, didn't you?"

"Of course. I told you about her granddaughter Europa, and her four-greats granddaughter Danae. But now I'm telling you something else. My son Epaphus, his daughter Libya, her son Agenor, his son Cadmus, and then his daughter Semele, my four-greats-granddaughter. Semele was special to me..."

Semele was a priestess of mine. A good one.

One day, I watched her slaughter a bull on my altar—wow, could she wield a knife. The bull didn't feel a thing: one minute, alive; the next, an offering.

Well, you know about bulls: they're big, and when you slaughter them, there's a lot of blood. Semele was good, but there's not much you can do to avoid getting bull blood all over you when you slaughter one. So after the offering, she jumped in the river Asopus to clean off.

I was watching, because… well, the offering was nice, but Semele in the nude was even nicer. I watched, and I thought, "here's this priestess, and she can handle a knife, and she looks great, too.…" You know what comes next.

But this time, it wasn't just lust. I really fell for her. Of course we did it that afternoon, but afterward, I found myself thinking about her, and I had to go back to her, again and again.

It turned into a relationship, which is pretty rare, let me tell you.

Unfortunately, I went back a little too often, and Hera twigged to what was going on.

So she appeared to Semele as an old crone, a potential worshipper, and befriended her. Eventually, Semele broke down, and told Hera I was her lover. Hera—sometimes, she can be a real bitch, you know?—pretended not to believe her, kept asking her if she had proof that her lover was really Zeus, and like that.

So one day, when I'm with Semele, she tricks me. Asks me to do her a favor. "Anything," I said, because I had real feelings for her. "Whatever you ask, I shall grant."

So she says, "Prove to me you really are Zeus. Reveal yourself in all your glory."

You know what happens in cases like that. She was enough generations removed from my descent that she really was mortal, so I begged her to ask for something else. But no, she was insistent: "Prove yourself to me."

I tried. Oh, how I tried. I showed her the smallest possible lightning bolt I could manifest. I called the sparsest, weakest thundercloud you can imagine. I tried to save her. But she was mortal, and mortals cannot look upon us gods without incinerating.

It was a horrible conflagration. Turned my stomach, not to mention breaking my heart.

But as she burned, I realized she was pregnant. Let me tell you, I was ready to incinerate Hera for that little trick.

But I grabbed the fetus, pulled it from the flaming Semele. It was too little, not ready to be born. What could I do? I sewed it into my thigh, where baby Dionysus came to term, and was born, a few months later.

Of course, I had to avoid Hera for those months: she would have noticed the lump on my thigh. And when it was the baby's time to be born, I went away to the mountains, hid myself, and gave birth to the baby.

But you know me; you know I wasn't in any position to be this new baby's mother. So I called in Hermes to help with child rearing.

From there, I'm not really sure how Dionysus grew up. Over the years, he and Hermes have given me several different stories: he was raised as a girl by King Athamas and Queen Ino; the rain-nymphs of Nysa brought him up; Rhea looked after him; once your Aunt Demeter and Uncle Hades said your cousin Persephone brought him up in the Underworld… I'm not really sure.

But I next met him after he'd grown up. He was going off to rescue his mother from the afterlife. After he brought her back to the overworld, I brought her up to Mount Olympus, set her up under a new name—Thyone—and now she presides over the frenzies Dionysus inspires. We don't see each other much, and Hera seems to have gotten over her pique, at least in that particular case.

"Which brings me to your mother. Oh, but look at the time. That's the end of your break. I'll tell you the rest some other time, but now, you have to go back to standing in your pool, Tantalus."

"..."

"And if you see Sisyphus on your way out, tell him I've got a story he needs to hear."

House of Asgard
"Build the Wall!"
Robert Greenberger

Loki tugged at his tie, adjusting the collar again and again. He studied his gaunt, pale visage in the mirror and grimaced. Two slender hands reached from behind and adjusted the Windsor knot with two quick moves and suddenly Loki looked prepared for his public. The hands then traveled slowly down his chest and his eyes met those of his wife Sigyn in the mirror. She was still incredibly attractive despite having given birth twice, but there was a hardness creeping into the set of her mouth, marring her beauty.

"You're all set for your meeting with the President," she said, stepping back, revealing her naked form. "Is everything arranged?"

Loki, now the President's trusted adviser, nodded once and turned into her embrace. He had his dalliances away from their marriage bed – it was in his nature – but still he returned to her time and again. She never rejected him and he truly loved her for that. It was why, once they settled on Midgard, they began making plans together. And now, things were about to come to fruition.

"And the Odinson?" Sigyn asked as she shimmied into a crimson sheath dress, completing pinning up her hair and she studied herself in the mirror. She gave her reflection a satisfied smile and turned to face him.

"I paid a massive amount of gold to the trolls to climb down Yggdrasil and terrify the Africans with frightening regularity. Once the President received word, Thor was dispatched. He'll be busy for weeks."

Loki kissed his wife passionately for a lingering moment then left their home at the Naval Observatory and crossed to the White House where he was quickly ushered into the Oval Office. There, studying a mountain of papers and reports was the President, his ever-present ravens on each shoulder.

"Good morning, my blood brother," the president said without looking up.

"Good morning, Mr. President," Loki said to Odin.

The silver-maned, one-eyed leader of the Free World looked up from the papers and studied the trickster. "You want something."

"No, not really," Loki said, taking a seat before the massive wooden desk. If the humans knew anything, it was wood craftsmanship. Odin reached into a suit pocket and withdrew some treats and fed the ravens, neither of which stopped staring intently at the trickster god. He both admired and hated them for that trait.

"But you've come to talk. I had a dream about you last night."

"Really? What did your knowledge foretell?"

"That you have a solution to a problem so let's have it. Tyr and I are meeting with the Joint Chiefs in fifteen minutes."

"You have an immigration problem," Loki said.

"The trolls, I know. I dispatched Thor to teach them about proper procedure," the all-father said.

"When you brought us down from Asgard, you addressed the world and said that things were getting out of control. You said you would start by taking control of Midgard's sole superpower and from there you would transform the world. Your promises were to bring peace to the warring nations, end famine, and ready men to assume their rightful place among the nine realms."

"We have waited many millennia for them to reach that point on their own. Clearly, they need our help," Odin said. Or at least the all-father had come to believe the months of whispers Loki had been placing in his two ears for the last few years.

"You cannot make this a better, safer country until you deal with the other illegal immigrants who are flocking to Washington like cockroaches drawn to the light."

"Indeed, Homeland Security says there has been a marked up-tick in such matters," Odin agreed.

"They must be kept out since we do not have endless resources to clothe and feed them. Sir, we have to protect that which we already have before allowing others entry."

"Why do you believe they are coming in such numbers?"

Loki cocked an eye at his father. "Why you, sir. They are coming for divine intervention, or for your blessing. Their lives are wretched beyond our borders and are coming, believing we will build this into a golden realm. You need to construct a fortification that will stop them once and for all. America has been plagued with these issues for too long and your divine presence is only exacerbating things. Build a wall, Mr. President."

Odin studied Loki's face, clearly seeking artifice or craft. Seeing none, he grunted once.

"For such a thing, I would need a master craftsman, an architect and engineer who can ensure it cannot be breached. The thickness would prevent boring through it and it would be too tall for mere mortals to scale. And only the foolhardy should try to tunnel beneath it."

"Most wise of you," Loki said and smiled. Odin continued to stare at him.

"You have someone in mind," Odin rumbled.

"Of course. You taught us all not to come to you with a problem without a solution. I know of a man whose reputation on this planet is without compare. Let me bring him to you so you and he may discuss the details."

Odin pondered the matter for a few moments then nodded. "Have him come Monday, when the Cabinet meets. 10 a.m."

Monday arrived soon enough and Loki ushered the gentleman into the room. He was large, broad, and clearly worked with his hands. He had dark hair and narrow eyes giving his rough face a shadowy look that caused the Secret Service agents to be extra careful in patting him down before allowing him into the Cabinet Room. The table was filled with various gods and goddesses filling in for their mortal counterparts. Baldur was eating a Danish while others drank orange juice or coffee.

"Master Craftsman, may I present to you President Odin and his cabinet," Loki said then stepped back, crossed his hands before him and relaxed against one wall.

"Do you not have a name?" Odin asked. Muninn nibbled on a pastry by his elbow while Hugginn stared at Loki.

"I do, Mr. President, but everyone seems so formal, what with the titles and all. I am Karl Steinmurer."

"Loki says you can build us a wall that would separate Mexico from the United States, keeping illegal immigrants out."

"Yes, Mr. President. He and I have been discussing this for some time and I took the liberty of drawing up plans that would not restrict waterways, rivers, and set up controlled gates for train tracks and highways. We'd embed fiber optic cables throughout along with motion detectors at the top and bottom. It's all here." With that, the builder withdrew from a deep pocket a small tablet, flicked it to life and handed it to the all-father. He squinted for a second then steadied his gaze. Satisfied, he handed off to his left, where Sif, sitting in for her husband the Vice-President, next studied it.

The tablet went from god to god as Odin addressed himself to the large figure. "Master Craftsman, we would pay for materials, but what would you charge for your labor? And how long would you need to complete this structure?"

"I would like three months to do the job right. As for a price, well, I have little need for cash or gold or even jewels."

Odin leaned forward, curious. "That's interesting for a mortal. What, then, would you ask?"

The Craftsman had been eyeing the woman on Odin's other side and the President turned and looked at the goddess of love and fertility.

"You are an impudent one," Freya, whose beauty was unparalleled on the seven continents or the nine realms, said.

"That may be, but a week with you is all I ask."

"A week?" she said with scorn dripping from her voice.

Loki stepped forward before Odin's wife could unleash her famed fury. "If I may, what he asks is very dear. The Aesir do not take lovers casually and give theirs away even less casually. To do so, it must be for a great reason."

"We must consult," Odin said.

"We must?" Freya repeated in a voice that chilled the air around her. The ravens flew across the table.

The builder was escorted into the hall, handed a pastry and coffee to tide him over. Then, Odin called for order. "You dare consider Freya as a payment for such service? Are you mad, Laufey Son?"

"No, but you have a problem that needs addressing. Others have promised a wall and failed to deliver. Build the Wall, Mr. President. Better yet, let him build it for you. Promise him anything, even Freya, since we both know there is no way he can construct so tall and wide a barrier in thirty days. Let him try and fail and we have that much of the work done for free."

There were nods from all around the table, except for Freya, who seethed at being discussed like a bauble. She glared at Odin, who clearly was taken with Loki's notion, even though everyone should be suspicious of him even when he declares the sky blue.

A deal was struck. The craftsman would be given thirty-one days but was restricted to his tools and his mule, a single man to do all the work. He readily agreed, which should have caused concern among the Aesir and Vanir gathered around the table but it did not. All swore an unbreakable oath on Gungnir, Odin's spear. Freya refused and none could blame her even though it was understood she must abide by their collective decision.

That evening, Sigyn greeted her husband and inquired of the meeting.

"It could not have gone better," he said as he settled into a chair, a flagon of mead before him. "He has his deal, Freya's virtue is on the line, and the seeds have been sown. Within a month, Odin will be disgusted and quit Midgard. His infallibility among the Aesir destroyed."

"Leaving it for us," she said, a hand curling around his ear and down his neck. He shuddered at her touch.

On the following morning, Loki, in his role of Advisor, visited Odin at the Oval Office. The all-father was feeding his ravens, who appeared breathing hard from their most recent flight.

"All well, Odin?"

"Huninn and Muginn tell me that the builder arrived at dawn on the eastern edge of the border. The mule was pulling twenty pallets of stone, mortar, cable, and other materials. He arrived by himself and set out to work."

"Then all *is* well," Loki said. "We shall keep your American worshippers safe from those coming from the south to seek your benevolence."

"For now. It is merely the first hour."

Each morning thereafter, the ravens returned with news of the progress. Vör, in her role as press secretary, deflected most questions from the mortal media, repeating that the Wall was being constructed as part of Odin's promises to keep America, and in turn, the Mexicans safe. The Craftsman, for his part, refused to address the press when they crowded near his workspace. His activity became a source of fascination to the humans, and they flocked near the space so much so that Tyr insisted barriers be erected to fairly allow the man to do his work unimpeded.

And each day, the barriers, the people, and the media had to be moved because another section of the Wall was completed. He was averaging sixty-four miles a day, working with such speed and efficiency that other contractors and workmen came to watch and study his methods. He never seemed to need to eat or take a rest or even use the bathroom. The man took no questions, engaged in no conversation, and each night, once the sunset and night fell, he somehow vanished from sight. And just as the sun crested the horizon, he would trudge back into view, the mule pulling the first of the day's palettes. No one was certain where the materials came from and since he disappeared the previous evening, he could not be trailed.

In short order, the Craftsman had become a hero to the Americans and a cursed figure to the human coyotes who profited from the misery of their fellow Mexicans.

Each day, Loki arrived at the worksite, usually disguised as a local bird, and marveled at the work. But as the time remaining was at the halfway mark, his joy turned to worry that he would need to find a way to deliver Freya, something he had not stopped to consider, a flaw which he mentally castigated himself.

"He builds quickly and efficiently," Loki crowed to Sigyn.

They were leaning over a balcony, surveying the calm Washington weather. The sun's setting painted the clouds in marvelous colors but the beauty was lost on the gods.

"If nothing untoward happens, we get the wall and he gets Freya," she said. Her hand caressed his shoulder before working its way down his spine.

"Thor remains preoccupied in Africa as more trolls continue to arrive," Loki said absent-mindedly. "Your deal with them was perfect."

Her hand stopped its travels and the next words died in his throat.

The following day, Heimdall was dispatched to survey the progress. Joining his expedition were Snotra, Vör, Hlín, and Freya and they watched from a safe distance. They were soon joined by the All Father himself.

"What do you make of it all-seeing one?" Freya asked Heimdall.

"He builds true and has honored his end of the bargain."

Freya shuddered at the implications. "Do you anticipate him being completed on schedule?"

"Barring the unforeseen, yes."

The look she gave Odin kept him silent for the remainder of the visit.

With a week left until the deadline, and under seven hundred miles of border remaining, Odin summoned Loki to the Oval Office. Loki chose a fine, dark suit, his hair slicked back, looking ever more mortal and ever less trustworthy.

"Loki, if this works, we will have protected the southern end of America. Need we build a northern Wall?"

Loki smiled tightly and answered, "These are troublesome times, blood brother. These savages seem to make up reasons to kill one another easier than I can lie and as you know, I lie very, very well."

"That you do," Odin agreed.

"Should we merely have a southern wall, America's enemies would surely try and come from the north. Until you can tame the whole world to your liking, these subjects need be protected so they may build your engines of peace without fear of attack."

"You speak wisely and echo Tyr's own thoughts," Odin said, his one eye never wavering from Loki. "Once America is rebuilt, we can begin to share our wisdom with the other nations."

"What do you think this man would charge to build a second wall? A month with Freya or two goddesses this time?"

"We can ask should he complete this wall on time," Loki said. That was the last they spoke of the matter until the night before the final day. The wall was less than seventy miles from completion and there was no reason for any of the gods to think the Craftsman would fail.

Freya grew more upset by the day until Odin could bear it no more. Frigg had grown cold toward her husband, spending her time consoling the goddess. That evening, he summoned Loki to the private residence above the Oval Office.

"Stop him," Odin commanded. "He cannot win Freya for even a second. You made this happen, now make it stop."

"We would lose face to the Americans and the remainder of Midgard's children. How do you propose to usher in a new era of global unity if your word cannot be trusted? We made the bargain and everyone swore on the spear. That bond cannot be shattered."

Odin let out a mirthless chuckle. "I watched, Loki, I saw how everyone *but* you swore on the spear. Your hand hovered over it, but never touched it. A technicality mayhap, but one we will now exploit. Find a way to thwart his efforts or I shall have you chained to an active volcano. We'll see how much Sigyn likes the heat."

Loki shuddered at the thought and nodded, vanishing from his presence.

At his own home, he fretted and paced the bedroom, Sigyn watching. "What can we do? I have no desire to visit you inside a volcano. We were to force Odin from Midgard."

"Hush!" he commanded, worried that all-knowing Heimdall might be listening. He saw and heard all but needed to focus to find specific information. He worried that Odin had tasked such surveillance.

"I have a command from the all-father, what shall we do? Everything was planned so we got the Wall and Freya was humiliated before Odin. Now I have to undo it all without exposing everything."

"Think hard and think fast," Sigyn suggested and then shut the door to her own chamber.

Loki thought until the first sunlight peeked inside his window. Given the westward travel, he knew he had three hours to find a plan and interfere. The sooner the Craftsman was interrupted, the better.

He changed into the form of a falcon and took to the skies, a plan finally taking shape.

Out West, in California, the Craftsman was emerging from the shadows, ready for the final day. Police and the National Guard had by then worked out a rolling set of barriers to keep the people and press at a safe distance while not impeding the mule's back and forth travels to bring more stone and cable and mortar for the structure.

Being the final day, there were more people than usual, including protesters on the southern side of the wall. It was already promising to be a long, hot and now loud day.

The Craftsman surveyed where he ended the previous day's labor and then set about to mix mortar and place the last of his stones into position. By the time that was completed, his faithful mule – stuffed imitations of which had become a best-selling item – was due momentarily with the first of the day's supplies.

As the last stone fell into place, he turned in anticipation of his companion's arrival. But as far as he could see, there was no mule coming. It was unshackled and dancing in circles on a meadow.

Running alongside the mule was a second mule, its manhood clearly signaling attention. The Craftsman bellowed for his animal but the calls were ignored. The two mules stopped running and nuzzled one another. They were now seen by the media but the mules didn't know anything about modesty or discretion.

The Craftsman gave up yelling and trudged off in the direction of the nearest stone quarry. Sure enough, an hour later, he returned with a single palette loaded with materials and he was sweating. Upon his return, neither mule was in sight and the crowd had returned its attention to the sun, which was nearing its apex, and the number of miles left to complete.

He was urged on by the throngs of Americans chanting, "Build the wall!"

As the hours wore on, the wall continued towards completing but at a far slower rate and the air was filled with the nattering sound of reporters telling their cameras that doubt had fallen on the work being completed on that day. Mortals were not privy to the bargain, the deadline, or the prize and if they were, their moral senses would have been horrified.

With an hour to go before sunset, Odin, Freya, and other gods arrived to see the deadline arrive.

The sun touched the horizon and the skies quickly lost their luster.

"You appear to have failed," Freya said, unable to hide her delight at the prospect.

"Indeed, the minutes vanish," Odin said, keeping his voice neutral. "Tell me, Master Craftsman, what was your true goal in building this? Freya mayhap be the most beautiful woman in all the realms but you did not do this for sex."

The Craftsman ignored the gods and, with sweat running in rivulets down his face, neck, arms, and legs, staining the ground beneath him, he shoved a rock into place and hastily spackled the crevices.

"More specifically, what did Loki promise you?"

That caught his attention and at mention of his name, Loki seemingly appeared from nowhere, standing discreetly behind the other gods.

"Australia," the man grumbled.

And then something happened. The Craftsman, already large for a human, shuddered just as the sun vanished from sight. The clothes ripped and fell away, mighty muscles sprouted along his back and legs and arms. His height grew until he stood fifteen feet then twenty feet in height.

"A Giant," one of the mortals behind them shrieked.

"I was to bed Freya and have Australia," the Giant said, his voice now deep and rumbling.

"Who made such promises?" Odin asked, but everyone knew full well the man behind it all.

Evan as Odin turned, Loki began to back away from the assembled gods but he neglected to look behind him for he walked right into the imposing figure of Thor.

"I see I have arrived in time," the god of Thunder cheerfully said.

"Thor! I heard you were still fighting trolls," Loki stammered.

"I was, but then peace broke out, long enough for me to smash a few more and settle a treaty," Thor replied.

"But how?" Loki was genuinely confused.

"You think yourself so clever but you also think you're the only smart one in the nine realms," Freya said. "When it looked as if I might actually be handed over to that... man, I decided to take matters into my own hands. Thor was gone for too long so it was clear he was being kept away and that smelled like something you had a hand in. So, I went to Africa and talked sweetly to the troll king. We reached an accommodation."

"You did," Loki said in a small voice.

"I did for am I not a goddess of not only love but of battle? That means I know how to both start... and stop them."

"You take us for fools, Loki Laufey Son," Odin said. "Between my wisdom and Heimdall's sight, we considered your motives and held private council. We concluded, and Tyr supported our thinking, that you wanted walls both north and south, not to protect America and its citizens, but to begin hemming us gods in. You are working with dark magical forces and seek to use the wall to diminish our power and trap us, make us vulnerable. Stay with simpler tricks, you're better at them."

There was no more to be said. Thor saw to it the giant was returned to his home while Magni was installed to oversee Loki's punishment: the long process of taking down the wall. He was not to use sorcery or recruit allies, something Odin thought would keep his adopted son busy and out of trouble long enough for him to move on to loftier goals.

The following day, with Loki at the backbreaking work and Sigyn banished back to Asgard awaiting Odin's judgment, the all-father convened his cabinet. No northern wall would be built and with war settled in Africa, they could resume once more bringing global prosperity to Midgard.

It would be nigh-impossible work but then again, it was also the work of gods.

Day Racer
Caw Miller

Maponos put his arm around the thin waist of a busty co-ed and guided her across the parking lot to a sleek, black Camaro parked in the middle of four parking places.

"Wait 'til you see my twelve-cylinder engine and huge crankshaft." Maponos ran a hand through his mullet to keep from running his hand across a portion of the co-ed that might get him slapped.

"She's too young for you," the Camaro said in a horsey voice.

"She's nineteen," Maponos said. "I'm only twenty-two."

"Twenty-two centuries," the car said.

"I'm always youthful, even now in 1980," Maponos said. "You're still a great horse, who now is a car with a computer."

"I'm a—" the car began.

"Like, what's going on here?" The co-ed wriggled out of Maponos' grasp. "Are you like a ventriloquist? That's like so not cool."

"No, honey. I told you I'm a loner on a quest to right wrongs and fight crime." Maponos smiled the crooked smile that melted girls' hearts. "My car talks. It's the finest car in the world and has seats that will caress your beautiful behind like a hand."

"Napa leather," the car said.

Maponos reached out to show how the seats would caress, but the co-ed took a step back.

"Are you like one of those guys who like makes girls take their shoes off before they like get in the car?" She crossed her arms, barricading her beautiful bosom.

"Yeah, but I have these really comfortable slippers for you to wear." Maponos offered the slippers.

"Napa leather," the car said.

The girl backed away. "Loser." She fled back into the mall.

Maponos slapped the roof of the Camaro. "ATEP, why did you chase that girl away? She was going to worship me."

"Tammie told me to keep you from frivolous flings so you could seriously search for your life mate," replied the car.

"What do you know about life mates? You're a car."

"Tammie and I are life mates."

Maponos opened the door and settled into the seat of the Camaro. He sighed as his bottom was carefully cradled. "I hate to break this to you, bud, but Tammie's your mechanic. You won't be mating with her."

"Tammie's mother thinks I am Tammie's lover because Tammie spends so much time with me."

Maponos sighed. "Tammie's mother wants grandchildren. Are you going to knock her up?"

"No, but I would be happy to drive children to and from day-care and primary school."

Maponos chuckled. "I'm sure you would, bud. I'm trying to get alone with girls so they can touch my body. Are you trying to do that?"

"Tammie has put her hands on my valve stems."

Maponos laughed as he started the engine. "If I didn't know better I'd think you just made a joke."

"Tammie says I am incapable of making jokes."

"You don't need to testify for me, bud." Maponos slammed the car into gear then squealed the tires when he pulled out.

"Maponos!" ATEP said.

"Don't tell me. I pulled out too quickly and you're going to tell Tammie on me because I'm stressing your delicate rear end."

"Well, that too, but Darren's on the line."

"Put him on screen and take over driving."

The radio retracted, revealing a small screen. "Hello ATEP, and you too, Maponos," the older man said.

"Very funny," Maponos said. "Everyone's a comedian today."

ATEP stopped at a traffic light.

"I need you to come in for a new mission," Darren said.

"Will do, boss." Maponos closed the cover over the screen. "ATEP, let's make like a banana and peel out."

ATEP pulled out in a slow, controlled manner.

Maponos sighed.

The black Camaro pulled up next to a glass-encased house cantilevered over a cliff. Maponos climbed out of ATEP and then checked his hair in the reflection in the car window.

"I'm going to see Tammie," said ATEP.

"Give her a kiss for me." Maponus snapped his fingers. "Shoot, you don't have lips so you can't kiss her."

"You are right. I will let her put her hands under my hood, though." ATEP lowered into the ground on an elevator.

Maponos brushed at his tight, black jeans, fluffed his mullet, and then strode into the mansion.

At a paneled wall, he placed his hand over a knot. The walls slid back, revealing a huge office with a bank of floor-to-ceiling windows overlooking Silicon Valley. Behind a huge desk sat a middle-aged, prim man who looked like he should have a white cloth over his arm and be carrying a tray of highballs.

Maponos dropped into a leather chair, one leg over the arm-rest.

"What's the sitch, boss?"

Darren smiled. "Nice to see you, Maponos. I hope you are well rested from your last adventure."

"If I was any more rested I would be arrested."

"Very amusing." Darren adjusted his necktie. "Do you know that Atepomarus Enterprises is a solar panel manufacturer?"

"Sunlight does occasionally shine up a dog's butt."

"Equally amusing. To promote our solar energy initiative, we are sponsoring a multi-day race by solar-powered vehicles. A terrorist called Lugnuts has threatened to sabotage the race."

"He doesn't sound too smart or dangerous."

"We have no information on Lugnuts. It could be a man, woman, or group."

"And you want me to win the race and sniff out the bad dude."

"Not exactly. I want you to be the marshal for the race and make sure the racers behave themselves, and keep an eye out for terrorists."

"I don't get to race? I have the best horse on the planet. I can't lose."

Darren steepled his fingers. "ATEP is not a toy but is a significant asset to the corporation. You will be a marshal in the race."

Maponos shrugged. "ATEP's going to be so disappointed. I don't know if I'll be able to keep him from showing off his twelve cylinders."

Darren smiled. "I guarantee there will be no cylinder displays. Let's go visit Tammie."

Darren pushed a button on his desk and an elevator opened in the wall. After descending one floor, the doors opened on an immaculate garage with sparkling wrenches on the walls. Maponos' eyes were drawn to a curvaceous woman with her head under ATEP's hood. He stroked his mullet and admired the view.

"More than her hands under his hood," Maponos murmured.

"Oh." The brunette stood up revealing a sultry smile and a spot of grease on her nose. "I've barely started."

"I thought it best if the news came from you," Darren said.

"Oh? Sure." Tammie rubbed her nose, smearing the grease. "I'm taking out ATEP's motor and converting him to solar electric for the race."

The garage spun. The floor smacked Maponos on the mullet.

Maponos returned to consciousness lying on his back on the spotless floor of the garage, his head resting on a technical manual and his feet raised on a toolbox.

"All right, there, Maponos?" Darren asked.

"I had the craziest dream," Maponos said. "My beautiful Camaro was becoming a Trans Am."

"Just solar," Tammie said.

The garage spun....

Maponos came awake lying on his back on the floor of the garage, a headache throbbing his brain.

"Really, Maponos, are you sure you aren't coming down with something?" Darren asked.

Maponos sat up. "I'm coming down with my beautiful horse being desecrated and gutted."

"I think it looks cute," Tammie said.

"ATEP, what do you think?" Maponos asked.

"Although Tammie says it makes me look darling, I prefer my shiny black paint."

Maponos rubbed a pink flower sticker on ATEP's fender. "Tammie's right. You're as cute as a Volkswagen Bug."

"I told you never to call me that," ATEP said.

Maponos used ATEP's fender to climb to his feet. "You're right, sorry, bud. You're as cute as a hatchback."

"Maponos!" ATEP said.

"Boys, don't fight over me," Tammie said. "Mapo, the solar conversion is temporary and there's a battery for back-up. After this mission I can give you back your manhood."

"You let me hit my head twice."

"You fainted four times," ATEP said.

Maponos rubbed his head. "Feels like ten times." He noticed that the back of the Camaro was filled with a large box. "Is that the battery? There's no backseat. Where am I going to make-out?"

"Get a room." Tammie pivoted and carried a wrench to the wall. "I'm tired of cleaning stains off the seats. When I take the batteries out, I'm putting in a rubber covered seat."

"Yes, well." Blushing, Darren stepped forward, proffering a folder to Maponos. "Here's your credentials. Report to Palo Alto and see my good friend Sully, the race coordinator. I know I always say this, but I really mean it this time: keep a low profile."

Maponos saluted. "Marshal Maponos reporting for duty."

"Bring ATEP back undamaged, for once," Tammie added.

After a look and sigh at the huge engine hanging in the lift, Maponos climbed into ATEP.

"Darken the windows," he said.

The windows darkened.

"More."

"If I go any darker you won't be able to see," ATEP said.

"I'm more concerned about if people can see me. I'm keeping a low profile, remember."

After leading the parade of race cars for a mile, ATEP pulled to the side and the race began. ATEP kept pace with the pole sitter.

Maponos glanced to the side and saw an older man driving the vehicle.

"Let's take a walk through the field of racers." Maponos pulled out the file for the car on the pole, a giant solar panel on a skinny body with three wheels. "Driven by ex-vice president Spiro Agnew. I make him suspect Numero Uno."

"Why is that?" ATEP asked.

"He's got to have better things to do than this race."

"That's your reasoning?"

"He also got kicked out of Vice President for accepting bribes. You got something better?"

"I will run algorithms on him and see if there are any connections." ATEP slowed and drove beside the second car in the race.

"Run your little heart out. I'm on to other potential villains, like the driver of this Chevy: Slick Johnson, a NASCAR driver. That sound like a fake name to you?"

"That is not his baptismal forename, but is his surname."

"What's a bump-and-grind NASCAR driver doing in this dog and pony show?"

"He's retired."

"Likely story. Keep an eye on him."

ATEP slowed to drive next to the third car.

"Next contestant is—" Maponos stared at the driver of the Fiat.

"Maponos, you're drooling on my Napa leather seat," ATEP said.

Maponos pulled out the eight by ten photo from the file. He kissed the black-and-white image. "Angelina Nova, former Miss Italy, kicked out for fighting. Is this file mixed up with Slick's?"

"No, Maponos."

"Was it mud wrestling?"

"No."

"Jello wrestling?"

"No."

"Spaghetti sauce wrestling?"

"Close. Miss Nova punched Miss Congeniality over a comment about the best shape of pasta noodle."

"That hardly makes her out to be a terrorist. I will keep my eyes on her."

"Your hands, too?" ATEP said.

"Absolutely. Next driver is some milquetoast from Cal Tech. He's got more pimples than a... scarlet pimpernel. Next."

"That's hardly a reason to rule out a suspect," ATEP said.

"You're the horse who lost his horse sense and now's a computer. You compute. I'm the person. I'll judge based on those hunches that people get."

Maponos looked out the window, then back to the file. "Next contestant is a driver from UCLA – a girl. Nothing to see there, even after you get past the thick goggles. Next."

ATEP slowed to pace the next car. "I think Honda is an up-and-coming car manufacturer."

"Maybe you can become life mates? I'm intrigued by the driver, Walter Suther. Eccentric millionaire noted for secrecy and technology. Big rival of Atepomarus Industries. This race would be the perfect cover to discredit a rival."

"I'll run algorithms."

A mousy, middle-aged man with glasses drove the next car.

"Next driver is Baylor U. professor, Lou Garman," Maponos said. "He's in a Continental? Is he crazy?"

"The large, flat roof, hood, and trunk lid are perfect for holding solar panels."

"That car's as heavy as a tank," Maponos said.

"It passed the speed and endurance trials."

"Eggheads are too wimpy to be villains." Maponos pulled out the last file. "The last driver's a student from Arizona State U., whose mascot is a sun devil, which means villain."

"Are you being humorous, again?" ATEP asked.

"It'd only be more obvious if he was wearing a black cowboy hat."

"Sometimes I wish you would grow up," ATEP said.

"Not a chance." Maponos tossed the files onto the passenger seat. "This case is ninety percent solved. Catch up to that hot chick and get right on her bumper, which I plan to do tonight after the Stage 1 banquet."

"I will maintain a safe following distance of three seconds."

Maponos sighed.

When the last car crossed the finish line for the day, Maponos sat up. "This was one of the most tedious times I can remember since the dark ages. Can't those dang cars go any faster? Let's get to the feast. I can't wait to see Miss Italy in a ball gown."

"I cannot drive you there. I'm solar," ATEP said. "Using my battery will give away the secret."

"How'm I supposed to get to the ball, then?"

"Well, you could do what you did before you captured me from the herds of Tír na nÓg – you could walk. That also might keep your black jeans from being so tight."

"Ha, ha. My ass has been divine since horny, teenaged Irish girls prayed me into existence. You, on the other hand, just ceased to be the finest horse in the world. Think about that while you're parked here all night."

Maponos climbed out, then slammed the door. He paced in angry little circles. ATEP had not been this useless since he was a velocipede and the first automobile putt-putted by, winning the race, then driving away with the trophy and the hot chick.

His mind doing donuts around the former Miss Italy, Maponos arrived at the starting line to find an uproar. Drivers flung insults, pointed fingers, and hurled racial slurs. This was what he had expected.

"All right, pipe down. What's the problem here?" Maponos demanded.

The pimply driver from Cal Tech rushed up. "Someone cracked my roof cell. It's causing an eighty percent decrease in efficiency."

"Did you see who broke it?" Maponos asked.

Pimplyface looked at his shoes.

"He put too much pressure in his cells," the UCLA driver said. "It likely was a hairline last night that widened as the cell cooled, or cracked when it heated up again this morning."

When Pimplyface did not disagree, Maponos knew the argument was won, even if he did not understand it. "That decides it. Unless you have proof of human interference, we have to assume it was that crack-thingy. Drivers to your cars."

Not long after the start of the race, the Cal Tech car was in last place and barely moving. The team resigned from the race.

Throughout the long day, Maponos napped. The ASU car took the lead on a daring pass that nearly wrecked Ex-Vice President Agnew.

"See? The sun-devil is a villain," Maponos said.

ATEP sighed.

When Maponos arrived at the starting line, the racers were again in an uproar. This time the ASU car had slashed tires. Maponos ducked into ATEP to receive a video call from Darren.

"Everything all right there?" Darren asked.

"A car is out for a broken panel, another for slashed tires," Maponos said.

"Hmm. Seems rather weak for terrorists."

"Absolutely. I think it's petty in-fighting between the racers. The problems keep happening at night. I'll stay up and keep an eye out."

"Better make it two," Darren said.

"Yes, both eyes," Maponos said.

"I meant you and ATEP."

"He can't," Maponos said. "Solar cars can't be out at night."

"That's a flaw in the plan for sure."

"As long as I'm parked in the correct position, I can watch much of the area and videotape until my battery runs out," ATEP said.

"Hm." Darren frowned. "That'll have to do. I hate my best agent being just a voyeur for this. Maponos, park ATEP with a view of as many tents as possible."

"What am I, a valet?" Maponos asked.

"You're a loner on a quest to right wrongs, who sometimes is a valet," Darren said. "Now get out there and screw Lugnuts."

Maponos climbed out of the car grumbling about not getting respect, echoing that hot new standup comic. He addressed the gathered racers and support staffs. "We'll start the race once the tires are replaced."

At three AM, Maponos was taking a leak behind ATEP when a woman's scream came from the tents. "Sorry about the splash, bud. I jumped at the scream."

"I hope urine does not etch the paint," ATEP said.

Maponos arrived in the middle of the tents to see Slick Johnson stumbling out of his tent, tears streaming down his face. "Someone smashed my panels." His voice was as high as a woman's.

"You screamed?" Maponos demanded.

Slick blushed.

"Oh for Pete's sake," Maponos said. "How bad's your car?"

"Undrivable."

"Everyone back to their tents," Maponos said.

Once everyone was out of sight, he slipped into ATEP. "Tell me you saw something."

"I wish I could," the car replied. "I've reviewed the recording multiple times and the most I see is Lou Garman chasing a moth. He returns right before you arrive."

"So who's out of the race?" Maponos asked.

"Two students and Slick," ATEP said.

"Who's left in the race?"

"Agnew, Suther, Nova, UCLA, and Garman."

"How are they related?"

"Those who are out are men."

"So this could be some sort of women's lib thing? Knocking out men so a woman can win?" Maponos said. "I figured a villain with the name Lugnuts would actually have nuts."

"I'll run algorithms," ATEP said.

"What men are left?"

"Agnew, Suther, Garman."

"Which one's the target for tomorrow night?"

"I'll run algorithms," ATEP said.

Maponos snapped his fingers. "I just noticed something. The young men are out of the race."

"Good observation, Maponos. In fact, they have been attacked in order of youngest to oldest. The next oldest male is Suther."

"You keep an eye on the ladies and I'll watch the next male victim – I can't believe I actually said that."

The race got under way without any hysterics.

"ATEP, take over driving." Maponos let go of the steering wheel and ATEP almost clipped Spiro Agnew's car.

"ATEP! Take over driving," Maponos said.

"Sorry, Maponos. I have control now."

"Good. Don't disturb me. I have thinking to do." Maponos opened a Playboy Magazine to the centerfold photo.

Later, Maponos was studying photos of what girls really did during sleepovers when the car bounced over a curb.

"ATEP, buddy, you sleeping at the wheel?" Maponos demanded.

A sigh whinnied through the speakers. "I've been thinking about what you said."

"You mean 'don't disturb me?' That means I don't have a hand for the steering wheel."

"No, what you said two nights ago about me being useless. Even before being converted to solar, I've been feeling outdated."

"I was just kidding, bud, feeling a little stupid myself right then and I took it out on you. You're still the finest horse in the world."

"Thank you for saying so, but I'm not—"

Maponos looked up just as a large, dark car clipped ATEP's fender, driving ATEP off the road and over a cliff.

"Shamrocks!"

Maponos regained consciousness upside-down, his body weight pressing his head and neck at a sharp angle. He wished he had listened to that radio commercial with the Fifth Dimension singing about fastening seatbelts. "ATEP. You all right?"

When the car did not answer, Maponos pushed buttons on the dash.

"ATEP, talk to me!"

Shouting and button pushing failed to get a response. Maponos climbed out of the upside down car, which looked to have been in a demolition derby. Maponos looked up at the cliff top, a good one hundred feet up. "A little help here?" he shouted.

"ATEP, buddy, are you all right?" Maponos walked around the car, looking in the windows and tapping the body, trying to get a response. "I hate to leave you like this, bud, but I've got to go for help. I'll be back as soon as I can."

Maponos sat in Tammie's pristine garage, next to the wreck of ATEP.

"Are you in there, bud?" Maponos asked for the hundredth time. "We've been together for 2,200 years. You can't leave me now. It's not even your worst crash. Remember that time in the Circus Maximus during that chariot race? Twelve horses crashed together and I swear that you came away with another horse's legs, but you got up. After a couple days, you were the fastest horse again. Or how about that time when I wanted to one-up Sleipnir and you had ten legs. You tripped so many times you broke every bone in your legs. Or, how about when you were a motorcycle and I tried to jump you from one roof to another? You crashed into a brick wall, then landed in the alley and shoved your rear wheel through your block, and my kidney. That had to be worse than this little tumble over a cliff."

Maponos rubbed one of the few smooth spots on the car's body. "I don't know if I can go on without you."

The car said nothing, showed no lights.

Hands caressed Maponos's neck and shoulders, becoming a massage.

"How are you holding up?" Tammie asked.

"Not well."

"I don't understand why I can't even loosen a nut or bolt. I need to change out parts, check his motherboard, but everything is locked up tight. Is this how a god dies?"

"I don't know. The only Celtic god that died was Balor. He was a Fomorian so I don't even know if that counts."

"I thought Balor was Norse."

"That was Baldur. Balor was a one-legged cyclops whose looks could kill, so he kept his eye closed, which allowed Lug, his son, to sneak up and kill him with a slingshot boulder to the eye."

"Oh." Tammie's hands drifted down.

Maponos moved to give her a better angle and bumped his favorite piece of anatomy on what was left of ATEP's side mirror.

A very odd sensation tickled Maponos' brain. He yearned to be worshipped, but this sensation made him feel unhappy inside. He turned around. Tammie grabbed his engorging crankshaft.

"You know, ATEP really cares for you," he said.

"But I can't love him like I can love you."

Maponos lifted Tammie's hands from his crotch and held them in her soft bosom.

"ATEP needs you right now, more than me. Sit with him, with your hands on him. He always liked that."

"But—"

Not knowing what to say, Maponos fled.

At sunrise, Maponos drove a gold Corvette to the starting line of the race. After recovering from their surprise, the gathered drivers and crews applauded.

"Alright. Quiet down. Today is the last day of the race. As you know I had a little accident yesterday and so had to go to a back-up car, and no, it's not solar, although it is bright like the sun." He winked at the Corvette. The car did not wink back. "I want a clean race, today. All passes must be made with plenty of room. Divers, to your cars."

Maponos removed the Corvette's T-top windows and placed them in the tiny trunk, then he sat in the low car. He realized that the car could not start itself. His keys were in his tight jeans and so were impossible to squeeze out of his pocket. "This is going to be a long day," he said. "I miss ATEP more than I would have imagined."

The Corvette did not answer, which made him even sadder.

When the race began, Maponos stayed near Walter Suther, the likely next target. Having raced for days, the cars stayed in their places, at their fastest paces, except for Lou Garman's Continental, which dropped back until it was right in front of Maponos.

"Now I can't see the cars in front of me," Maponos said.

The Corvette did not answer.

On a slight uphill, the Continental pulled to the left and drifted back until the driver was visible. Maponos waved but Lou Garman did not wave back, instead a huge man with freckles made an obscene gesture. The redheaded man lifted a huge, gnarly slingshot from the seat and pulled back a small boulder.

Maponos tromped the gas pedal. The Corvette leaped ahead of the boxy Continental. Spinning the steering wheel and stepping on the brakes, Maponos spun the Corvette around directly into the path of the much larger car. A quick step on the gas spun the rear tires, lowering the front of the car. Maponos dove across the passenger seat as the Continental drove up over the Corvette.

Maponos climbed out of his ruined car and ran to the driver's side of the now upside down Continental.

"Lug! Why are you trying to kill me?"

The Fomorian upstart grabbed the sides of the shattered window and pushed outward, ripping the Continental in half and freeing himself from the wreckage. He swelled to his proper, giant size.

"I'm killing all of the Celtic pantheon until I reign supreme. A bag of sugar in the gas tanked Atepomarus. You're next." Lug raised the slingshot.

"Aren't you afraid of my power?" Maponos stalled and exuded his power.

"What is your power?"

"Always youthful."

"I'm so frightened. My power is killing gods and you're next. Any last words?" Lug pulled back the boulder.

Maponos smiled at the swarming teenaged girls. "Girls, that man threatened to hurt my face."

"Get him!" the girls screamed.

"This isn't over," Lug shouted while fending off the scratching fingernails of the girls.

Maponos strode to the partially flattened Corvette. He ducked to check the flattened front tire.

A boulder tore a slash through the roof. Maponos looked through the channel and right into a boulder on Lug's slingshot. Girls lay scattered around the giant.

Maponos ducked and a boulder smashed through the car. He skittered to the far end of the car and a boulder sheared off the bumper where he had just been hiding. Boulders shredded the Corvette, leaving Maponos little cover.

Maponos combed his mullet. "This could be the end, and I never found true love."

A black vehicle darted between Maponos and Lug. A boulder bounced off the windshield. Maponos squinted. The vehicle was too tall to be a car, but too sleek to be a Jeep. It had large, black wheels.

"ATEP, is that you, bud?"

"Yes, Maponos," said ATEP in his characteristic horsey voice.

"What did Tammie do to you?"

"Nothing. I transformed into a new, more useable shape. I am a car with four-wheel drive."

"Like a cross between a car and a truck? How many cylinders now? How big is the crankshaft?"

"Eight cylinders. I'm mainly powered by solar, now, with a co-gen electric engine and battery back-up."

"Only eight? Is there a backseat?"

"Yes."

"Thank Cernunnos." Maponos rushed from behind the Corvette and into ATEP's open door.

A boulder shattered on the windshield, rocking ATEP.

"You get any weapons in your upgrade?"

"No, I'm a glorified horse. But soldiers used to pray to you, remember?"

"They prayed to me for bravery, which they confused with youthful bravado. I got many young heroes killed for their reckless actions like frontal assaults on overwhelming odds. I was never a soldier. Those were the female battle gods."

A boulder blasted the windshield, making a small crack.

"You need to do something soon," ATEP said. "My windshield can only sustain two more impacts."

A boulder bounded off the windshield, making the crack larger.

Lug smiled and loaded another boulder from a bulging sack tied to his belt.

"All right. Pummel that Corvette into some sort of weapon."

While fending off boulders with his sloped back window, ATEP repeatedly crashed into the Corvette until it resembled a club. "Now what?"

"I'm going to get that Corvette and charge Lug in a reckless frontal attack. You shield me and distract him."

"I don't like the sound of that." Another boulder bounced off ATEP's back window. "I have a sunroof."

"I like it. A glorious charge on my great horse one last time. It's been a pleasure working with you. See you in Tír na nÓg." Maponos leaped out of ATEP and snatched up the car club. Springing while tearing off his shirt, he dropped through the sunroof.

"Charge!"

After an impressive burnout that filled the air with smoke and the stench of burnt rubber, ATEP darted toward the giant.

A boulder bounced off the windshield, and Maponos swung the club like a baseball bat to drive the missile right back at Lug. It pierced Lug's eye and the Fomorian fell like a redwood.

ATEP skidded to a stop. Maponos jumped out and onto Lug's chest. He waved the club over his head and screamed a battle cry in Ancient Gaelic.

Around him, the recently recovered young ladies swooned.

When the wind stopped blowing his mullet, Maponos leaped down. He considered the crumpled Corvette. "A car club. Pretty useful."

"Well done, Maponos. I knew you could do it," ATEP said.

Maponos leaned on ATEP's fender. "Thanks, bud. I couldn't have done it without you. Hey, what's up with this crazy black paint?"

"Infused solar panels. Every part of my body can collect solar energy."

"Hot," Maponos said, but he was hardly listening because the young ladies were awakening from their swoons.

"Who wants to worship me?" he said.

The girls rushed forward. Maponos ushered the first three into the back seat. He chuckled.

"Rubber covered backseat." ATEP whinnied.

III's Company

Brian Koscienski and Chris Pisano

"Helen, will you get a load of the kids these days? Look at these girls and how short their togas are!" Menelaus groused, looking through his living room window to the sunny day of the outside world. "I swear I can see the one girl's Vesuvius!"

"Mene, you wouldn't know a Vesuvius if one erupted on you," Helen replied, sitting on the couch, her legs tucked under her floral print, over-sized toga.

Lips pursed, Menelaus turned from the window and scowled at his wife. With her back to him and the window, she ignored his re-action while she flipped through the papyrus pages of her magazine, *Modern Pompeii Woman*. Talking to her crown of curls, he said, "That's not true. I just don't need to see a Vesuvius every time I go to the gro-cery store."

"I think it's exciting."

"You think a trip to the grocery store is exciting."

Helen closed her magazine and turned around onto her knees on the cushion. She snapped at her husband, "I do not, Mene! But it's the only excitement that you offer me anymore! You used to be excit-ing. You used to be willing to sail across the sea to whisk me away. You used to say I had a face that could launch M ships."

"You still have a face that could launch M ships."

"I do?" she cooed. "You really think so?"

"Sure. If we went to the docks right now, M ships would leave!" He grinned, open-mouthed, at his clever comment, but made sure to turn his head away from Helen, so she would not see him.

Helen promptly swatted the top of his gray-haired head with the rolled up magazine. She turned back around, slapped the magazine on the coffee table, and then crossed her arms over her chest. In a half-whine, half-pout, she said, "Well, this is going to be one heck of an anniversary."

Menelaus put his hands in his toga pockets and slouched. "Sorry, Helen. I didn't mean to upset you on our special day."

Standing, she shooed the stray wrinkles from her toga. As she walked by, she continued, "You're lucky the kids upstairs are hosting a party for me, and Mercury is cooking. I have to use the powder room. While I'm there, you better run upstairs and confirm that everything is going to plan."

Menelaus stood silently; content to watch his wife leave the room. Once she did, he peeked down the hallway one last time, and then rushed to the liquor cabinet, the one place Helen would never suspect Menelaus to hide her anniversary present. He pulled out the ornate box he had stashed there. Just as taken aback now as he was the other C times he'd checked on it, he whispered to himself, "Everything is going to plan."

On the verge of giggling, he closed the cabinet and left the apartment, box in arm. After bounding up the stairs two at a time, he knocked on another apartment door. Minerva, a short perky woman with shorter black hair and an even perkier smile, greeted him. "Hi, Mr. Troy! What's up?"

Menelaus frowned. A half-XII pixies flittered close to the ceiling, playing pan flutes and harps and tambourines in a modern cacophony, while Venus and Mercury moved offensively around the room to the up-tempo beats. In her short toga, the very same style Menelaus griped about earlier, Venus's butt cheeks took turns peeking out from underneath, while her bouncing breasts flirted with escape. Mer-

cury all but marched in place while snapping his fingers, his head bobbing to the beat of Venus' chest and her off-center, blonde ponytails. *It
wasn't fair*, Menelaus grumbled inwardly. When he was young, goddesses weren't built like that, and their attention certainly wasn't
wasted on the wrong type of men. Men like Mercury, whose winged
feet made him look more at home with the pixies in the air, not with
two beautiful roommates. Of course, if Mercury wasn't the type of
man he was, if he were a man's man, then Menelaus would never allow him to live here with two such divine creatures.

"Turn that racket off!" Menelaus snapped. "I'm the landlord of
a respectable building, and I want to keep it that way."

The song and dance stopped. Venus looked confused; Mercury
looked guilty. Minerva shooed the pixies away out the nearby window.
"What's wrong, Mr. Troy?"

"What's wrong? What's wrong? You're hosting my anniversary
party tonight. Instead of getting ready, you're acting like my worst tenants."

"It's all good, Mr. Troy," Mercury said. "We were just testing
the new sound system. All the decorations are in the girls' room and
the meal is cooking in the kitchen."

Venus' bottom lip pouted out and her eyes shimmered with the
start of tears. "We're not really your worst tenants, are we?"

Menelaus looked down and dragged one of his sandals across
the floor. "No. You're not."

Venus squealed and flounced across the room and hugged him.
Sour faced, Menelaus pulled away. "Okay, okay. I'm a great landlord."

"Is that why you're here?" Minerva asked. "To let us know
how great you are."

Menelaus frowned, unsure about the level of sarcasm. "No. To
see how the party planning is coming along. And to hide this from

Helen." He presented the box. Mercury took it from him, but it was Venus who couldn't keep her hands off it. Caressing the lid, her eyes bugged out over its magnificence. "Pretty."

"Don't open it!" Menelaus yelled, startling Mercury, causing him to fumble the box. Minerva went for the box as well, trying to keep it from falling to the floor. Menelaus drew his lips to his teeth and impotently wiggled his fingers as if they were involved in the fight against gravity. Finally, Mercury got the situation under control and placed the box on the coffee table, and raised his hands in the air. Everyone backed away in unison.

"Okay," Menelaus started. "No one open the box. It's for Helen. No one even touch it." He continued to back away to the door, pointing his finger at the residents. After one final poke to no one and everyone, he exited.

Venus reached for the box.

Minerva slapped her hand. "Venus! You heard Mr. Troy! Do not open the box. It's for Mrs. Troy."

Venus bounced on the balls of her feet while flapping her hands at the wrists in a mini tantrum. "But Minerva!"

"Venus! No!" Minerva scolded.

With one final foot stomp, Venus stopped. "Fine. I'm going to pick out a toga for the party."

"Me, too," Minerva said, following Venus to their shared bedroom.

Mercury laughed and shook his head as he aimed for the kitchen. Time to check the fig pie he was baking for the party. Before he could make it to the kitchen, a knock came from the front door. He looked to the girls' bedroom in hopes that they heard. Judging from the giggling, they had not. No help from them. Praying that his fig pie didn't need any further assistance, he bounded across the living room and answered the door. "Hello?"

There stood a teenage girl with perfectly even pigtails. As she gazed upon him, her smile grew. "You're cute."

"Actually, my name is Mercury. And you are?"

She sauntered in, her hips rolling with far more experience than her years would imply. "I'm Pandora."

Confused as to why she invited herself in, Mercury asked, "Can I help you?"

In a guttural purr, she replied, "I bet you can."

"No, I mean, are you looking for someone in particular?"

"I'm here to see Menelaus Troy. He's my uncle."

Mercury jumped back as if her hair had turned to snakes. "Your uncle? How can such an adorable girl be related to him?"

Doe-eyed, Pandora took a step closer. "You think I'm adorable?"

One more step backward, Mercury answered, "For a girl. A young, little girl."

Pandora advanced, her sultry voice returning. "I'm XVIII years old. I'll be graduating soon."

"Graduating? You're still in school? See, you're still in school and do school things with school people. I'm long out of school. I'm a chef and do chef things like make fig pie … fig pie? My fig pie!" With that, he bolted from the living into the kitchen.

Alone in the living room, Pandora wandered around, looking at the decorative tapestries and urns. Then something shiny on the coffee table caught her eye – the ornate box. As she slinked over to it, she glanced in all directions to make sure she was still alone. Satisfied with the situation, she reached for the box.

And opened it.

A tornado of horror erupted from the box. Shielding her face with her hands from the whipping winds, all she could see were glimpses of fangs and wings, glowing eyes and calloused skin. Shrieks of agony that could be mistaken for ecstasy mixed with cries of pleasure that could be pain. Fighting through the torrent of despair, Pandora strained to reach out with one hand. Nearly blind, she groped along the coffee table until she found the lid and slammed it down on the box. Huffing and puffing, Pandora looked around the room for any evidence of whatever she had unleashed. Nothing. The room was empty until Venus and Minerva ran in from their bedroom.

Eyes wide, Minerva asked, "What happened? What was all that noise? It sounded like every evil thing ever being released into the world!"

Pandora composed herself to express nothing but innocence. "I don't know. I just got here."

"Me, too," Venus said. "I don't know either. And I don't know who you are."

"I'm Pandora."

Eyes wide, Minerva noticed Pandora's proximity to the box. "Why are you standing so close to the box?"

"What box?" Pandora's coyness fooled no one.

"Did you open the box?" Minerva asked, voice rising in timbre. "Please tell me you didn't open the box."

Pandora shrugged a shoulder. "I didn't open the box."

"Did someone say the box was opened?" Menelaus asked, standing in the open doorway. He barged into the apartment, straight for the coffee table. "I heard you kids making all kinds of noise, and it woke me from my nap. It's getting so a man can't even get XL winks around here!"

"Mr. Troy ...?" Minerva started, but stopped as Menelaus leaned over and opened the box.

The now empty box.

"Who opened the box?" he wailed.

"She did," Pandora answered, pointing to Venus.

"I did?" Venus asked.

"Yep."

Minerva stepped in front of Venus to come to her defense. "She did not!"

"I didn't?" Venus asked.

"No, you didn't," Minerva reassured her.

Venus stepped in front of Minerva and stomped her foot down and pointed to Pandora. "Yeah! I didn't open the box. She did."

Menelaus turned to his niece. With a simple smile and wide eyes, she was the perfect statue of innocence, as if sculpted by Pasiteles himself. Shaking with rage, Menelaus turned back to the girls and waved his index finger. "How dare you blame my niece for this. I asked you to do one simple favor and you couldn't do it and then have the nerve to blame a little girl."

Pandora batted her eyelashes and interjected, "Yeah. I'm only XVIII, you know."

"You're lucky I don't evict you right now," Menelaus continued as he grabbed Pandora by the hand and led her to the door. Before he left, he finished with, "Tonight's party better be perfect, or I *will* evict you!"

Venus started to cry, a tearless bawl, just as Mercury exited the kitchen carrying a pie with blackened edges. Waving away the wisps of smoke, Mercury said, "Don't cry Venus, I might be able to salvage a little from it and call it a tort. And I still have time to make another pie."

Venus sobbed even louder.

Mercury reeled back. "Okay, so you don't like my fig pie. Sheesh!"

Minerva flattened her brow and shot a look of contempt to Mercury. "It's not your fig pie, Merc. Pandora opened Mrs. Troy's box and now if we don't throw the perfect party, we'll get evicted."

Looking back to his burnt pie, Mercury said, "No wonder Venus is crying about my pie."

"Merc!"

"I'm sorry, Minerva, but unless you can think of a way to get Pandora to tell the truth, then all our hopes rest on my baking ability."

"Oh!" Minerva shouted. "I have an idea!"

Venus stopped crying and looked to Mercury as Minerva ran to her bedroom. Mercury simply shrugged his shoulders and blew at the smoke emanating from his pie. With a small vial in her hand, Minerva ran from her room to the kitchen. "Follow me!"

Venus and Mercury did as their roommate requested, entering the kitchen just in time to see Minerva open the last of the cabinet doors and grab a large ramekin. "Ta-da!"

"A crazy person in my kitchen?" Mercury asked as he looked in wonder at all of the open cabinets.

"No, Merc! You said you could salvage some of the pie and turn it into a tort. We'll do that, but we'll add some of this," Minerva said, handing the vial to Mercury.

"And this is?"

"You don't listen, do you? Just last week, when Venus and I had a girls' night with Veritas, she gave us this truth potion."

Mercury held the vial close to his face. "I remember. I remember asking you to never fix me up with Veritas."

Minerva slapped his shoulder. "Merc! Be serious. Add some of the potion to your tort. Venus and I will take it downstairs to the Troys. We'll offer it to Pandora as an apology."

"Do you think it will work?" Venus asked, watching Mercury scoop the center of the pie into the ramekin.

"It has to," Minerva replied, "Because we don't want to try to find another place to live."

Mercury glazed the top of the tort with the potion, stuck a fork deep into it, and handed it to Minerva. "Good luck girls."

Venus and Minerva ran down the stairs to the Troys' apartment and knocked on their door. Menelaus answered, grumpy scowl already upon his face. "What do you want?"

Minerva audibly gulped. "Well, Mr. Troy, Venus and I felt bad about the incident earlier, so we wanted to come down and apologize to Pandora."

"Okay. Come on in. Mrs. Troy is in the bedroom getting ready for the party. She'll be out any minute."

"We wanted to apologize with tort!" Venus said, barging into the apartment past Menelaus. She went straight to Pandora, who sat on the couch flipping through the latest issue of *XVII* magazine. Venus presented the ramekin. The teenager didn't even bother to look at it before saying, "No thanks."

"Oh, come on. It's yummy."

This time Pandora looked up, her voice changing from bored to angry. "I said no thank you."

Venus waved the ramekin in front of her face. "Are you suuuuuuure you don't want to try a bite?"

Pandora's face turned red, but before she could release her rage, Menelaus circled around the couch and plucked the fork from the ramekin. "I don't mind if I do."

Venus moved the ramekin just as Menelaus tried to garner a piece. He tried again, but only stabbed air as Venus pulled the tort away. Looking nervous, Minerva whispered, "Venus? What are you doing?"

Frustrated, Menelaus approached with the fork primed and said, "You're not leaving until I have a piece of tort."

Venus moved the ramekin to her face and used her fingers to scoop the tort into her mouth. Her eye lashes fluttered as she chewed, cheeks distended by fig tort. Her fingers continued to slide around the ramekin collecting the dessert remains and shoving them into her already stuffed face. With one last gulp, she started licking the ramekin until Minerva yelled at her, "Venus! What are you doing?"

Blurry-eyed from the side effects of the potion, she mumbled, "I didn't want Mr. Troy to ruin the surprise about Mrs. Troy's anniversary present."

Menelaus waved his hands about while looking over his shoulder. "Shhh! Shhh! Enough surprise present talk. You two gotta leave if you're going to be talking about that."

"Yes, Mr. Troy," Minerva said as she guided Venus out the door by the shoulders.

"I gave Prometheus fire because he told me that I'm pretty," Venus said as she staggered up the stairs.

"I know, sweetie," Minerva replied as she opened the door to their apartment.

They entered the living room just as Mercury exited the kitchen, wiping his hands with a rag. "I just put a new pie in the oven. How'd it go with Pandora? Did she confess to Mr. Troy?"

"No," Minerva answered, guiding the stumbling Venus to their bedroom. "She didn't want the tort, but Mr. Troy did. Venus ate the whole thing so Mr. Troy wouldn't let slip what he got for Mrs. Troy for their anniversary."

"Jupiter cheats on Juno! With humans! And you turned a human into a spider because you lost to her in a weaving contest, Minerva!" Venus sang.

Minerva shoved Venus into the bedroom. She followed her inside, but before shutting the door, she explained. "I won that contest! The blind goddess Justitia could have stitched better than that human girl."

Mercury laughed. Once again he aimed for the kitchen to check on his fig pie, and once again, a knock at the door distracted him. He debated about ignoring it, but his best friend yelled through the door, "Hey, Merc, it's me Laverna. You home? I got a great story."

Mercury opened the door to greet Laverna. Gold medallions rested on the thick patch of his chest hair, and he had belted his toga to expose a large triangle of skin nearly down to his waist. "It's not the story of how you sold Apollo a lemon, is it?"

Wincing as if physically struck, Laverna entered the apartment. "Hey, that used chariot was perfect – *perfect* – when I sold it to him. He never asked if it was rated to carry the sun!"

"So, if he had asked, you would have told him the truth?"

"What? No! But then he would have a good reason to be mad at me. But that's not why I'm here. I went on a date last night."

"You go on a date every night. Why was last night's different?"

"Because it was with Greedy Gorgon."

Mercury curled the fingers on both hands to mimic cups and held them in front of his chest. "Greedy Gorgon? You mean the one with the really big medusas?"

Laverna clapped his hands and rubbed them together. "The one and the same."

"Oh yeah? How'd it go?"

"Well, there was a lot of wiggling."

Mercury inched closer to Laverna, a co-conspirator ready to learn a big secret. "Yeah? And?"

"There was a lot of squirming."

Mercury moved even closer, his voice dropping. "Yeah? And?"

"Snakes, Merc! She had snakes for hair!"

Mercury reeled back. "Really?"

"Yes, really!"

"How have we never noticed that?" Both men looked at Mercury's hands, still in the same position as they were at the beginning of the conversation. Ashamed at his own shallowness, Mercury shook his hands and then hid them behind his back. "Okay. But did you seal the deal?"

"No! I tried. I begged. I promised her a golden fleece. She was too mad at me for never noticing her snakes."

Mercury laughed.

"It's not funny, Merc. I felt like Xerxes going up against CCC angry Spartans."

"No, I know it's not. I have a woman problem of my own."

Wringing his hands together gleefully, Laverna smiled and advanced. "Really?"

Mercury frowned. "It's not like that. It's Mr. Troy's niece, Pandora."

"Ooooooh! Juicy."

"Ha, ha. Mr. Troy got Mrs. Troy a decorative box for their anniversary. He had us keep it until the party, but told us not to open it. But his niece opened it and then blamed Venus for it. Then the girls tried to slip Pandora some truth potion, but apparently that didn't work."

"Well, that's a problem."

"Yes, but not the real problem. The real problem is that she can't keep her hands off me."

Laverna laughed. "Mr. Troy's niece can't keep her hands off you? I can't believe that."

"Believe it," came from the doorway. There stood Pandora, leaning against the frame, twirling a fork in her hand. Once she had the attention of both men, she put it in her mouth and slowly pulled it out. "Venus and Minerva forgot their fork. Uncle Menelaus told me to return it. He says he didn't want to do it himself, because this apartment is too weird."

Mercury stepped behind Laverna for protection. Laverna stepped forward and extended his hands toward the kitchen. "By all means, come on in. Why don't you drop it off in the kitchen. Mercury will show you where it goes."

Pandora put the fork back in her mouth and sauntered into the apartment, never taking her eyes off Mercury until the kitchen door closed. Mercury grabbed Laverna by the shoulders and shook. "Are you crazy? I can't go in there by myself. Alone. With her."

"I have an idea," Laverna said. It was his turn to grab Mercury by the shoulders, but he added a half rotation spin. He then guided Mercury across the living room toward the kitchen. With one final shove, he sent Mercury stumbling into the kitchen.

After crashing into the sink, he turned to run back into the living room, but Pandora moved to block the door, now swirling the fork in her mouth. She pulled it out and purred, "So, where should I put this fork?"

Mercury gulped. "Ummm, dirty forks go in the sink."

Pandora sashayed around the small table in the middle of the kitchen. At the same pace, Mercury circled the table as well, using it as a barrier between Pandora and him. Once at the sink, she dropped the fork. The tip of her tongue glided across her upper lip. "What's the matter? You look tense."

"Tense?" As he stammered, Mercury clasped and unclasped his hands, folded them over his chest, and immediately moved them behind his back. "Who's tense? I'm not tense, you're tense. There's no reason to be tense, no tension here."

Pandora resumed her way around the table, and Mercury continued to retreat accordingly. "So, Mercury, do you know what I've been studying in school?"

Mercury tried to speak, but found that he couldn't. Instead, he shook his head vigorously.

"Massage. I'm studying to be a masseuse."

"Masseuse?" Mercury squeaked.

"I'm the top of my class."

"Top?" Mercury's voice hit an even higher pitch.

""Top," Pandora replied as she hurried around the table.

Brain mired by the connotations, Mercury froze, powerless. Pandora slid behind him, placed her hands onto his shoulders, and plied her craft. His base desires culminated into an unstoppable force that crushed his reason and common sense. She guided him to sit in a chair by the table. Tracing her fingers across his face, she walked around to the front of the chair. Fingers combing through his hair, she straddled his lap. Puckering her lips, she cooed, "Very top of my class."

Eyes half shut, his lips seemed to pucker on their own as well as if they were sentient entities that moved only by lust. As her face moved closer, his ankle wings flapped faster. He knew this was wrong, but for the life of him, he couldn't remember why. Instead, in duck-lipped baby talk, he repeated, "Vewy top of your cwass."

Until the kitchen door flung open.

Laverna pushed Menelaus, stumbling, into the kitchen. Menelaus griped non-stop about being there against his will. Then he saw the scene before him.

"What's going on here?" Menelaus yelled.

Pandora jumped from Mercury's lap. "Uncle Menelaus!"

Jumping from the chair, Mercury repeated, "Uncuw Menewaus!"

"Get out here!" Menelaus yelled, pointing to the living room.

Under the scornful watch of Menelaus and unchecked glee of Laverna, Pandora and Mercury scurried into the living room. Curious about the commotion, Venus and Minerva exited their bedroom. Venus, still wobbly from the truth potion, needed Minerva's assistance to stand. "What's happening out here?"

"Laverna here ruined yet another nap for me by dragging me from my apartment all the way up here, and when I get here, I find Pandora on Mercury's lap!"

"It's Mercury," Pandora squealed, pointing to the accused. "I just wanted to return the fork and he wanted *more*! He … he … pulled me … onto his lap and tried to kiss me."

Crossing his arms over his chest, Menelaus scowled at Pandora. Nodding toward Mercury, he asked, "*He* pulled you onto his lap?"

"Yes."

"*He* tried to kiss you?"

"Yes."

"You're lying, Pandora. And I think you lied about the box as well. Go downstairs. I'll deal with you in a moment."

Fists clenched, Pandora stomped all the way out of the apartment.

"Thank you, Mr. Troy," Mercury said.

"I knew you couldn't have done what she said, Mercury."

"You did?"

"Yeah. Because you're ... you know." Pantomiming his words, he put one hand on his hip and cocked it while extending his other hand, wrist going limp.

Mercury rolled his eyes, upset that he had to lie about his personal choices, but satisfied that his living arrangement was no longer in jeopardy – until Venus spoke up.

Eyes half crossed, she swayed as she said, "That's not the reason."

Menelaus turned to Venus and asked, "It's not?"

Minerva tried to put her hand over Venus's mouth, but the blonde goddess kept smacking it away.

"What's going on here? What's wrong with her?" Menelaus asked.

Mercury sighed. "The girls put a truth potion in the tort they brought down earlier and tried to get Pandora to eat it. They didn't want you to eat it because they were afraid you'd tell Mrs. Troy about the box, so Venus ate the tort."

The ridges along Menelaus's forehead deepened as he pondered what he just heard. He turned to Venus and asked, "Okay. What's the truth then? About Mercury?"

She smacked Minerva's hand away one last time and said, "Mercury is the nicest god in the world. He couldn't have tried to kiss Pandora because he would never try to take advantage of someone like that."

Face softening, Menelaus walked over to the box and picked up the lid from the coffee table. Minerva said, "We are sorry that the box is empty."

Menelaus smiled and said, "You are all good kids. You tried to help each other, you tried to tell me the truth, and you wanted to make sure Mrs. Troy's surprise wasn't ruined. You make me feel good about kids these days. The box isn't empty. It is full of hope." He punctuated his statement by gently placing the lid on it.

Putting his hands in his toga's pockets, he meandered to the door. Before he left the apartment, he said, "Thank you. I'm looking forward to the party tonight."

After he left, Mercury, Minerva, and Laverna all heaved a sigh of relief. Mercury looked to Venus and said, "So, Venus, are there any other truths that you want to share?"

"Yeah! Laverna's been tricking us all along. He is really a she."

Minerva and Mercury gawped at Laverna. With a carefree shrug, Laverna said, "A great used chariot came in today. Anyone wanna take a look at it?"

The friends all shared a laugh.

The Love Fune
Izzy Squared / A Catch for Katachi / Whose Sea is it, Anyway?
Lee C. Hillman

Captain's Log, the tenth day of Minazuki, the month of water, in the fifty-third year of the third cycle since the ascension of the Empress Fujira (the year of the dragon): We have put in to port at Hamamatsu after a successful and propitious voyage. Our passengers have disembarked and we are about to board our next group of guests. I have looked over the manifest; this cruise will include some of the most prestigious passengers we have hosted since the day the celestial sun herself, Amaterasu, graced the Chrysanthemum Princess *with Her loveliness. The signs are favorable for an auspicious journey....*

Captain Uwatsutsu, he who possessed the surface of the sea, descended the stairs from the bridge to the promenade deck, where key members of his crew were already awaiting their guests' arrivals. The ship's purser, Daikokuten, stood by with clipboard in hand, ready to take charge of any precious cargo that might need special attention. Ōkuninushi, their doctor, was there to lend the proceedings an air of confidence and well-being. And outshining them both, the heavenly goddess of revelry, Ame-no-Uzume, director of activities, beamed forth a smile as radiant as sunlight upon the waves. Uwatsutsu felt a haiku forming. He committed it to memory so that he could calligraph it later. For now, there were passengers to welcome.

"Greetings, honored Captain," Daikokuten said as he saw him approach. They exchanged bows.

"The signs were quite favorable this morning," Dr. Ōkuninushi offered brightly.

"Yes, I consulted them as well, my friend," said Capt. Uwatsutsu. "We have quite the company of noble personages today, Daikoku. Uzume, I hope we will be suitably entertaining."

"Aye-aye, Captain!" the goddess said with a wink.

The first group of passengers boarded and bows were duly exchanged. Then a resplendent couple climbed the gangway, but they were so occupied in argument that they barely noticed the Captain and crew.

"I still don't see why I can't just kill them," the wife said to the husband.

"Because, my love, one doesn't simply kill with no rhyme or reason," he insisted.

She stopped in her tracks, the long train of her layered kimonos swirling around her feet. "That's the most ridiculous thing you have ever said," she told him. "That's exactly what I do. That's the nature of death itself." She turned imperiously to the Captain. "Do you not agree that death is random, indiscriminate, and inevitable?"

Uwatsutsu considered his answer carefully. "Well, Lady, it is for mortals, of course," he agreed with diplomacy. "But here on the *Chrysanthemum Princess*, we consider it a standard of service to deliver our passengers safely into every harbor--very much alive, if that's how they joined us. But you are looking remarkably well yourself, Lady Izanami," he continued with a respectful bow.

The goddess of death turned a baleful eye toward him, but returned the bow gracefully. "Izanagi," she said to her husband, "you never told me our Captain would be a god of the water."

"This one is but a humble servant of the surface, dear Lady," the Captain said softly. "I believe you are well acquainted with my brother of the deep, Sokutsutsu. But nevertheless, I hope you both will do me the honor of dining at my table tonight." He did not nod toward Daikoku to confirm the invitation; he could be certain that the purser would make all the necessary arrangements.

"That is most kind," Izanagi replied. "We should be honored."

"I do not eat worldly food--anymore," said Izanami. The disappointment of her tone had a tinge of regret to it.

"My lady," put in Daikokunyo, mysteriously appearing now in her female alter-ego, "not to worry. We have extensive kitchens--I oversee them myself. I can assure you, there is fare fit for your needs."

"There, you see, my love?" Izanagi said eagerly. "I knew this trip would refresh you."

"It has not done so yet," she observed sourly. "But let us go to our stateroom. I hope it is on a lower level. I have been above the earth for too long."

They moved along as Daikokunyo summoned a steward to assist them.

"She's a ray of sunshine," Ōkuninushi muttered under his breath.

"I don't blame her," said Uzume. "How would you feel if your lover followed you to the underworld, failed to rescue you, and then abandoned you there?"

"That's an oversimplification," said the doctor. "But I suppose I'd feel perturbed, if you put it that way. Still, I don't think I'd take it out on a thousand people per day."

"And Izanagi exhausts himself bringing life to fifteen hundred a day, just to make up for her," Uwatsutsu pointed out. He felt the need to avert a battle between his crewmembers. "Let us hope that the powers of our little vessel set them back on the path to love."

As he said this, another important immortal approached them all. This deity was formless, a collection of wisps of smoke in varying colors and levels of transparency. The tendrils were held together by the clothes they wore. A mask with a bland expression covered what should have been a face.

"They prefer the pronoun 'they,'" Daikoku whispered in the Captain's ear as the deity bowed in greeting.

"Kuninotokotachi," said Uwatsutsu reverently, opting for a more formal address and appropriate bow. "We are most honored. We hope you have a very pleasant voyage."

Rather than speak, the deity projected their response so that they all felt their answer. "I am here to observe," they said. "My pleasure has little to do with the matter."

Uwatsutsu blinked, but unfazed, he said, "Nevertheless, we shall endeavor to make your time aboard as comfortable as possible. Please do not hesitate to ask if there is anything my crew can do to improve your experience." He almost asked if the ancient one would dine at his table, but swallowed the invitation at the last moment. He wasn't certain that one of the oldest gods known to anyone even ate food at all, much less would deign to join other gods and goddesses, some of whom Kuninotokotachi had summoned into existence, at something so mundane as a meal. Luckily, Uzume was way ahead of him, as usual, with her innate knack for pleasing the passengers.

"Kuninotokotachi-kami, if you will kindly honor this humble servant, it would be my great pleasure to conduct you to your stateroom."

The being bowed again and allowed Uzume to show the way.

"I had no idea they were planning to sail," the doctor said after the two had gone. "I wonder how they feel about Izanami and Izanagi being aboard. After all, they are, in a way, their creator."

"Who knows?" the Captain said in astonishment. "I've never seen a hidden kami--well, one doesn't, does one? That's rather the point. I wonder what they meant by observing? It's going to be a most intriguing voyage."

Two days later, Captain Uwatsutsu had cause to regret his words. "Intriguing" was hardly the term for it--maddening was more accurate. Their course should have been straightforward, and the seas calm for their trip southeast. But where they should have sailed within striking distance of the first port on their journey, instead, they seemed to be heading into a choppy area, and no land in sight. It required much of his energy to keep the waters from buffeting the huge ship, and their rudder aiming straight. But at what? The volcanic mountain at the center of Mikuna-jima should have been visible off the bow. In fact, they should have put in the day before. What devils were playing havoc with his command of the ocean?

He left the bridge in the charge of his first officer. In his cabin, he poured a quantity of water into a basin and added salt. He stirred it with a finger, and before the pool could swirl three times, he lit a stick of incense. "Brother," he called into the water. "Naketsutsu ko ono Mikoto, I need your help. Will you speak with me?" A moment later, the water rose out of the basin in a wave form. It spilled out over the low table, its leading edge curling and growing until it took on the shape of a man in armor.

"Uwatsutsu, it has been a long time, my brother," said the watery figure. "How may I assist you?"

Uwatsutsu explained the unusual agitation of the sea. "I...I have lost our first island port," he admitted in shame. "I feel sure that if the seas were less troublesome, I could read our course."

"My portion of the oceans are in order," Naketsutsu answered. "There is nothing about the middle of the sea that should be causing you difficulty. Have you consulted the stars? The compass?"

"Both indicate we are where we should be," said the Captain, "but the island cannot be seen."

Crests of water broke over themselves in a motion rather like a shrug. "Perhaps you have a trickster on board. Anyone suspicious in the manifest?"

"None that I can think of, but then--"

"There are so many," both of them said together. "Yes," his brother continued. "The land of eight million deities offers infinite possible explanations. Well. Perhaps our eldest brother can provide an answer."

Uwatsutsu suppressed a grimace. "I had hoped to avoid involving him."

"So do not involve him, and solve your problem another way. Have you any dragons aboard?"

"Many," said Uwatsutsu.

"Ask one of them to scout for you."

"That will not do," said the Captain. "Imagine the dishonor of requesting that one of our passengers leave the *Chrysanthemum Princess* to perform such an errand!" He shook his head. "No. I shall have to find the port by other means. Thank you, my brother. Pardon my intrusion."

"It is no intrusion, Uwatsutsu," said his brother's image affectionately. "We who dwell below do not hear from you often enough."

"I regret that my duties keep me very occupied," Uwatsutsu said. "But now I must once again attend to them."

"Of course," said Nakatsutsu. The water flowed backward into the bowl as the connection broke. Uwatsutsu brewed a cup of tea while he thought of what to do. Perhaps his brother had a point, and someone on the ship could help--though not, as the other suggested, by flying overhead. He needed to consult two particular officers on his crew: his bartender, and his purser.

His purser, Daikokuten, was currently facing a challenge of his own. At Uzume's request, he had partnered with her in a four-handed game of shuffleboard against the powerful couple, Izanagi and Izanami. Their mixed doubles were also a mixed success, for Izanagi and Izanami, or the "Izzies" as Daikokuten had irreverently come to think of them, bickered constantly. It was all he and Uzume could do to keep smiling in the face of the couple's arguments.

"That disk has to go off," Izanami pointed out to her husband as he set up.

"Yes, my love," he said. He lined up his cue and pushed.

The ship hit a bump of choppy wave and the whole deck shifted. Instead of hitting the troublesome disk, Izanagi's shot slid into the "off" box on its own, missing his target completely.

"Please, that was not your error," Daikoku said immediately. "I insist that we replay your shot."

"*Domo*," Izanagi muttered, and retrieved the disk.

"Oh, nevermind," Izanami complained. "It doesn't matter. There's far too much sun today to remain outside."

Daikokuten scanned the skies. Heavy clouds covered the horizon and the turbulent sea reflected only the greyness from overhead. Uzume, standing beside him, blushed. She had also turned down her customary rosy glow, but she could only do so much. "Would you care for a parasol?" he asked politely. "Please forgive my not asking sooner."

"No, thank you," she replied imperiously. "I shall go below. Izanagi, you may remain." Whether or not he wished to stay seemed immaterial to the goddess--but the way she glanced at Uzume suggested that perhaps she felt uncomfortable at being encouraged to enjoy herself.

"Please forgive her," Izanagi said after she had descended to the lower decks. "She used to be so lovely, when she was alive."

"It can't be easy to take charge of the underworld," commented Uzume with sincerity. "Perhaps she simply needs to rest and relax."

"I had hoped, with so many other immortals here, she might enjoy the respite," Izanagi said quietly. "So far, she seems determined to find fault in everything."

"Maybe she enjoys finding fault," Daikokuten murmured, almost to himself. "Maybe she's happy when she's unhappy."

Izanagi cast a tired smile toward the crewmember. "Alas, you are probably right." He placed his cue back on the rack by the board. "I understand that this ship also has a Go master. If you will excuse me, I shall avail myself." He bowed a little stiffly and took his leave.

Daikokunyo shook out her hair before tying it into a low knot at the back of her neck. "Between us, I think she's jealous of you," she said to Uzume.

"I know. That's why I asked you to accompany us as Daikokuten. I wish she'd lighten up."

"I'm just glad she hasn't decided to start killing the passengers."

"Well, as most of them are immortal, it's a bit difficult."

At that moment, the Captain found them.

"Ah, Uzume, you're here, too. Good. I may need both of you to help me."

"Captain, is this because of our, er, navigational issue?" Daikoku asked, with a furtive glance around to make sure no passengers were listening.

"Yes. I think someone or something on this ship is preventing us from finding the port. Daikoku, please bring the manifest to the bar. I wish to consult Omoikane."

"Aye-aye, Captain," she said, and went off on her errand.

"Captain, while I've got you, there's another problem I've been meaning to talk to you about," Uzume said.

"Yes?" he invited.

"It's Kuninotokotachi," she confided. "The other passengers--they may not find romance, but at least they mingle. They mix. Kuninotoko-tachi... doesn't."

"They said they were here to observe."

"Observe what, though?"

"Uzume-chan, not everyone is designed to pair off," Uwatsutsu reminded her. "I know you live for the idea of matchmaking--"

"It's not that, Captain," she said as they made their way be-lowdecks to the bar. "It's my job to make sure everyone here is having fun."

The Captain shrugged. "Perhaps they want to spend time among others. They've had millennia to themselves, after all."

"But that's just it," she insisted. "If that's what they want, then why come on a cruise and spend the whole time indoors, apart from everyone?"

"Perhaps old habits die hard," Uwatsutsu said. "But Kuninotoko-tachi--"

"Is right behind you, sir," Uzume squeaked.

"Kuninotokotachi-kami-sama," the Captain exclaimed, whirling around. "You honor us."

"You are looking for me?" the entity asked telepathically.

"Er...after a fashion. That is--I was hoping to draw upon your in-sight, so that we might repair whatever is causing us to veer off course. Our instruments must not be working."

The deity turned their masked head toward the bulkhead. It was as if they were looking through the ship's walls directly out at the hori-zon. "But you are not off course," they projected. "This ship has circled the island twice."

"What?" Captain Uwatsutsu sputtered. "There must be some mistake. The island's nowhere in sight."

Kuninotokotachi pivoted in a slow full circle. Without the mask, or the robes, it would have been impossible to tell which way they were pointed. "Ah," they whispered, aloud, so soft that it was nearly silent, and yet it blew a breeze through the corridor that raised the hairs on Uwatsutsu's arms. The god continued in the Captain's mind, "I understand the confusion. I can see everything that is and everything that is not, whereas you can only see one reality at a time. Yes. There is someone--or more than one someone--playing with you, Captain."

"There is?" he choked. "I mean--yes. Thank you. Of course there is. But do you know who, kami-sama? And what can we do about it?"

Kuninotokotachi was still for a long time. Finally, the Captain perceived their answer. "Let us go to the bar, and discuss it."

Down in the ship's best dining room, Omoikane poured out wisdom and advice along with the finest mixed drinks on board. His current client was keeping him busy dispensing hot sake and pressed honeysuckle blossoms. From the appearance of the being, Omoikane had been at it for some time. The only other occupant at this hour was Hōtei, of course. The god of luck waved his fan toward the bar, but it seemed to do little to improve the other customer's morose mood.

"Sometimes I almost think I've got it," the small dragon said to the bartender. His speech was slightly slurred, but it could have been his forked tongue causing the sibilance. "But then, I lose my nerve."

"Hm. And you've tried leaving offerings," Omoikane responded, filling the dragon's outstretched sake cup again.

"All the time!" insisted the dragon. "I made a poem and put it into the wind," he continued solemnly. "That's why I took this cruise, even. To see if I could...get closer."

"But you haven't tried to speak to him?"

"I'm a fire dragon!" the dragon pointed out. "I don't think he'd want anything to do with me."

"You never know--Oh!" Omoikane snapped to attention as the Captain and Uzume entered.

The dragon spirit hopped off his bar stool and immediately leaned against it to steady himself. Then he squeaked, though presumably that was more in response to the multi-colored shadowy figure behind the Captain.

"Morikasai-tutsu, isn't it?" Captain Uwatsutsu identified the diminutive spirit.

"I--yes, I--it's a pleasure to meet you, Captain. Please excuse me," he continued quickly, backing away from them all before ducking out of the bar.

"Odd little fellow," the Captain commented to Omoikane.

"He's all right. Just a little lovesick," said the sage. "Katachi-kami-sama," he then said, bowing to the ancient god. "This is indeed an honor. What can I do for you, Captain?"

Just then Daikoku joined them again, clipboard in hand.

Meanwhile, it seemed Kuninotokotachi had telepathically brought Omoikane up to speed, because the bartender said, "I'm not sure why you think I can help."

"You're the god of wisdom," Uwatsutsu told him. "If anyone can view this list and decide who might be a likely suspect--"

"Captain, you're assuming it's someone on board," Omoikane said.

"Well, if we don't then we have an infinite number of potential culprits," the Captain groused. "So let's begin with someone who is taking this voyage. Who has a reason *not* to put in to the island?"

"That assumes it's deliberate," Omoikane mused, but he took the page Daikoku detached from the clipboard and looked it over.

"Loads of water-spirits," said Daikoku, handing another page to Uwatsutsu. "Any one of them could be keeping us at sea."

"But why?" the Captain said aloud. "Kunino--" The question died on his lips, for the object of his address had disappeared.

"They really don't like to mix in," Omoikane reminded him.

"Obviously."

"Don't you think they ought to, though?" Uzume asked.

"That is not for us to say," Omoikane observed.

An hour later, they had compiled a list of five suspects. "I want to handle this quietly," Captain Uwatsutsu instructed his crew. "But quickly, before anyone realizes how far behind schedule we are."

They each took one name and agreed to find and question them. Uwatsutsu asked them all to meet at his cabin half an hour before the dinner bell to discuss what they discovered.

While Omoikane summoned backup for the bar, Daikoku and Uzume left to seek their chosen passengers. Uwatsutsu pocketed his assignments and directed his steps to sick bay.

"It's a little early for your physical," Ōkuninushi joked when he opened the hatch to his visitor. "Feeling all right?"

"No, but I've written my own prescription," said Uwatsutsu, and explained what he needed. In a few minutes, they both exited the infirmary, heading in opposite directions.

The Captain's target was a demigod of the Hiuchi-nada Sea, a kami used to much calmer, but colder, waters. He was found sunning himself on a chaise near the largest swimming pool on the ship.

"Hiuchiko-san," Uwatsutsu greeted him. "I trust you are enjoying your holiday?"

"Oh, very much, Captain, only--" The demigod broke off. "Forgive my impertinence, but aren't we supposed to be at Mikura-jima by now?"

"A mere adjustment to the cruise timetable," said Uwatsutsu. He played the delay as a planned one, watching the demigod all the while to see if he showed any sign of knowledge otherwise. It would not be outside the realm of possibility that the demogod brought up the problem for the same reason. It was tiresome to bluff, but necessary, at least for the moment, to eliminate the passenger without accusing him.

Unfortunately, the demigod betrayed no hint of deception. "Oh, well, I hope we will still have time to explore the island," he said with a frown. "I've got a cousin I was going to meet. We so rarely get to see each other."

"I did not know you had a cousin there," said Uwatsutsu politely.

"Oh, yes. Shirataki-hime," said the sea spirit. "She lives at the base of a long waterfall."

"Lovely. When did you last see her?"

"Oh, not for a few centuries. I was really looking forward to catching up with her."

"I see. There should be time, never fear," said the Captain with a confidence he did not feel. He brought the conversation to a respectful conclusion. This little fellow was not their mastermind, and thus it made no sense to prolong the interview.

Half an hour before dinner, the crew met back at Uwatsutsu's cabin. As he put the final touches into tying his obi, they conferred on their detective work.

"Mine was completely innocent," said Ōkuninushi, "but I wound up giving her a potion for seasickness."

"You gave a water spirit a prescription for seasickness?" Uzume asked, aghast.

"Ironic, isn't it?" he chuckled. "But she's unused to this type of motion, being a river goddess. It's inconceivable that she could be keeping us at sea."

"What about you, Daikoku?" asked the Captain.

"Uh, well, I don't think he's responsible, Captain," said the purser. He blushed. "At least, I hope not. He's a river dragon, but he's really...very charming."

"Daikoku, are you saying--" Uzume asked with excitement.

"I have a date tonight," Daikoku confirmed, nodding.

"Oh, wonderful!" Uzume clapped. "I so hoped you'd hit it off. He's quite handsome, don't you think, and--"

"If you please!" Captain Uwatsutsu interrupted. "Daikoku, we are meant to be conducting a serious investigation, not--not pursuing our own interests in romance."

"Yes, Captain," he said.

"And Uzume, I'm surprised at you. This is not the time for matchmaking. Did you arrange it so that Daikoku could talk to this river dragon, as a means of introduction?"

"Sorry, Captain," she said, not sounding it at all. "But I don't see why we can't do both things. Eliminate the suspects and pursue romance, that is. After all, one purpose of the *Chrysanthemum Princess* is to provide opportunities for deities and spirits to--"

"To find romantic partners, yes," the Captain allowed warily. "But that does not apply when we are trying to solve a problem. I expect you all to put the safety and security of this vessel ahead of personal engagements."

"Aye, Captain," they all said together.

"I should have thought that went without saying," he grumbled. They assented again, but he continued: "Now how can we know that Daikoku's assessment is not clouded by his attraction to this dragon?"

"Oh, because he can't abide salt water," Daikoku revealed. "He specifically said that his aunt recommended the cruise, and he agrees it's diverting, but being surrounded by so much saline has him a bit out of sorts. He kept sneezing, in fact--you might give him some powder for that, doctor."

"Of course. Well. That's two down, then," said Ōkuninushi.

"Three, actually," Uzume added. "Mine's not guilty, either. She's a very nice old spirit from a hot spring in Hasetsu. She and her husband, a bath spirit, are both on the ship together. There's nothing suspicious about them at all."

"Hm," said the Captain. "And mine was not at fault. Omoikane, that leaves yours."

"Nope," Omoikane said, shaking his head. "My candidate isn't responsible either, Captain. Though he is a bit shifty, he was quite fixed on how much he's looking forward to reaching Kugoshima. He has no reason to delay us at this point in the journey."

"I don't understand," Uwatsutsu said in frustration. "Kuninotokotachi indicated we would find the cuplrit on board the ship. So if these five were the most likely perpetrators...."

"Captain, if I may--I said before, they are only the most likely if we presume that they had power over water, and if they are causing our problem deliberately." Omoikane straightened his kosode lapel a bit fastidiously. Uwatsutsu suspected the movement was to give the bartender something on which to focus besides meeting his captain's eye.

"You did indeed, Omoikane-kami," Uwatsutsu allowed. "Very well, have you any suggestions as to who might be causing this situation accidentally?"

"Many," replied Omoikane serenely. "I propose that our criteria ought to include those whose interest lies at sea, rather than in port."

"That could be almost anyone, Ōkuninushi observed.

"Or almost *everyone*," agreed Uzume.

"I have an idea that might help us," Omoikane announced. "With your permission, Captain, I shall implement it over dinner."

Sure enough, at just that moment, the dinner gong sounded.

"If it will resolve our problem, Omoikane, permission is gladly granted."

The dining room teemed with guests when the crew arrived. Uwatsutsu took his place at his table, Izanami to his right and Izanagi beside her. To his left sat Yuki-onna, the goddess of snow, a perennial passenger at this time of year. As he and the crew knelt onto their zabutons, servers swarmed the tables with trays of plated dishes. Years of practice had inured Uwatsutsu to the strange concoctions that passengers sometimes required, but the dish served to Izanami could not have been more revolting. By contrast, Yuki-onna's simple bowl of rice and lily petals seemed particularly inviting. Nonetheless, he suppressed his disgust at Izanami's platter of dried beetle carapaces, worms, and flies' wings, and raised his glass of plum wine to lead a toast.

To his shock, Omoikane rose fluidly to his knees and begged everyone's attention. "My fellow travellers," he said, "I ask you to charge your glasses tonight for our Captain. He is far too modest to say it himself, but it has been only by his intrepid skill that he has kept us from calamity today."

"Discreet, Omoikane," Uwatsutsu hissed under his breath. Omoikane must have known his action would anger the other, though, for he winked at the Captain's table. "I am sure many of you are wondering why we have not yet made our first landfall," he continued. "The answer is somewhat distressing, but please have no fear. Our Captain has everything under control. In truth, we are being pursued by none other than Umibzu himself." This caused a ripple of concern around the room. "I don't wish anyone to be alarmed--there is no danger to anyone aboard, so long as our illustrious Captain remains at our helm, so to speak. I have it on good authority that this evening when the moon is high, in the hour of the dog, the Captain intends to send our would-be hunter back into the deep where he belongs. Once Captain Uwatsutsu banishes the great beast back below, we will be safe to make landing at Mikura-jima." Omoikane raised his glass in salute. "Still, it would be improper to share rice and wine with you all without acknowledging the efforts of our benefactor. I give you, the Captain."

"The Captain!" they all echoed. Immediately, the dining room devolved into a susurrus as everyone discussed Omoikane's bombshell.

"An interesting development, Uwatsutsu-san," Izanagi commented around his wife. "Won't banishing the beast result in capsizing our vessel?"

"No one's capsizing--"

"Indeed. I've seen no evidence of a shadowy sea-monster this voyage, my dear Captain," added Yuki-onna. "The only thing I have noticed that is different on this trip is that the island is not where it ought to be."

"How do you know?" asked Izanami, ignoring her dish, but intrigued for the first time since embarking.

"My Lady," Yuki-onna explained, "I sail every year at this time. It is my custom, while awaiting my season's return. I have been in these waters almost as much as the crew, I daresay. Uwatsutsu, what, may one ask, is going on?"

"I might ask my bartender the same question," Uwatsutsu replied. He signaled the god in question with the tip of his finger, and Omoikane joined them to kneel at his elbow. "All right. What's your plan?" he asked the other.

"Captain, our passenger is a fisherman of sorts. There is something in the water that holds his interest--not Umibzu of course," he continued. "Something else. I believe if you summon it, we might accomplish our objective."

"You mean to summon what the seeker wishes to find," Izanagi guessed.

"Hai, kami-sama," answered Omoikane.

"And...you suspect that if your seeker believes we are imperiled, he will be nearby when the true object of his search is brought to light," commented Izanami.

"Hai, kami-sama," answered Omoikane.

"Why didn't you tell me this before supper?" Uwatsutsu growled through gritted teeth.

"Because, Captain, you would not have appeared suitably chagrined at my revelation."

"Hmph," said Uwatsutsu. Omoikane, as usual, was probably right.

Now all he had to do was summon--what? "Er. Omoikane, what is our fisherman trying to catch, do you think?"

"Oh, no one much. Only Ryūjin."

"The great dragon?" Uwatsutsu said. "Well, compared to Umibzu, that is not necessarily better."

"He's at least reasonable," Omoikane countered.

"Well!" said Yuki-onna, giggling merrily. "Who would have guessed, after all these years, that this cruise had such adventure to offer?"

"It's certainly more exciting than my realm," mused Izanami. Uwatsutsu breathed a silent sigh of relief, and spotted Izanagi from the corner of his eye, visibly relaxing as well. The Captain was still annoyed by Omoikane's deception, but if Izanami was finally taking an interest in something beyond misery, perhaps it was all worth a little deception.

Several hours later, Uwatsutsu and Omoikane walked along the promenade deck. They were followed by a number of spectators, all watching over the railing for any sign of the inky, ghostly figure of Umibzu. Uzume hurried to catch up to them.

"Captain, before you start, there was another matter I wanted to consult you about."

"Yes, Uzume?"

"Well...in a word, Kuninotokotachi-kami-sama."

Uwatsutsu halted, causing a minor traffic jam behind him. "What about them now?"

"It's only that I'm still worried they're not getting the most out of their trip," she said. "Even Izanami has shown a glimmer of enjoying herself, if tonight's any indication. Usually by now I've figured out what will serve everyone. But in Kuninotokotachi's case--"

"They're standing right behind you," Omoikane pointed out.

"Oh, dear!" Uzume exclaimed.

The entity reached out a glowing tendril of smoke. The wisp opened in a lacy pattern not unlike a stalk of wheat, or a delicate hand. All three of them felt the being's assurance: "I am not displeased with my journey, daughter. I said I came to observe. That is what I am doing. All is well." They then directed their mask toward the Captain. "And you, Uwatsutsu, are you prepared to speak to Ryūjin? He may not be happy to join us at this time of night."

Take that up with Omoikane here, thought the Captain, but aloud he said only, "My duty is to serve this ship, kami-sama. If this scheme of Omoikane's is our way out, then yes, I am prepared."

With that, he crossed to the railing and gestured over the water with one hand. Below, the water swirled into a deepening whirlpool, but one that did not disturb the vessel at all. As the sinkhole widened, a huge shadow became discernible, a dark spot under the moonlit wave. The passengers let out a collective cry of concern. Then the head of an enormous dragon broke through the swirling water, followed by the rest of its body, at speed. He hurtled into the sky, high enough to eclipse the moon. He hung suspended for a moment, then dived back into the water, his tail undulating as he plunged. His feathery, scaly fluke sprayed the onlookers with water as he dipped. Then he came back up again, just his upper body this time, and held his head level with the Captain's.

"Why do you call me?" the giant dragon rumbled.

"Great Ryūjin, we have a favor to ask," Omoikane said. "We are unable to find Mikura-jima. Something or someone on board is, inadvertently, I believe, keeping us at sea."

The dragon rested his great chin on the boat's railing. Water dripped off his beard onto the deck, and the vessel tipped to starboard under the weight of his gigantic head.

"Ryūjin, my ship," Uwatsutsu said tightly.

"Ah. Uwatsutsu! My apologies, cousin," the dragon said, lifting his head again. He glanced toward the position of the island. "It is true, Mikura-jima is missing. But what has it to do with me?"

"Yes, I'd like an explanation as well," said Uwatsutsu.

Omoikane answered. "Of course. Kami-sama, there's one on this ship who wishes to meet you. He has been so desirous of meeting the great Ryūjin that he took this cruise, but has been unable to bring himself to go further. He's spent most of his time in my bar, where, as you know, Captain, our dear friend Hōtei is practically a resident. Hōtei has been trying to improve the fellow's situation. That's his job, after all, isn't it? Bringing good fortune and happiness to people. I believe Hōtei's enthusiasm, combined with our passenger's own apprehensions, have caused us to drift out of our reality. Kuninotokotachi-kami-sama, that's why you suggested the Captain go to the bar, wasn't it? And did you not say to the Captain that the land is here, only that it is in another version of the universe?"

Kuninotokotachi nodded.

"I think that we have been transported to a reality in which Mikura-jima does not exist," Omoikane said.

"What?!" a small voice squealed, far in the back of the crowd of onlookers. "No, no, no...Omoikane-kami-sama, that can't be true! This is all...because of me?"

Morikasai-tutsu pressed forward, while the others parted for him. He was so short that the movement resembled a rodent running through high stalks of reeds--they parted but for no visible reason, until he burst through the first row to stand beside the Captain and his wise barkeep. Faced with the enormous dragon, he dropped to his knees and touched his forehead to the decking. Then he burst into tears. "I'm not ready!"

"No time like the present," Omoikane told him. "Ryūjin, allow me to introduce to you, your admirer: Morikasai-tutsu."

Still bowing low, little Morikasai-tutsu whimpered pitifully.

"Morikasai-tutsu," said Ryūjin sharply.

The dragon was chastened into rising onto his hind legs. "Hai, kami-sama," he said, coughing out a tiny puff of smoke.

"Fujin brought me a poem composed in my honor, by someone named Morikasai-tutsu. Was that yours?"

"Um...hai?" he replied, trembling.

The sea dragon chuckled, and the vibrations made the whole ship shudder. "Morikasai-tutsu. Would you like to come visit my palace?"

"V-very much," he said.

"Then let us go now, and let these people be on their way. I would speak with you on...the merits of fire and water."

The much smaller dragon climbed onto the railing and from there clung on to Ryūjin's neck. As he settled, Ryūjin launched again high up into the sky, setting up for a dive. His scales glittered with every color of the rainbow, catching and reflecting every bit of moonlight. To the exclamations of the passengers, he lunged back into the center of the whirlpool. The waves immediately closed in on themselves in his wake, and before the spray could fall back into the sea, the waters subsided. The moon illuminated Ryūjin's dark shadow for a few seconds until he disappeared. Then, just ahead, they made out the greenish shape of a volcanic mountain.

"The island!" said Daikokunyo. "We're back in business!"

"Come, Omoikane," said Captain Uwatsutsu. "I think we ought to have a word with Hōtei."

Captain's Log, the thirteenth day of Minazuki: We made port at Mikura-jima early this morning. After the excitement of last night, nearly all our passengers were pleased to go ashore and enjoy the pleasures of dry land for a while. I have prayed for favorable winds to get us back on schedule as soon as we are underway once more. I'm also happy to report that our mystery yielded additional benefits. Ame-no-Uzume cannot stop smiling at the thought of Daikokuten and their new boyfriend. I hope I don't lose a valuable crewmember and excellent purser, but I am pleased to see them so enchanted. And they are not the only ones....

"Did you know that the couple in the cabin next to ours have been on this cruise over twenty times?" Izanami said to her husband as they walked the gangway back on board. "She showed me the most charming little shop on the island. Oh, and she's friends with Kenash Unarabe--the Ainu vampire queen. You know I have always wanted to meet her...."

"You seem in much better spirits, Lady, Lord," said Uwatsutsu in greeting.

"Thank you, Captain. I think all those years of dwelling in the lands beyond simply took some time to shake away. I feel much revived." She took Izanagi's hand. "In fact, we may have to make this trip every year, as Yuki-onna does. She swears it keeps her young."

"She's an old wom--" Izanagi began.

"Youth of spirit,

Better far than body's age,

Brings wisdom and grace," Uwatsutsu extemporized, hoping it would disrupt what might have become a new argument.

"Just so," Izanagi amended. Quietly to the Captain, he added, "And meddling into the affairs of the other passengers doesn't hurt, I'm sure." Then to Izanami, he continued, "Come, love, let us go and plan our evening. Do you still wish to go to karaoke tonight?"

"Yes, I do!" she said enthusiastically. "I am fairly certain I could absolutely crush 'One Way or Another.'"

Laughing, they headed toward the stairs and their stateroom.

Captain Uwatsutsu glanced around at his crew. They had certainly set their course for adventure this time. Perhaps it had had a rocky start, but this was shaping up to be another successful voyage.

Life's sweetest reward,

Flows out and floats back, smiling:

Love on friendly shores.

Green Eyed Monster
Jeff Young

In what was becoming too typical a landfall, the Zeus Deuce came to a halt on the precipitous edge of the cliff. Minor landslides cascaded into the valley far below. Two landing struts were only a few meters from the edge of the drop. Osiris wiped the sweat from his green brow. "We just made it."

Seated farther back on the bridge, Dr. Anubis crossed his arms, looking up at the ceiling, and rolled his eyes. His tongue flicked out and smoothed down a few stray bits of fur on his long muzzle. 'Just made it, indeed.' Osiris was a show off and a dangerous one at that. Granted, the Zeus Deuce seemed to have a marked propensity toward disastrous breakdowns, but it was unlikely that the auto-lander and the lidar both failed at the very same time. In fact, the pilot was probably being a hot shot to impress Dr. Geb's Crusoe's daughter, Isis.

As if to prove his point, she sat up in her chair, straightened her throne-shaped crown, and then proceeded to bat those big brown eyes at Osiris. "You were amazing."

Managing to turn a deeper shade of green, he waved off her compliment. "No, just another ordinary landing."

Anubis watched the whole interchange, seething. If only they realized that a calm steady hand – such as his – on the wheel would leave them in less dangerous situations. Couldn't they see that he was the one who was capable, who had a firm grasp of the situation and rock steady nerves? Not criminally reckless like a certain officer who acted as green as his skin tone. Anubis realized he was chasing his own tail and forgetting the important part: he would have to do something about Osiris. Later, once they all realized how perilous his feck-lessness was, the others would come to thank Anubis. Yes, they would.

One by one, the crew descended the ramp to the planet below. Anubis stood in the doorway, awaiting whatever disaster might befall such inept explorers. Why hadn't they sent the Automaton first? They were fools and deserved each tragedy they earned. In fact, where was the blasted machine? The silence from behind made him leap forward and stumble a few feet. He turned about to stare at the large metallic form looming over him. "You chrome-plated assassin, you nearly made me jump to my death!"

Pushing past both the Automaton and Anubis, Dr. Geb's youngest, Weneg Crusoe, came tearing down the ramp and threw over his shoulder, "Aw, come on, Dr. Anubis, Ro-Butt didn't mean any harm. He just doesn't make much noise."

Anubis stared down his snout at the automaton. "Henceforth, you will make some sort of noise when you are approaching. Creak or clank or squeak or something. No more sneaking up on me!" One of the tubular arms brought its clamp hand up to the rotund glass dome that served as a head in mock salute. Then it forced its way by him to roll downward. Anubis was treated to a view of its odd, rounded shiny posterior, where its batteries were stored. No wonder Weneg called it Ro-Butt. *You'll get yours too, you metal bastard*, he vowed. Anubis considered the scene below, taking in the pastel colored vegetation, lumpy boulders, and clear blue sky. Well, no one was in the throes of death yet; perhaps it might be safe to explore.

A few moments later, he came upon the Automaton at the edge of the cliff. Was it staring downward? It was hard to tell, but the opportunity was hard to resist. In fact the more Anubis considered it, the more he convinced himself he shouldn't resist. He put a boot right on that chromed fundament and gave the machine a firm push. There was a second of flailing arms and it went tumbling over the edge. He took a moment to savor the image, then cried out, "Oh, the horror! The horror! That fool machine's just tumbled over the edge!"

Predictably enough, the others came running to find him, head in hands on his knees. He pointed downwards. Dr. Nut Crusoe, Geb's spouse, gathered him up in a smothering motherly embrace, patting him on the head. Anubis did his best to stop his foot from jittering. Geb stood at the edge, shaking his head. Weneg leaned over his hands on his knees muttering, "That's a long way down." The girls dissolved into expected hysterics and Osiris gave him a look with a raised eyebrow. Predictable, so predictable.

Anubis forced himself away from Nut's ministrations, pushing her star-covered arms aside. "Well, we can't leave him down there like that, poor thing." There was a short period of gaze shifting and then everyone was looking at Osiris.

He coughed and, putting his hands akimbo, managed to flex his green biceps. "I guess I am the man for the job, considering my rappelling experience. Let me go get my gear."

Watching him cannily, Anubis thought, *Yes, you go, little man. Yes you go. If something horrible were to happen on the way down or the way up, well that will just be a bonus.*

"Well, that's all of it," Osiris commented, setting the box down on Anubis's chair.

Looking up from the main body of the Automaton, which covered most of his work desk, Anubis flicked his hand through the air, "Fine, fine."

"I'm off for a shower. That was hard work." Osiris turned and left the room.

Anubis glared at his retreating back. Was that meant to imply that he wasn't pulling his own weight around here? Wasn't fixing this piece of motile electronic idiocy work? Never mind that he'd caused it. If Osiris was taking a shower, that would keep him busy. Anubis knew for a fact that Geb and Nut had retired to the Rover – and when the Rover was a rockin' it didn't pay to come a knockin'. Creation gods, one Big Bang and all they could think of to do was try to have another one. He'd taken care of Isis earlier by stealing her throne crown and cutting all of the legs to different sizes. She'd be forever trying to get it to sit properly on her head. That left Bast. He grabbed the box of Automaton parts and emptied it onto the floor. Sticking his head out of the doorway, Anubis called, "Here kitty, kitty."

Moments later, she was no longer an issue. All he'd done was toss the box in front of her and she'd leapt inside, curled up, and gone to sleep. Once again in his laboratory, he considered the bulk of the Automaton, but concluded that problem could wait a little longer. Right now, he needed something else. Anubis turned on the manufactory and considered the menu. With this machine, he could make anything he needed, but what exactly did he need? There was something tugging at his memory. He'd seen it once long ago, perhaps in a commercial back when humanity had been obsessed with television. There was nothing for it; he would have to search the records. He settled into his chair and started up the monitor. The answer was in there somewhere and it was sharp. He was certain of that.

Anubis was half asleep when what he was looking for appeared on the screen. An Asian gentleman waved his arms rapidly, his cutlery slicing through the air with a whish. His tall chef's hat balanced on his head, he proceeded to apply his weapon to vegetables of all sorts, to his own shoe, and finally, he sliced through a metal can. Anubis sat upright. This was the weapon he had been searching for.

"Hey Doc, whatcha watchin'?"

Anubis flicked off the screen with a disingenuous grin. He'd accounted for everyone except the smallest crewmember and Weneg had caught him out. "Just a little light entertainment, my boy. Nothing for you to concern yourself about."

"Oh, sure," Weneg said and picked up a servomotor from the floor to toss from hand to hand. "Want some help putting Ro-Butt back together again?"

Pushing himself out of the chair, Anubis caught the part in mid-air, then turned to place it on the table. "I am of course a Master Cyberneticist, so I require no help in repairing the Automaton. While I do understand that you are a genius, my dear boy, we should each be allowed to play to our strengths. Speaking of play, is there not something that you can enjoy? Perhaps somewhere else?"

"Everyone else is busy now."

Anubis considered that. Perhaps he'd succeeded a bit too well in ensuring the others were occupied. Then he spied the large sack lying in the corner. Osiris had used it to carry up the main body of the Automaton and then tossed it aside. The boy was trusting; perhaps Anubis should take advantage of that. A brief glance at his watch confirmed that sunset had just passed. Perfect. "My dear Weneg, have you ever heard about the fine sport of hunting for the elusive Snipe?"

In mere moments, they'd exited the ship and walked out into the dusk. After a brisk walk and having located a suitably large tree,

Anubis positioned the young god at its base. "Now when the Snipe runs down the tree, you need to pull the top of the bag closed and hold on, Weneg."

"How will I know when I've got one?"

"You'll know my boy, you'll know. Now be quiet. We wouldn't to scare one off. A little patience and you'll have your very own Snipe."

"Wait, where are you going, Doctor?"

"You wouldn't want me scaring the Snipe off would you? I must absent myself so that you have the best chance of success."

Back at the foot of the ramp to the Zeus Deuce, Anubis dusted off his hands. That took care of all of them. Now he could get to work. Two, yes, he would have the manufactory create two of those fine blades. Then a little judicious reprogramming of that mechanical reprobate and perhaps, just perhaps, something unfortunate might befall a certain officer. He wasn't going to find it easy being green, no not at all, once Dr. Anubis finished with him.

A bit later he considered the small remote in his hand and its single glossy red button. Anubis tapped it with one claw. In front of him, the reassembled Automaton brought its tubular arms up and began flailing about madly. Perfect: add two very sharp pieces of metal that were cooling after their emergence from the manufactory and his trap was ready to be sprung. He permitted himself a brief evil grin before tucking away the remote into his tunic. Now all he needed was the right time and place.

Anubis sat up with a start. He'd fallen asleep in his chair. He ground his paws into eyes and yawned widely, shaking himself. He looked around the laboratory with the concerning thought that he'd forgotten something. Despite his cursory survey, he couldn't remember. After making his way to the ship's mess area and grabbing a cup of coffee, his unease continued. There was something amiss. He reached into his pocket and pulled out the remote. He hadn't lost that. He whistled imperiously and after a moment the Automaton appeared, this time actually preceded by the squealing of its treads on the decking. Excellent: that problem was resolved. Still, his unease persisted. Only then did he remember Weneg. Ye gods, he'd left the young one outside all night on some unexplored planet. Turning, Anubis slung his coffee cup into the sink and set off running. The Automaton stood there for a second, spun around on its axis and then set off in pursuit.

At the top of the ramp, Anubis whipped his gaze back and forth. Weneg was nowhere in sight. He slapped a splayed paw across his face. He was never going to hear the end of this. At least the Automaton was with him to help him search. He swung about to command it forward and found himself face to face with Osiris. Anubis was certain that a number of expressions chased themselves across his face before he was able to force his features into a mask of concern. "Weneg's missing," he yelped.

Osiris glared at him and then pushed him aside to run down the ramp. "He was mumbling about going outside last night," Anubis cried after him. He might as well try to cover his ass now. Who were the adults going to believe – him or a child? That thought brought him up short. This time when he turned about the Automaton was behind him. "What are you waiting for? A written invitation? Get after him!" Once again, Anubis was shoved aside as the Automaton thundered down the ramp. Taking a deep breath, he proceeded downward at a lope.

A short while later, he was leaning forward, paws on thighs, panting. He wasn't built for all of this heroic dashing about. Anubis leaned against a tree, a very familiar tree in fact. The leaves about its base were all thrown about as if a struggle had occurred here. What had he gotten that dear boy into, he wondered. That was the point at which Anubis realized there was a pant leg just visible around the other side of the tree. Fortunately, it was still attached to young Weneg. The large sack he'd given Weneg was stretched to busting over something that also appeared, like its captor, to be sleeping. Selecting a nearby twig, Anubis poked the boy, "Wake up, Weneg. We need to get back before the others find out about your Snipe. We can just let that be our little secret, can't we?"

Weneg rolled a sleepy eye at him and then threw both arms up in the air to stretch. That meant he no longer had control over the sack and its occupant. What burst forth from the bag looked like a cross between a baboon and a wart hog. It whined like a rusty chainsaw, threshing its tangled mass of teeth and tusks before leaping into the air straight onto Anubis's chest. Using him as a launch pad, it thrust itself forward right into the path of the oncoming Osiris. Anubis had a brief glimpse of bright blue butt cheeks as the Snipe set off in pursuit of Osiris. A second later, the Automaton arrived. "They went that way," Anubis cried, gesticulating madly.

All three vanished into the underbrush. Anubis risked a brief sigh of relief and then something occurred to him. It was all about timing. Turning away from Weneg, he reached into his tunic and pulled out the remote. He pushed the button once. Then he pushed it several times more, just to be sure. It sounded like flailing, it certainly did, but with all of the noise the Snipe was making it was difficult to be sure. One could only hope.

Whirling about, he found Weneg staring at the empty sack. "I had him."

"Some things, my dear boy, aren't meant to be," Anubis responded. "Perhaps, it would be best if we returned to the ship. So you don't have to share your embarrassment at failing, maybe we can keep this between ourselves? Now stay behind me, I believe that Osiris may have startled your Snipe and we don't want to annoy it any further."

Weneg dutifully followed in Anubis' footsteps until they came down the path to a clearing. What awaited them brought Anubis to a sudden halt. He swung about and grasped Weneg by the shoulders. "Don't look, my child. It is quite awful. You must go back the other way to the ship and get the others. Tell them it's an emergency. Now, run!" Anubis pushed him away.

After his footsteps faded, Anubis turned about. "Oh, the horror," he said aloud, but his tone was anything but frightened. In fact, it carried a touch of awe. He did spare a moment to pull out the remote and tap the button again, which brought the Automaton's flailing to a sudden stop. It shook the blood from its knives and concealed them in a compartment in its side. Anubis looked about the clearing. Bits of Osiris were everywhere. The Automaton and its sharp knives had carved him up like an unsuspecting carrot. Anubis tipped his head to one side. Where should he be standing when they found him? Decisions, decisions. Ah, there, right there was the perfect spot.

That was where they found him when the crew rushed headlong into the clearing, skidding to a stop on some slippery Osiris bits. Bast promptly turned aside and hacked up a hairball while the rest of their complexions began to resemble that of the victim. Isis broke down in sobs. Anubis watched all of this peering through fingers that covered his face as his body shook in false spasms of grief. He even squeezed out a few tears, just to be certain.

"What in Set's name happened here?" cried Geb as he tried to nonchalantly wipe his boot on the nearest patch of grass.

"Weneg can tell you. There was a beast, a horrible beast with the strangest blue backside and a mouth that looked like a grinder. It jumped upon me and then chased Osiris down the path. It must have torn the poor man to pieces." Anubis pointed toward the pair of paw marks that marred the front of his tunic.

Stunned, Weneg could only nod numbly and mumble under his breath, "Oh, Snipe. Snipe what have you done?"

Surprisingly, it was Nut Crusoe who overcame the shock first. She reached into the thigh pocket of her breeches and produced a small flail-shaped device. Selecting the largest bit of Osiris at hand, she shook it over top of the flesh and then considered the hieroglyphs that appeared on the handle. "We can still save him! Girls, back to the ship. I'll need the GG and material to wrap up the body. Go, now!"

Bast and Isis quickly responded and were soon running through the brush back to the Zeus Deuce. Nut began to carefully gather the pieces of Osiris together. Weneg thoughtfully offered his Snipe bag for the collection effort.

Geb made his way over to stand next to Anubis. "It's their show now," he confided.

Giving the Captain a quizzical look, Anubis asked, "Whatever do you mean?"

With a smug expression on his face, Geb responded, "Mostly it was Nut's idea. She does really hate to see any of our pantheon pass into the great beyond, so she came up with the concept for GG. Since my two lovely daughters are both geniuses, it only made sense that they would help her realize her ambition. Bast is studying molecular medicine and Isis will be working on her thesis soon concerning the five parts of the soul and prolonging their existence in emergencies."

The confusion on Anubis' face prompted Geb to continue, "Together they developed God Glue. It's a wonderful substance that works with the Ka and maintains the Ba of an injured god. Of course this is a rather extreme case, but since Nut was still able to detect Osiris' Ka, we should be able to 're-assemble' him."

There was no need for Anubis to feign disbelief, as his reaction was quite natural.

Geb slapped him good-naturedly on the arm. "My ladies are quite the bunch and the GG, well, everybody wanted a piece of developing that property. We had so much money it allowed me fund the program that created the Zeus Deuce. You didn't think that was paid for by a government program, did you? Not hardly."

While Anubis rubbed his sore arm, Geb walked over to the nearest area of carnage and began to pick up pieces of his pilot. "Come on Doctor, it'll be just like puzzle time on Sunday nights after dinner. Pitch in and start picking up."

Holding up his paws, Anubis whined, "I'm so very sorry. When I was knocked down, I got dirt all over my pads. I'm afraid it wouldn't be very sanitary for me to be touching any of Osiris's bits."

Geb waved understandingly and turned to drop his pound of flesh into the sack that young Weneg held open.

Anubis shook his head and turned away. What a fool he'd been. He'd underestimated the women of the crew. That was the problem: the entire family were geniuses, even if some of them didn't always act like it. Well, he'd learned his lesson. Next time, he'd just do in all of them. He wasn't the Lord of the House of the Dead for nothing. While all these thoughts rolled about his head, the Crusoes continued their task like a litter crew. Only after they'd filled the sack and Bast's coveted box and returned to the Zeus Deuce did he move. Anubis looked down at the bits of Osiris that lay under his boot. He kicked the flesh back into the weeds. His adversary wouldn't be needing those any more. The whole exercise hadn't been a complete failure after all.

Osiris lay in state on the dining room table, wrapped up like some giant holiday present. There'd been some understandable consternation when the project neared completion and Geb had made an offhand remark about things never going back together quite they way they should when one was doing DIY. Consequently, Nut wasn't speaking to the Captain at the moment. Anubis ducked out of the proceedings as soon as possible.

Turning into the main corridor, Anubis ran headlong into the Automaton. "Blasted piece of mechanical idiocy, what are you, furniture? Out of my way!"

The machine's wheels squealed on the deck plating as it backed up a few paces and came to a halt. At that point, Weneg's voice came from behind the Automaton. "Hey Doc, this looks like something you made. What does this red button do?"

A loud click echoed down the hallway. The arms of the Automaton flexed. Two very sharp knives slid out of its carapace with a snick. The limbs of the machine accelerated , becoming a blur. "Peril, Weneg Crusoe, Peril!" it bellowed, voice like a klaxon, as the wheels in its base began to rotate.

Anubis turned. The corridor extended into the distance, becoming indistinct and vague. Then he was running. After a few strides, he realized he'd never make it like this and dropped to all fours. As his paws skittered along the deck plating and his muscles began to burn with exertion, he spared one second to wonder if there just might be any more God Glue left at all. Then he ran. He ran like a dog.

Out for Justice
Michael D'Ambrosio

Nemesis, an exotic island beauty with perfect skin, strutted across the courtyard on Olympus with sharp, piercing eyes and long dark hair. Under a leather jacket, she wore tight jeans with black boots and a red tank top that accented her perfect figure. A voice from the palace called to her, "Nemesis, where are you going?"

Nemesis replied without stopping, "No time to chat, mother. There is someone on Earth who requires a lesson in humility." She snapped her fingers and a black Harley chopper appeared in front of her with flames painted on the gas tank and reflectors on the spokes that looked like eyes. Nemesis sat gracefully on the bike, eager to take flight.

Oceanus, Nemesis' mother, approached her in a white flowing robe. "Would this someone be Harvick Speckle?" queried Oceanus.

"As a matter of fact, it is," Nemesis responded. "His arrogance precedes him and it's time to teach him a lesson."

"And that's all you are interested in?" she countered.

Nemesis grinned deviously and answered, "I have been challenged by Father to prove myself. I am the goddess of Retribution and Indignation. Mr. Speckle is about to learn humility."

"Remember, you are mortal when on Earth," Oceanus cautioned sternly. She was unhappy that her husband Zeus would lure Nemesis into such a challenge with such risk.

"Of course," she replied confidently and rode into the billowing white clouds.

A gray-bearded Zeus stepped out from behind the pillars and chuckled to himself. He knew his daughter all too well and believed she needed a lesson in humility herself. Oceanus stared at him with an expression of scorn.

A severe thunderstorm storm struck New York City. Thunder and lightning sent everyone scurrying for cover. Nemesis appeared in the sky on her motorcycle and rode one of the lightning bolts to the ground. The storm dissipated as quickly as it formed.

Nemesis savored her first trip to modern day America and was anxious to humble the highly successful attorney Harvick Speckle. The thought of depriving him of his fame and wealth made her shudder with excitement. She imagined how he would cower and fall to his knees, begging for mercy, when she dispensed her punishment on him.

Nemesis waited patiently for the black Lexus LS460 to turn the corner and then raced after it. When the Lexus stopped at the next red light, she pulled up along the driver's side and stared through the window at Harvick.

Harvick was captivated by her stare. He lowered the window and smiled at her. "Do I know you?" he asked politely.

Nemesis stared as if she saw right into his soul. Harvick felt the power of her gaze and waited anxiously for her response. None came. The light changed and she raced ahead. A noisy local bus, #79, passed Harvick on the right. Distracted by the sound of its engine, he slowed up to focus on Nemesis. His mind raced as he pondered the chance that they had met previously.

When they approached the next light, two teenagers stepped into the crosswalk. They paid no attention to the oncoming traffic. Nemesis frantically tried to stop the bike, but lost control on the wet street. The motorcycle slid out from underneath her, striking the two teens. She tumbled and slammed her head against the curb.

The teens lay injured in the street. Several pedestrians rushed to their aid. Harvick called nine-one-one and went to Nemesis' aid. She lay motionless on her back with a small blood stain on the curb behind her head. Harvick placed his suit coat over her for warmth and waited for help.

Two police cars arrived, followed shortly by an ambulance. One paramedic tended to the teens while the other hurried to Nemesis. A police officer pulled Harvick away from the scene and questioned him about the accident. A second police officer directed traffic away from the scene.

Another ambulance arrived and two paramedics came with a gurney. Harvick looked on with concern. The paramedics placed Nemesis in the ambulance and drove off.

Harvick questioned the police officer, "What will happen to her?"

The police officer rested his hands on his hips. "She's in a lot of trouble. Riding without a helmet," he expounded. "Her bike isn't registered and has no license plate. She also struck two pedestrians in the crosswalk."

"The kids did enter the crosswalk against the light," Harvick explained. "She didn't have a chance."

"Well, the judge will have to decide on that."

Harvick considered if he should get involved on Nemesis' behalf. A flatbed tow truck pulled up next to the bike. Once the driver secured the bike on the flatbed, the tow truck pulled away.

Harvick asked the police officer, "Will she be charged for injuring the kids?"

"Depends," he replied as he jotted down notes about the accident on his notepad. "I imagine the parents will file a suit though. Do you know the woman?"

"No, never saw her before."

"Well, she'd better have a damn good lawyer," the police officer quipped. "New York City doesn't take too kindly to bikers who break the law."

Harvick frowned and returned to his car. He knew the police officer was right: Nemesis was in a lot of legal trouble. Turning onto Fifth Avenue, he considered that it was a loser of a case with no reward in it. Then he recalled the look she gave him: those coal black eyes. There was something mysterious about her and, more than likely, she wasn't local. "No one rides a bike around New York City without a helmet," he thought to himself and chuckled. His curiosity pushed him to know more about her.

Later in the evening, he sat at his desk with a glass of Scotch. He should have gone home hours ago but the accident haunted him. Once more, he debated what to do. Harvick set the glass down and folded his hands. He decided he would take on Nemesis' case. "I know I'm gonna regret this," he grumbled.

Harvick paused outside Nemesis' room in ICU. The nurse instructed him that only family members were allowed to see her.

"Has anyone been here to see her?" he asked.

"No," replied the nurse. "And who are you?"

"I'm her attorney, Harvick Speckle. I need to speak with her."

Nemesis opened her eyes when she heard his name. Despite her disdain for him, she would give him a chance to prove her wrong.

"Well, Mr. Speckle, you can't," the nurse informed him. "She's been sedated."

Harvick continued to pressure the nurse with legal jargon. The nurse warned him to leave or she'd call security. Harvick glanced in the room at Nemesis and then turned away.

"Wait," called Nemesis weakly. "Send him in."

The nurse relented. When she turned around, Harvick was already in the doorway. "You may enter, Mr. Speckle, but only for a few minutes. She needs to rest."

"I understand," he replied appreciatively. "Thank you." Harvick approached Nemesis.

He studied her facial features. She had a bruise on her cheek and a bandage wrapped around her head. Monitors were connected to her arms and head.

"What brings you here?" she asked after an awkward moment of silence between them.

"How about 'thanks for stopping to help' or 'what's your name?'" he suggested.

Nemesis turned her head to him slightly and repeated her question. "What brings you here?"

Harvick pulled up a chair and sat next to her bed. "In case you aren't aware, you're in a lot of trouble. They plan to arrest you if you're found guilty when you get out of here."

Nemesis bit her lip, knowing she was helpless in her mortal state. She recalled that her mother warned her to be careful but she never expected something like this to happen. "What can I do?" she inquired humbly.

"I can help you if you'll let me."

She didn't expect this from Harvick and suspected an ulterior motive. "And how would you do that?" she asked.

He leaned forward and spoke softly. "You aren't from around here, are you?"

"No, I'm not," Nemesis responded dejectedly. "How is my bike?"

Harvick shook his head in disbelief. "Forget the bike. How are you?"

"I'll live," she answered somberly. "I want that bike back, though. It's my only way out of here."

"First things first," Harvick told her in a firm tone. "I need to know your name and address."

Nemesis was in a real quandary. How could she navigate through this mess with no Earth identity or address? Her previous visits to Earth occurred in much earlier times and frivolous details like identity weren't an issue. "My name is Nemesis," she reluctantly revealed.

Harvick smiled at her. "Nemesis as in the hand of justice and retribution from Greek mythology or is that your biker name?" he kidded.

"Named after the one and only in mythology," she said proudly.

"And how about an address?" he inquired.

"Look, Mr. Speckle, this isn't my first fall on the bike. Not long ago, I had another accident and I don't recall much of my life before that," she lied.

Harvick wondered if he met her before, perhaps an old girlfriend or client. Then he rejected the notion. "Does that explain why you had no helmet on or registration for your bike?"

"Maybe," she lied again. "I really don't know."

The nurse entered. "Time to leave, Mr. Speckle," she ordered.

Harvick took Nemesis' hand in his. "Relax and get better," he advised her. "I'll see what I can do."

Nemesis smiled at him. She was pleased by his compassion for her and wondered if she and Father were wrong about him. *He is quite attractive*, she thought. "Thank you, Mr. Speckle."

"Don't thank me yet. I'll be back to check on you soon."

The nurse ushered him out of the room.

Nemesis was impressed with him. He was different than other men she had met on Earth.

Later that night, Oceanus appeared in her room. "Well, my daughter, it seems you have landed yourself in quite a mess."

"It's fine, mother. Where is Father?"

"Forget him. I can help you if you like," she offered.

"Thank you, Mother," replied Nemesis humbly. "I was foolish not to heed your words.

Oceanus touched Nemesis' forehead. The pain subsided but she was still weakened. The monitors beeped and chattered as the displays showed that her condition improved.

"I owe you my thanks," Nemesis replied appreciatively. "I feel much better."

Oceanus touched her arm affectionately. "By the way, how is Mr. Speckle?"

Nemesis was startled when her mother mentioned him. "He's, uh, just what I expected," she stammered. "I don't regret coming here to give him his just due."

"Are you sure about that?" Oceanus countered.

Nemesis frowned and turned away. Oceanus smiled and vanished from the room.

Harvick went to the auto repair center and paid ahead to have Nemesis' motorcycle repaired within a few days. Then he went to meet with a friend in the judicial system to discuss Nemesis' situation. It was agreed that his only option was to convince a jury that the injured teens were responsible despite Nemesis' lack of knowledge of the law regarding her motorcycle.

Harvick then visited the parents of the minors and discussed the situation with them. He informed them that the teens actually caused the accident and that he'd be willing to forgo a suit against them if they dropped their suit. The parents of one minor spoke with their son and agreed to drop their suit. The other family was determined to take Nemesis to court, despite Harvick's offer.

Two days later, Harvick arrived at the hospital to see Nemesis. When he reached the nurses' station, he was shocked to see her room empty. Fearing she had passed from her injuries, he frantically summoned one of the nurses. "Nurse, where is the woman who was in that room the other day?"

The nurse gestured for him to keep his voice down. "Her condition improved dramatically, so she was turned over to the police this morning."

"Thank you," he said, baffled by Nemesis' quick recovery. The nurse nodded toward the door and ushered him out of the ICU. He stepped into the hall and called the police station. When he learned that Nemesis was being held in a cell, he made several calls to obtain her release.

The police station was only six blocks away so Harvick walked. Inside the station, the desk sergeant handed him a form to fill out. He posted her bail for a thousand dollars; not a big deal for a bigshot lawyer like Harvick in New York City.

"You'd better hope she isn't a flight risk, Mr. Speckle. Judge Samuels will be very unhappy if she doesn't show tomorrow."

Harvick scribbled information on the form, along with an explanation that Nemesis suffered from some memory loss. Harvick tipped the man twenty dollars and whispered to him. The sergeant gratefully accepted it and assigned one of his men to escort Harvick back to Nemesis' cell.

Nemesis sat dejectedly on the bench while four other women argued and fought. Harvick felt bad, seeing her subjected to this humiliation. He suspected she was much more than some ordinary woman on a bike. *Perhaps she was a Senator or even royalty from another country. That would explain her ignorance of the bike laws*, Harvick considered.

The policeman unlocked the cell door and shouted, "Come on, Ms. Nemesis. You're free to go."

Nemesis hurried from the cell to hug him. "I can't believe I'm saying this but I'm so happy to see you, Mr. Speckle."

Harvick brushed her bangs away from her eyes. Their eyes locked briefly and, again, he felt as though she saw right into his soul. He nervously backed away.

"Please, call me Harvick. Now let's get you out of here."

When they left the precinct, Harvick informed her that she needed to appear before the judge in the morning. When he learned that she had no place to stay, he offered to let her stay at his apartment for the night. Pleased by his generosity, Nemesis welcomed the opportunity to learn more about him. She suspected that is where he would show his true self and receive his judgment.

Nemesis showered while Harvick made calls regarding her motorcycle. He arranged for his mechanic to deliver the bike to his parking space under the apartment when the repairs were finished.

When Nemesis entered the living room wearing only a bra and panties, Harvick nearly fell over at the sight of her. "Please, have a seat," he offered nervously. "Some wine?"

Here we go, thought Nemesis. *He helped me and now I have to sleep with him. Judgment time.* "I'll have one glass," she answered coyly, feigning her eagerness for him. She sat next to him and wondered how far the game would go before he revealed his true self.

Harvick poured two glasses of pinot noir and handed her one. Nemesis studied her glass of wine and asked, "What shall we toast to?"

Harvick suggested, "How about to your healthy recovery and the hope that your missing memories return?"

Nemesis was concerned. This wasn't at all what she expected from him. "Very well, Harvick." They tapped glasses and sipped.

Harvick related to her everything that took place between himself and the two families. While he spoke, she looked about the apartment. When he finished, she inquired, "You live alone?"

"I do," he replied somberly. "I prefer my solitude."

"So there is no Mrs. Speckle?" she asked curiously.

"No, I'm single and probably will be for some time." After a moment of unease, he changed the topic. "Let me tell you what you can expect tomorrow."

"What a shame," she remarked jokingly. "A handsome man like you with a successful practice and no woman?"

Harvick sipped again and looked sadly at the glass. He swirled the wine as he recalled a painful memory. "There was someone once," he confessed. "She broke my heart."

264

Now Nemesis was shocked. His demeanor wasn't arrogance, but heartbreak. "I'm sorry. What happened?"

"She didn't think I was good enough. That drives me to be the best at everything I do every single day. Now, can we talk about your case?"

Nemesis placed her hand on Harvick's thigh. "You've done a lot for me," she said, baiting him once more. "How can I ever repay you?"

With all sincerity, he responded, "Wear a helmet and get your bike registered."

Nemesis stood up in front of him with hands on her hips. "You're kidding me!" she exclaimed giddily. "I'm standing here in front of you, literally throwing myself at you and all you can say is 'wear a helmet and register your bike'?"

Harvick tried not to focus on her shapely body and replied, "If you thought I brought you here to sleep with you, then you're wrong. I'm only trying to help."

Nemesis was caught with no backup plan. "So you did this for me out of the kindness of your heart?" she asked, still amazed by his actions.

"No, I did it because I could help. Wait until after we see the judge before you decide how you feel about me."

"Fair enough," Nemesis answered. "But what if we lose?"

"I'll do my best to get you out of this," he assured her. "Don't think about it."

"But you never lose," she reminded him. "You're the best lawyer anyone could wish for."

"I wish my life was as good as my legal practice," he revealed somberly. "I'd trade my successes away in a heartbeat to have someone special in my life."

"That's sad," she replied and hugged him. Harvick shied away, suggesting they get some rest. He directed Nemesis to his bedroom, while he made up a bed for himself on the couch.

Nemesis lay awake, wondering how she and Father had been so wrong about him all this time. Then Oceanus appeared in front of her with a concerned expression.

Nemesis was startled. "What are you doing here, mother?" she asked uneasily.

"Just checking on my daughter."

"I'm fine, thank you."

Oceanus sat on the edge of the bed and inquired, "Is Mr. Speckle taking good care of you?"

"Why do you ask?" she countered, somewhat embarrassed.

"This doesn't look like retribution on your part if you ask me," she teased.

"Oh, it's coming," she assured her. "Just wait and see."

"Be careful, my child," she warned. "Perhaps your father is teaching you a lesson." She vanished before Nemesis could respond. *That son of a bitch!*, she thought. She was angry that her father would do this to her, but then smiled and went to sleep.

The next morning, they appeared in court. The judge read the charges and listened briefly as Harvick entered his motion to dismiss. The family of the injured teen sat in the front seat listening anxiously for the judge's remarks. The judge denied the motion, set a court date for two weeks, and suggested that Harvick find something a little more concrete to support his defense.

Harvick and Nemesis walked slowly down the street. Neither one spoke as Harvick was lost in his own thoughts. Nemesis contemplated what she would do if they lost her case. Without her bike to return to Olympus, she was doomed on Earth as a mortal.

Harvick's phone rang and he answered. After a brief discussion with his assistant, he agreed to come in to the office shortly. Escorting Nemesis back to his apartment, he apologized that the case couldn't be resolved quickly. Nemesis didn't mind and looked forward to knowing him better.

The next two weeks were bliss for them as their friendship grew. The day before the hearing, Harvick walked past the location of the accident. He stared at the spot where Nemesis was injured. The #79 bus passed again, annoying him with its loud engine. Then his eyes widened with hope as he realized he had his answer. He rushed after the bus and boarded it at the next stop.

"Excuse me, sir," he interrogated the driver while breathing heavily, "but were you driving this route on the day of an accident a few weeks ago. Do you remember the girl on the motorcycle?" Harvick handed him a twenty for his patience.

The driver remained at the stop as passengers eked by to board and exit. "Yeah, where she hit the two kids, right?"

"That's the one," he replied excitedly. "The light was green when you crossed the intersection, right?"

"Of course. If I got caught running a red light in one of these buses, I'd lose my job."

"Would you sign a statement to that effect and attesting that you saw the accident and the light was green?" he asked the driver.

"Well, I didn't actually see it happen but I saw the woman and the two kids in the street through my rear view mirror."

Harvick stared at him, waiting for the important part. "Oh, and the light was green," the driver added.

"That'll do," Harvick replied confidently. He took a notepad from his briefcase and requested the man list his contact information and his statement. Once he had it, he hurried back to the office.

His assistant, Jessie, noticed that his attitude was much improved. "Something happen I should know about?" she asked playfully.

"Nope. Everything's under control."

"Good, because your nine o'clock is waiting," she informed him.

Harvick smiled and proceeded to his meeting.

When Harvick returned to his apartment in the evening, Nemesis was in tears. Harvick sat next to her and placed his arm around her for comfort. "It's gonna be okay. I promise I won't let you down."

She blurted, "It wasn't supposed to be this way."

"What are you talking about?"

"You were supposed to be a jerk," she uttered between sobs.

"And the problem is?" he countered.

"You're so much better than I thought."

"And?" he pressed.

"I'm ... I'm falling for you."

Harvick's jaw dropped. He was at a loss for words. He had developed feelings for Nemesis but he had to be a professional until after the trial. Against his better judgment, he responded, "Is that so bad?"

Nemesis took him in her arms and kissed him. Harvick tried to refrain, but couldn't resist her.

Zeus stared down from Olympus disappointedly at the two of them. Oceanus crept up from behind and taunted him, "Something wrong, Zeus?"

"I'm just admiring how our daughter is setting him up for the greatest heartbreak of all time."

"Maybe it's really love," she suggested. "Maybe she knows more than you give her credit for."

Zeus glared at her and walked away. He had a plan in case this happened.

The next morning, Harvick and Nemesis walked hand in hand to the courthouse. Before entering, he took Nemesis in his arms. "I never thought I'd say this again to anyone but I'm in love with you."

"And I'm in love with you as well," she replied giddily. "We shouldn't be doing this, should we?"

"I don't care."

The two kissed and entered the courtroom. Harvick immediately went to the attorney for the injured teen. He whispered in his ear and showed him the affidavit from the bus driver. The attorney nodded and the two approached the bench. They spoke to the judge briefly and then returned to their respective tables. The judge dismissed the case.

Harvick gestured for Nemesis to follow him. She was baffled by what transpired but followed him out to the steps. "It's over," he told her happily. "We won."

Nemesis jumped in the air and hugged him. "I can't believe you did it!"

"It was the bus driver that did it," he revealed. "Once I remembered he went through the light just before you did, I knew I had proof of your right-of-way. C'mon, let's celebrate."

When they returned to his apartment, he led her into the parking garage.

"Where are we going?" she asked curiously.

Harvick pointed past his Lexus to her motorcycle. It was immaculate after the repairs. Nemesis ran to it and sat on it. "Care for a ride?" she asked him.

"No, motorcycles aren't my thing. But I want you to enjoy this."

With a sheepish, grateful grin, Nemesis started the engine and rolled the bike into the aisle. Harvick stood with arms folded and smiled at her. Then Oceanus appeared behind him and winked at her daughter. "Harvick, I love you," she shouted and rode to the garage exit.

Zeus frowned from above and launched a lightning bolt at her. The bolt struck her and she vanished.

Harvick was horrified. He rushed to the spot where she vanished. With only burnt concrete left to indicate where she once stood, he was awestruck in disbelief.

Nemesis parked her motorcycle in the courtyard on Olympus, tears on her cheeks and her head down in fury. Zeus appeared and remarked proudly, "I didn't think you could destroy the man like you did. Well done!"

"I was wrong!" she cried, "and so were you to interfere!"

Zeus shrugged his shoulders and remarked, "Time heals all wounds, even a broken heart."

Oceanus arrived and hugged her tightly. "You're father's an ass," she uttered angrily. "He baited you into that."

"I'm leaving here, Mother, and never returning."

Oceanus urged, "Follow your heart, my child."

Nemesis rode off into the clouds. Determined, she rode another bolt of lightning to the ground.

Harvick knelt by the charred concrete with a tear in his eye. He was startled when Nemesis skidded to a stop in front of him. "Get on," she ordered. "We might not get a second chance."

"What happened to you?"

"Some things are better left unsaid. Now hurry."

Harvick anxiously settled into the seat behind her and wrapped his arms around her waist. Together they drove off toward the country.

Oceanus watched from on high and smiled proudly at her daughter. Zeus joined her and quipped, "That's my daughter."

Oceanus slapped his face and remarked, "You are such an ass!"

Many Hands Make Light

Aaron Rosenberg

Monday, 8:00am
Spiritual Plane

"Okay, where are we?" Brahma asked, rubbing his hands together. The forwardmost of his four faces stared out over the other gods who had assembled around the long table with him, as was their custom.

"Well," Saraswati offered, holding up a hand even though Brahma always insisted that these meetings were informal events. It was her first hand, the one holding the pustaka or book, which made sense, as she was consulting its text even as she spoke. "We have the Celestial Address today at five pm, of course."

"That's AST?" Ganesha interrupted with a twitch of his ivory tusks.

Saraswati frowned at him. "Naturally." AST stood for Ayodhya Standard Time, since Ayodhya was the holiest site in all of India.

"You never know," Ganesha protested in his own defense, flailing his trunk about him. "I mean, it's going out to the entire physical world, maybe we decided to start it earlier so people east of there could still get to bed on time?" No one took the comment very seriously, but that was the case with half of what Ganesha said. For such a popular deity, he could be extremely silly at times.

Beside him, his daughter and aide Santoshi Mata patted his arm gently, half support and half remonstrance. "They've got it cov-

273

ered, Ganesha," she muttered softly. He grumbled but subsided.

"Right," Brahma said, moving forward as if this little exchange had never taken place. He stroked his long white beard. "We need to get all the regalia out of mothballs, then." He waved his hand at the others, but looked primarily at Ganesha, who served as his second when it came to most tasks. "See to it. Lord Vishnu will be here at four to gear up. Anything else?"

"Shiva has been making noises about wanting to do the Address," Hanuman offered from his perch near the table's far end. "He claims it's his turn."

"He always thinks it's his turn," Karthikeya burst out, slamming a hand down on the table. Everyone except Brahma jumped. "When's that jumped-up demigod gonna learn that it's never his turn as long as Vishnu's still in charge, which will be for all eternity?" the war god demanded, his already red face shading even darker as he got worked up. Again. "Just once," he growled, reaching for Vel where it leaned against the table beside him, "I'd like to—"

"Karthikeya." Brahma didn't raise his voice—he rarely did—but his sharp tone lashed like a whip and the war god shut up mid-rant. "Put it down." Without even conscious thought, the red god released his hold on the Divine Lance and subsided back into his chair. "I'll speak to Shiva," Brahma continued. "It's fine. Anything else?"

"There's some demons down along the Ganges," Hanuman offered.

"There's always demons," Brahma replied. He scanned the table, then nodded. "Right. Get to work."

And with that, the gods dispersed to take care of business.

9:15am

"We have a problem," Hanuman declared as he stepped into Karthikeya's abode, careful not to tread on the peacock's tail.

"What?" the war god demanded. "Is it Shiva again? Because I'll—"

"It's not Shiva," the monkey minister replied quickly. He knew better than to let Karthikeya get all worked up on that particular subject—or, for that matter, most others. "It's Ananta."

"Ananta?" Karthikeya slid down from his peacock's saddle and peered down at Hanuman. "What about it?" His hand had already tightened on Vel's haft, probably without even realizing what he was doing.

Hanuman gulped but had no choice. "It's gone on strike," he answered quickly, hoping to get the news out and leave before the war god decided to focus his displeasure on the bearer of said news.

"What?" Naturally, that plan didn't work, as Karthikeya's brow lowered. "What do you mean, it's gone on strike?" he asked, his voice going from bellowing to deadly quiet in a heartbeat.

"It says it wants more pay and better hours," Hanuman explained. "It's refusing to coil until that happens."

"It. Is. Refusing. To. Coil." With each word, the spear shook in his hand, the long, gleaming tip hovering dangerously over Hanuman's head. "This is preposterous!" Karthikeya finally burst out. "It cannot be allowed! We need that cursed snake!"

"Ah, that's the other thing," Hanuman managed to squeak out. "The name."

"What name?"

"Its name." Hanuman sighed and looked down at his hands to avoid the war god's fierce gaze. "It wants to only be addressed by its full name from now on. Ananta Shesha-naga," he supplied helpfully.

"Because officially it's the Shesha Naga, the king of all snakes, and so it feels that—"

"I don't care what it wants!" Karthikeya screamed, raising Vel and thrusting the spear forward so that its point slammed into a broad wooden column some twenty feet behind them. The column featured deep punctures all up and down that one side, proving that it had borne the brunt of the god's displeasure many times. *Better it than me,* Hanuman thought, but was wise enough not to say. "It is the chosen seat of our lord Vishnu!" the war god was still shouting, drawing Hanuman's attention back to him. "He must make the Celestial Address while reclining upon its infinite coils, and so he shall, or I will slice those coils into so many pieces we'll all be dining on Ananta Unagi for the rest of forever!"

"I'll speak to it," Hanuman promised, already backing toward the celestial portal that led back out of this sub-realm. "I'm sure we can work something out."

Vel flew through the air behind him as he turned and ran for the portal, the spear impaling another pillar on the portal's far side. The image of it quivering there, mere feet from his head, was the last sight Hanuman had before he fled the war god's realm, but beneath the ever-present fear he couldn't help but wonder—why did their meetings always have to end this way?

10:47am

"So, there may be a slight issue with the Address," Santoshi Mata began as she entered Ganesha's sacred den.

"What's that?" he asked, not even glancing up from the scroll he was reading.

"I don't know what to wear," the young goddess blurted out. "I mean, I'll be on the lotus, of course, and I'll have my sword and trident, but should I wear the white, which is traditional but I don't want Saraswati to think I'm copying her even though she shouldn't be the only one who gets to wear that color just because it symbolizes her purity and insight since it's not like she's the only one with those traits around here and—"

"Santoshi." Ganesha sighed and set the scroll aside, looking up at her even as he rubbed his trunk against his cheek just below one eye.

"Yes?"

"Is this the issue you came to see me about?" he asked. "Or was there an actual problem and you're just hitching your sartorial concerns onto that?"

"It's not like you care," she replied with a pout. "You'll just wear your same old ceremonial robes, of course. As long as your tusks are polished, you're fine. But I'm a lot newer at this, you know! I don't have an established iconography of my own yet! And how am I ever supposed to develop one if no one will help me develop my own distinctive visual style?" When the elephant-headed god sighed, though, she shifted topics. "It's Kaustubha," she replied, referring to the sacred jewel Vishnu wore about his neck. "It's missing."

"Missing?" Now she had Ganesha's undivided attention. "What do you mean? Where is it?"

"If I knew that, it wouldn't be missing," she replied—eminently sensibly, she thought. "It should be in the sacred storeroom with all the rest of the regalia, but I just went to inventory everything and it isn't there."

"That damned—" Ganesha muttered, rising to his feet.

"You know who took it?" Santoshi asked, following her father as he strode toward the door.

"Oh, I've got a pretty good idea," he replied over his shoulder. "Don't worry, I've got this." Then he was gone.

Santoshi Mata stared at the door as it slid shut again behind him. "I didn't even get to the rest of the list," she stated, but there was no one left to hear her.

11:23am

"Hello? Saraswati?" Santoshi Mata called out softly. The elder goddess was seated by the River Ganges, strumming gently on her veena, and Santoshi hated to disturb her but with Ganesha gone, she didn't know where else to turn.

"Hello, Santoshi Mata," Saraswati replied without turning around, still strumming. "What can I do for you?"

"Well, it's just—" the young goddess wrung her hands together. And she only had the two! "I was inventorying the regalia," she started. "You know, for the Address? And, um, we have a few small . . . hiccups."

"Hiccups?" The goddess of knowledge and learning swiveled about so that she could study Santoshi fully, though her lower hands continued to tease soft music from the instrument she held. "What sort of hiccups?" She was always so poised, Santoshi couldn't help thinking. Always so calm and regal. Everything a goddess should be. While she always felt that she was busy flailing about everywhere, getting worked up over everything.

Like right now. She bit her lip to keep it from trembling as she answered: "Well, there's a problem with Kaustubha, but Ganesha says he's handling that." She paused, and Saraswati nodded for her to continue. "But the rest of the regalia, it, well, I guess whoever was supposed to be maintaining it hasn't been doing so properly? Maybe not since the last Address? Because things aren't exactly shipshape over there."

Saraswati frowned ever so slightly. "You're saying there are problems with the rest of the regalia?" she asked. Santoshi nodded. "Explain, please."

So of course Santoshi did. "The sankha, for one," she said.

"The sacred conch, yes," the other goddess clarified. "The representation of Om, the first sound of creation and the beginning of matter. What about it?"

Santoshi could barely get the words out. "It's moldy."

"Moldy?" The barest hint of a furrow appeared on Saraswati's perfect brow. "The sacred conch is moldy?"

Santoshi nodded. "And that's not all," she exclaimed. "The Padma? It's wilted."

"The lotus that symbolizes glorious existence is wilted," the older goddess repeated.

"Yes," Santoshi confirmed. "Which is weird, right? Since it also symbolizes fertility? But it's all brown now, and dried out."

Saraswati sighed, her hands finally stilling on the vela. "Anything else?"

"Um, the gada?" Santoshi said, her voice barely more than a whisper.

"What about it?"

"It's . . . sort of . . . dented?"

Now the older goddess actually raised one of her upper hands to rub at her forehead. "The mace that represents the elemental force from which all physical and mental power derives is dented."

Santoshi nodded. "Yes."

"I see." Saraswati studied her. "And the chakra?" she asked, referring to the sacred discus that represented the Sun and the cycle of time.

"Oh, that's fine," the younger goddess answered, and was rewarded with a weary but still lovely smile.

"So we need a new lotus," Saraswati pointed out, "and to clean out the sankha, and to repair the gada. Is that right?" Santoshi nodded. "And all in"—she consulted a watch that appeared suddenly on one of her upper wrists—"the next four and a half hours."

"I . . . guess so, yes," Santoshi agreed. She was relieved that the older, wiser, more experienced goddess seemed to have taken charge of this mess.

"Right," Saraswati stated, unconsciously imitating Brahma as she rose to her feet. "You see to the conch. I'll figure out a way to get the mace fixed. And I'll send Garuda out to find us a fresh lotus. Good?" The younger goddess nodded. "Great. Okay, let's go, chop chop."

The younger goddess scurried off to handle her assigned task, and once she was gone Saraswati allowed herself a second to scowl at the empty air. "Why does this sort of thing always happen?" she demanded of no one at all. "And why does it always wind up landing in my lap?"

She got no reply, of course. And after a second she sighed, gathered her skirts and her tools, and turned away from the soothing gurgling of the river, intent upon the problem she had agreed to tackle.

She only hoped she'd be able to figure out a reasonable solution in time.

12:01pm

Ganesha put on his best poker face as he approached the peak of Mount Kailash. Fortunately, having an elephant's tusks and trunk made his expressions difficult for most people to read even when he wasn't trying to hide them. But it was true that your parents and your spouse were the most likely people to be able to divine what you were thinking at a glance, and Ganesha was on his way to see one of the former right now.

As he'd expected, he found Shiva sitting cross-legged at the mountain's summit. The god of destruction sat unmoving, eyes closed, snake motionless, trident resting across his lap.

And sitting there atop the trident's tines was a silken pouch that clearly contained something large and round.

Something much the same size as Kaustubha.

As Ganesha approached, one of Shiva's eyes—the one in the center of his forehead—blinked open and studied the elephant-headed god.

"Ganesha," Shiva said.

"Father," Ganesha replied, adding a respectful bow. That out of the way, he dispensed with pleasantries. "You know why I'm here." He gestured with his trunk at the pouch.

"Oh?" Shiva shifted his shoulders slightly, a smirk forming on his lips. "I'm afraid I don't know what you mean."

"No? So you're telling me that isn't Kaustubha sitting in your lap?" Ganesha demanded.

The smirk widened. "Is Kaustubha missing? Oh, that's unfortunate! And right before the Celestial Address, too! Such a shame! That probably won't look so good to all the faithful, will it?"

"Look, let's cut to the chase, Dad," Ganesha insisted. "I get it.

281

You think you should get to deliver the Address. But it ain't gonna happen. Not now, and if you keep behaving like this, not ever."

"I am the Lord of Destruction and Change!" Shiva roared, all three eyes open now, rising to his feet in a single fluid motion, his trident in one hand and the pouch securely in another. "I am a member of the Triumvirate! It is my right!"

"Your right?" Ganesha tilted his head, scratching at his trunk as he studied his father. A thought had occurred to him. "Okay, then," he said amiably. "It's all yours."

That took the wind out of Shiva's sails. "Wait, what?" the dark god sputtered. "Really?" He flicked his long, matted locks back out of his face as he scrutinized his eldest son. "I can give the Address?"

"Absolutely," Ganesha agreed. "I'll tell Vishnu myself. He'll sit this one out, and you'll address all the faithful." He paused. "Of course, you'll need the full regalia, right?"

"Yes, yes," Shiva agreed eagerly. "All of them!"

"The sankha," Ganesha recited, ticking each item off on his fingers, "the chakra, the gada, the Padma. The Srivatsa, that might be a little tricky," he admitted, referring to the curl of hair on Vishnu's chest, which showed his immortality. "But we'll think of something. Ananta to sit on." He stopped and regarded his father as innocently as he could manage. "And Kaustubha on your chest."

"Yes, I—" Shiva's voice trailed off as he registered what Ganesha had just said. "What?" he managed weakly after a second.

"Well, you can't just carry the sacred gem around in a sack, right?" Ganesha pointed out. "You'll need to wear it properly if you're really gonna do this thing. Show everyone that you've got what it takes." He squinted at his father. "You do have what it takes, don't you?"

For a second, neither of them spoke. Ganesha blinked at Shiva, and Shiva glared back at him. Then, finally, Shiva thrust the pouch out. "Take it," he muttered. "Just take it and go."

"Are you sure?" Ganesha asked, his own hands still firmly at his sides. "Because if you really want to do this—"

"Take it!" And Shiva all but hurled the pouch at his son's chest.

"Well, if you insist," Ganesha agreed, grabbing the pouch before it could bounce off him. "Thanks." And, humming softly through his trunk, he turned and walked away again. He was careful not to run, or to glance back, but every inch of his back and shoulders and neck prickled from the force of his father's parting glare.

Clearly the next family dinner would be just oodles of fun.

1:15pm

Santoshi Mata was waiting for Ganesha when he returned to his den. "Did you get it?" she asked eagerly.

"Did you doubt me?" he replied, hoisting the pouch with a triumphant grin.

"Yes!" She clapped her hands, then froze. "I mean, yes for getting it, not yes for me doubting you, because of course I didn't doubt you, you know that I have the utmost faith in your abilities. Still— yes!" Then she frowned. "How did you get it? It was Shiva who had it, right?"

"It was," Ganesha confirmed. "And I told him he could keep it—and do the Address—provided he wore it properly."

"Oh." Santoshi broke into a big, beaming smile. "Because of course, Shiva can't wear Kaustubha," she supplied.

"That's right," her father agreed. "Only Vishnu can. It's the divine pearl, with 'the beauty of the lotus and a radiance equal to the sun,'" he quoted. "Only the leader of the gods is powerful enough to withstand that much heat and brilliance."

Santoshi nodded eagerly. "And Shiva himself said that, didn't he? So if anyone knew he wouldn't be able to wear the sacred gem, it was him!" She clapped her hands together again. "Nice!"

Ganesha executed a short bow, cheerfully accepting her admiration as his due.

"How's everything else?" He asked, slinging the pouch onto his desk with a casual disregard Santoshi considered completely inappropriate for a treasure of such magnitude.

"Okay, I guess," his daughter replied, blowing a strand of hair out of her face. "I mean, who knew it would be so hard to get mold out of a shell? It's not like you can just put it in the wash, but still, they shouldn't even be able to get moldy, should they? But I guess they are organic, and might have remains of whatever shellfish wore them originally, so it kind of makes sense—"

Ganesha had dropped into his desk chair and put his feet up on the desk—dangerously close to the pouch, in fact—and now was staring at her with an all-too-familiar expression of mingled confusion and amusement. "Santoshi," he started, but she barely heard him and didn't stop.

"I found Garuda," she continued instead, "and he said it was fine, he was happy to go get a new lotus but it had to come from Mount Meru of course so he headed out right away and he isn't back yet and I hope he hurries because we need to make sure it's suitable." She paused for a breath, and Ganesha tried again, but still she kept on, picking back up with, "And Saraswati is taking care of the mace, she said, though I don't know how exactly, but it's not like I'm going to question her, after all. So I think we're good there. Still—"

This time Ganesha actually put some force into it. "Santoshi!" he bellowed.

"What?" she replied. "Why are you shouting? I'm standing right here!"

Her father rubbed at his trunk. "Yes, you are," he agreed, "and you're going on and on and I don't have the faintest clue what you're talking about!"

"Oh." She considered that for a second before smiling brightly. "Well, don't worry about it, then." And with that she turned and strolled away.

Ganesha stared after her. "Because that's going to work," he muttered, throwing his hands in the air. But then his eye caught sight of the pouch and he leaned back in his chair, hands going behind his head, and started humming again.

He'd taken care of the hard part, after all. Let Santoshi and the others deal with the rest.

4:03pm

"Got it!" Garuda declared as he burst into the conference room. The mighty eagle had his massive wings spread wide, and clutched tightly but gently in his long talons was a perfect white lotus.

"Great!" Saraswati replied. She took the flower from him, careful not to bruise a single petal, and examined it. "It's perfect," she agreed finally. "Nice one, Garuda."

The king of birds swelled with pride. "Thanks." He shrugged modestly. "It wasn't so hard." Then, tilting his head this way and that, he glanced around the room. "What about the rest?"

"I got the mace fixed," the goddess answered, lifting the gleaming weapon with both hands and setting it gently on the table in front of her. She shook her head. "It wasn't easy finding a smith who was qualified to work on it, much less one who'd agree to touch it or who could make the repairs that quickly, but I did. Now it's good as new."

While they were talking, the others were filing into the room. "Here's Kaustubha," Ganesha reported, holding up the silk pouch. "Safe and sound, and believe me, that wasn't as easy as you might think."

"I have the sankha," Santoshi Mata stated, hurrying in behind the elephant-headed god and holding up the conch, which gleamed in the heavenly light. "It might smell a little like soap, but it's certainly clean now, inside and out."

"Here's the chakra," Karthikeya reported, waving the holy discus before setting it on the table. "All good there." The way he gritted his teeth when he said that suggested that he would have liked for it to have been otherwise, so that he'd have had an excuse to fight someone.

"What about Ananta?" Brahma asked as he walked in—lotus flowers forming beneath his every step, as always, which gave the housekeeping staff a constant headache—and taking his place at the head of the table. How the Creator even knew about the situation with the snake was beyond anyone's guess, but somehow he always did.

"All set," Hanuman replied, slipping in right behind Brahma and circling around to the table's far end and his usual seat. "I spoke with it at great length." That produced a few knowing chuckles around the room—Hanuman was renowned for his impeccable grammar, his great knowledge, and his propensity to demonstrate both, at length, at every available opportunity.

"And you got it all sorted out?" Karthikeya demanded. "No more of this strike nonsense? Because if you didn't knock some sense into that overgrown worm, I will!"

"I took care of it," the monkey minister promised. "Ananta Shesha-naga has agreed to continue at its appointed task . . . in exchange for a few minor concessions."

Brahma speared the monkey with his gaze. "Such as?" he asked dryly.

"Use of its full name and title, for one," Hanuman replied. "A week off every other year, second. And third, an additional bushel of fish each week, plus one of crabs and other assorted shellfish each month."

Brahma considered that a second, then nodded. "Fine." He looked around the room, studying each of the assembled gods and goddesses in turn. "We're all set, then."

"Are we?" A deep voice inquired. Everyone glanced at the doors, which had just swung open to reveal a tall, majestic figure standing in the entrance. The dark-skinned male entered, his every movement the perfect depiction of grace, power, and nobility, his four hands folded in front of him, his eyes powerful but kind as he nodded to each of the others, making his way past them.

The leader of the gods paused several times along the way, however. "An excellent choice, Garuda," he told the king of birds. "Nicely done, Santoshi Mata, and don't worry, I like the scent of jasmine," he complimented the youngest goddess, and "Saraswati, you never disappoint," to the more senior goddess, who glowed with pride. "Ganesha, cleverly handled as always," he told the elephant-headed god, "and Karthikeya, I appreciate you keeping your cool. This time." Then he reached Brahma.

"Lord Vishnu," Brahma intoned, rising to his feet and bowing so low that the tip of his beard scraped the lotus blossoms on the floor. "All is in readiness for your Celestial Address."

"Is it?" Vishnu pondered that, even though it was clear he already knew the answer. Then a warm smile spread across his handsome face. "Excellent." He clapped both sets of hands together. "So let us begin."

As the supreme deity turned his attention toward the table and began collecting each item of his regalia, Brahma glanced past him and met the gaze of the other gods. With a single nod and the faintest hint of a smile, he managed to convey a well-earned 'well done, everyone' and the rest of the gods relaxed. They'd done it again, and just in time.

It had been a good day.

"Oh," Hanuman muttered as they filed out after Vishnu.

Ganesha, who was beside him at the back of the group, half turned. "What?" he asked softly.

The monkey minister sighed. "I forgot to update the speech," he admitted just as quietly. "It doesn't have Ananta's full title yet."

Ganesha groaned. The two of them glanced at each other, and then quickened their pace and pushed past their fellow gods in hopes of catching up to Vishnu in time.

Author Biographies

Cliff Ackman

Like most sit-coms, not much has changed since the last episode. Cliff Ackman is still gainfully employed as a statistical analyst. Two cats still do their best to prevent him from writing, playing board games, and producing amateur films. (They are not always successful.) He tries to be kind, polite and erudite. If you have comments, questions or thoughts; he can be reached at Cliff006@frontier.com

Russ Colchamiro

Russ Colchamiro is the author of Crossline, *Finders Keepers, Genius de Milo,* and *Astropalooza,* and is editor of the new anthology, *Love, Murder & Mayhem,* all with *Crazy 8 Press.* Russ lives in New Jersey with his wife, two children, and crazy dog, Simon, who may be an alien himself. Russ also contributed to several anthologies, including Tales of the Crimson Keep, Pangaea, and Altered States of the Union. He is now at work on a top-secret project, and a Finders Keepers spin-off. For more information, please visit www.russcolchamiro.com, follow him on Twitter @AuthorDudeRuss, and Facebook at www.facebook.com/RussColchamiroAuthor. Russ encourages you to email him at authorduderuss@gmail.com

Michael D'Ambrosio

Michael, a life-long resident of the Philadelphia area, is well known for his Fractured Time Trilogy, Space Frontiers Series, Night Creeps Series and his Pain Series. Queen of Pain, the second book in the Pain Series and sequel to Princess Pain, is due for release in May, 2017, from AZ Publishing. Michael also writes screenplays, adapting several from novels. More on Michael's appearances and projects can be found at www.fracturedtime.com . Michael can often be found at sci-fi conventions across the country.

Keith R.A. DeCandido

Keith R.A. DeCandido's other stories featuring Cassie Zukav have appeared in Apocalypse 13, Bad-Ass Faeries: It's Elemental, A Baker's Dozen of Magic, Buzzy Mag, Out of Tune, Ragnarok and Roll, Tales from the House Band Volumes 1 & 2, and Without a License. Other recent work: the Marvel's Tales of Asgard trilogy, Orphan Black: Classified Clone Report, A Furnace Sealed, Mermaid Precinct, three Super City Cops novellas, and stories in Aliens: Bug Hunt, Baker Street Irregulars, Joe Ledger: Unstoppable, Nights of the Living Dead, Stargate: Homeworlds, and more. Keith is also an editor, musician, martial artist, pop-culture writer, and baseball nerd. www.DeCandido.net.

Michael Jan Friedman

Michael Jan Friedman is the author of 76 books, nearly half of which are set somewhere in the wilds of the *Star Trek* universe. He has also written for television, radio, and comic books. His novelization of *Batman & Robin* was, for a time, the #1 best- seller in Poland (really). You can follow Mike on Twitter @Fried- manMJ; on Facebook (Michael Jan Friedman), or on his website, MichaelJanFriedman.net.

Robert Greenberger

Robert Greenberger is a writer and editor, having spent time on staff at Starlog Press, DC Comics, Marvel Comics, *Weekly World News*, ComicMix, and Famous Monsters of Filmland. His written works span fiction and nonfiction with original and media tie-in stories for a wide variety of ages. A cofounder of Crazy 8 Press, he continues to write original works. Bob is also a certified High School English teacher. For more find him at bobgreenberger.com or @bobgreenberger. He makes his home in Maryland with his wife Deb and dog Ginger.

Elektra Hammond

Elektra Hammond emulates her multi-sided idol Buckaroo Banzai by going in several directions at once. She's been involved in publishing since the 1990s—now she writes, concocts anthologies, and edits science fiction for various and sundry. When not freelancing or appearing at science fiction conventions, she travels the world judging cat shows. She is an associate member of SFWA. Elektra lives in Delaware with her husband, Mike, and more than the usual allotment of felines.

Eric Hardenbrook

Eric is a fan, an author and an artist, usually in that order. Eric lives in central Pennsylvania with his gorgeous wife and daughter. He writes to try to get the stories out of his head. When he's being a fan, he helps run *Watch The Skies* and assists in the publication of their monthly fanzine. He can be found (at least some of the time) at *The Pretend Blog*. When not working on those things, Eric enjoys the occasional video or board game and is an old school role player.

Lee C. Hillman

Lee C. Hillman died at the age of thirteen months. Since her mysterious return to life, she has busied herself conquering worlds too numerous to mention. She is also an author and editor in the "Bad-Ass Faeries" series, and a contributor to the "Defending the Future" series. She writes fanfiction under the moniker "Gwendolyn Grace," and is an actor, singer, songwriter, student of comparative media, member of the Society for Creative Anachronism, past producer of Harry Potter conventions, and self-professed "big damn geek." From 2008-2015, she co-wrote and moderated the shared fanfiction/role-playing game, HP Alternity, found on Dreamwidth.org.

Larry Ivkovich

Larry Ivkovich's short stories have been published in over twenty online and print markets. Published novels include urban fantasies The Sixth Precept and Warriors of the Light from IGWG Publishing. A finalist in the L. Ron Hubbard's Writers of the Future Contest, Larry was also the 2010 recipient of the CZP/Rannu Fund award for fiction.

Brian Koscienski and Chris Pisano

This story presents the unholy dichotomy between the blistering writing style of Brian Koscienski, who resembles Sasquatch with mange, and the dynamic gothic world of Chris Pisano, the last known Cro-Magnon man. When angry villagers wielding torches and pitchforks aren't chasing them, Brian and Chris make the world a better place through stories, novels, three magazine lines, and even bawdy haiku. Join these two in their latest novel, "The Devil's Grasp," a novel about five ensorcelled gemstones. Anyone possessing all five will have the power to call forth and control the demons that haunt Hell itself.

Caw Miller

Caw Miller has been published in the anthology TV Gods, in Daily Science Fiction, in the Bram Stoker nominated anthology Dark Tales of Lost Civilizations, and in other anthologies. His map-filled, e-novel General Drummer Boy is for sale on Amazon.

KT Pinto

KT Pinto's motto is "If you can't be good, be naughty. If you must be naughty, be safe." When she has spare time from adulting, KT writes short stories and novels and reviews sex toys. Find her on Facebook, Twitter, and Youtube.

Aaron Rosenberg

Aaron Rosenberg is the author of the best-selling DuckBob SF comedy series, the Dread Remora space-opera series, and, with David Niall Wilson, the O.C.L.T. occult thriller series. His tie-in work contains novels for Star Trek, Warhammer, World of WarCraft, Stargate: Atlantis, and Eureka. He has written children's books (including the award-winning Bandslam: The Junior Novel and the #1 best-selling 42: The Jackie Robinson Story), educational books, and roleplaying games (including the Origins Award-winning Gamemastering Secrets). He is a founding member of Crazy 8 Press. You can follow him online at gryphonrose.com, on Facebook at facebook.com/gryphonrose, and on Twitter @gryphonrose.

Hildy Silverman

Hildy Silverman is the publisher of Space and Time, a 50-year- old magazine featuring fantasy, horror, and science fiction (www. spaceandtimemagazine.com). Her short fiction publications include, "The Darren" (2009, Witch Way to the Mall?, Friesner, ed.), "Sappy Meals" (2010, Fangs for the Mammaries, Friesner, ed.), "The Six Million Dollar Mermaid" (2013, Mermaids 13, French, ed. and a finalist for WSFA Small Press Award), "The Bionic Mermaid Returns" (2014, With Great Power, French, ed.), "The Great Chasm" (2016, co-authored w/David Silverman, Altered States of the Union, Hauman, ed.), and "A Scandal in the Bloodline" (2017, Baker Street Irregulars, Ventrella & Maberry, eds.).

Maria V. Snyder

Meteorologist turned novelist, Maria V. Snyder's been writing fantasy and science fiction since she was bored at work and needed something creative to do. Over a dozen novels later, Maria's been on the *New York Times* bestseller list, won a half-dozen awards, and has earned her Master's degree in Writing from Seton Hill University where she's now part of the MFA faculty. Readers are welcome to check out her website for more information at http://www.MariaVSnyder.com.

Ian Randal Strock

Ian Randal Strock (www.IanRandalStrock.com) is the owner and publisher of Gray Rabbit Publications, LLC, and its sf imprint, Fantastic Books (www.FantasticBooks.biz). He is the author of many short stories appearing in *Nature*, *Analog*(from which he won two AnLab Awards), and several anthologies, and of much nonfiction, including *The Presidential Book of Lists* (Random House, 2008), *Ranking the First Ladies* (Carrel Books, 2016), and *Ranking the Vice Presidents* (Carrel

Books, 2016). He was put off by the delayed gratification in not answering the show's title when it first aired, but got hooked by the non-linear story-telling in *How I Met Your Mother* while it was in reruns.

Jeff Young

Jeff Young is a bookseller first and a writer second – although he wouldn't mind a reversal of fortune. He is an award winning author contributing to the anthologies *Writers of the Future V.26, By Any Means, Best Laid Plans, Dogs of War, Man and Machine, If We Had Known, In an Iron Cage, Clockwork Chaos, Fantastic Futures 13, Gaslight and Grimm, The Society for the Preservation of C.J. Henderson & TV Gods*. Jeff's own fiction is collected in *TOI Special Edition 2 – Diversiforms*. Jeff also edited the *Drunken Comic Book Monkey* line, *TV Gods* and this book you're holding.

Artist Biographies

Jelena Djordjevic
Pages 24, 136, 216, 240
Jelena Djordjevic, award-winning comic artist and illustrator from Nis, Serbia. Works on the comic series The Pros and Hordentown at the moment. More information about Jelena can be found at http://besnglist.daportfolio.com/

Dillon Fisher
Page 98
Dillon specializes in Character/Animal design. He graduated Cumberland Perry Area Vocational Technical School for Graphic Design, as well as Harrisburg University of Science and Technology for Video Game design. When not drawing, Dillon spends his free time collecting Monster Movie merchandise. You can see more of Dillon's work at (Facebook.com/DillonFisherArtwork)

Dawn Griffin
Pages 84, 160, 272
Dawn Griffin, out of Havertown, PA, is a designer/illustrator/cartoonist, A.K.A. Certified Creative Workhorse. She specializes in "cute, funny & sophisticated" all-ages material. Her comic strip Zorphbert & Fred has been posted online with a growing readership, and now is published in 3 volumes. Dawn also illustrated the Abby's Adventures kids' book series, which promotes self-esteem in girls ages 3-8, and now boasts 4 books. Wanting to give back to the online comic community, she co-founded the Webcomic Alliance, offering free articles, tutorials, videos and a podcast about the business of digital comics. Her next endeavor: inventing the 30-hour day. And maybe a coffee IV. http://dawngriffinstudios.com

Breanne Havener
Page 116
After her studies at the Art Institute of York, Breanne Havener is most known for her illustrative mural work which can be seen in her Facebook page titled 'Breezy's Murals and Paintings'. However, she has also taught

art classes to mentally different preteens for the Carlisle Arts Learning Center, led workshops for the elderly for the Harrisburg Latino Community Center, aided in a beautification project for the Save the Bay Foundation, and designed color guard sets for her Alma Mater. She would like to thank her mentor, renowned artist and professor, Nancy Mendes MFA.

Brian McCranie

Pages 42, 58, 110, 126, 254, 290

A native of Georgia, Brian was raised in the town of Macon just south of Atlanta. He is a self-taught Illustrator, starting early in life he created his first comic book by the age of 8 in a school classroom. Though crude and unpolished, Brian would continue to keep working at refining his craft. In 2012 Brian would go full time into freelance illustration. Here he worked on a varied array of projects until he decided to start work on The Sum of Light a creator owned project inspired by the works of H.P. Lovecraft. Most recently he can be found in various RPG manuals, notably Shadowrun.

Miguel Mora

Page 176

Miguel is a comic artist, illustrator and graphic designer, and has worked since 1999 for some Ad companies and as a freelancer. Published comics works in México and outside, in EUA in the Heavy Metal Magazine. He has taught in BA level in the IEST (Instituto de Estudios Superiores de Tamaulipas), University in Tampico-México.

Nicky Wagman

Pages 6, 76, 198

Nicky has been telling stories with pictures all her life and her gradeschool teachers have the defaced homework assignments to prove it! She studied comic books at the Savannah College of Art and Design and works at Comix Connection in Mechanicsburg, PA, where she continues to study the artform every day. Recently she has begun writing with words too and has published an ebook novella titled *The Faerie Godmother's Apprentice Wore Green*. Here she's thrilled to again have the chance to draw some of her favorite myths in modern updates and hopes the oracles predict more *TV Gods* soon!

FORTRESS PUBLISHING, INC.

is

Brian Koscienski ..............C.E.O./C.F.O./President/Editor-in-Chief/Writer/Megalomaniacal Genius
Chris Pisano ....C.O.O./C.C.O./Vice President/Writer/Spiritual Philanthropist
Christine Czachur...................C.I.O./Publicist/Project Manager/Mayhem Coordinator/Booth Babe

OTHER EXCITING PRODUCTS FROM FORTRESS:

THE REALM BEYOND MAGAZINE

64 pages devoted to the best in science fiction, fantasy and horror from spellbinding writers from around the world. After a few issues of this magazine, you will doubt everything you know about this realm of existence. This magazine is a can't miss for the true speculative fiction fan!

SCARY TALES OF SCARINESS

Vampires! Werewolves! Zombies! Join writers Brian Koscienski & Chris Pisano as they face down creepy creatures and mad monsters while they stumble their way through fifteen comedic tales of horror and suspense. They match wits with the devil! They go toe-to-toe with a slasher! They even fight a spider! Will they save the world? Or doom it? Or simply make monkeys out of themselves? Whatever their fate, whatever the outcome, they do it all without dropping a beer...

CEMETERY MOON

64 pages devoted to the best in horror, suspense and gothic from spellbinding writers from around the world. After a few issues of this magazine, you will doubt everything you know and give pause before every shadow. This magazine is a can't miss for true horror fans!

Visit us at:

www.fortresspublishinginc.com